THE PROGRAM

A DICKIE FLOYD DETECTIVE NOVEL

DANNY R. SMITH

Copyright © 2022 by Danny R. Smith

All rights reserved.

No part of this book may be reproduced in any form or by any electronic or mechanical means, including information storage and retrieval systems, without written permission from the author, except for the use of brief quotations in a book review.

ISBN-13: 978-1-7349794-7-3

Cover by Jon Schuler

www.schulercreativelab.com

❦ Created with Vellum

For Hudsy and Baby G

"Nothing less than brilliant storytelling!" — Frederick Douglass Reynolds, author of *Black, White, and Gray All Over: A Black Man's Odyssey in Life and Law Enforcement*

"Another outstanding work from the author of the Dickie Floyd novels." — Kay Reeves

"Danny R. Smith has woven the ideal story once again, filled with characters who jump off the page and into your heart. Outstanding! Very Highly Recommended." — Michele Kapugi

"Smith outdid himself! His in-depth development of Josie in this episode of the franchise really made this book enjoyable." — Jeff Schauer

"One of those books you can't wait to finish and makes you angry when you're done." — Dennis Slocumb

"Best book I've read in the past several years." — Bud Johnson

"Few writers can take you into the minds of police and criminals. None do so as well as Danny R. Smith." — Phil Jonas

PROLOGUE

THE FIRST TIME RUDY PRADA FOUND JESUS HAPPENED SHORTLY AFTER he'd walked into Angel's Market on Third Street in East Los Angeles, two blocks from King Taco and a half mile west of the sheriff's station, a gun in his jacket pocket.

His day had started just before noon when his girlfriend, Veronica "Vero" Lara, stuck the barrel of a snub-nose .38 against his cheek and interrogated him about a hoochie mama named Sylvia, having found her name and number scrawled on a cocktail napkin in purple ink and tucked into his jacket pocket, along with the blued-steel heater she'd used to nudge him from his slumber. Rudy, handsome and silver-tongued—irresistible to ladies who favored soft-core bad boys—had assured Vero that his homeboy Mikey had worn his jacket the night before and that both the gun and the hoodrat's number were his. Then he made love to her, retrieved his gun, and left the house. He walked to the nearby King Taco where he picked up an order of *tacos al pastor* and ate them as he meandered down the sidewalk on his way to the liquor store where he would pick up a can of beer to wash them down. At the register, Rudy dug into his jacket pocket for his cash, and as he brought out the bills, the .38 fell out. The Korean woman behind the counter, who, along with her husband, had purchased the store from Angel Gutierrez two years prior, panicked. She hit the silent alarm to signal a robbery-in-progress, but then she had no idea how to undo the chain of events she had set in motion after Rudy picked up the gun, put it back in his pocket, apologized, and paid for his beer. He was standing outside the liquor store, basking in the early afternoon winter sun, and drinking his beer, when a sheriff's patrol car came around the corner and veered toward him. He shoved the beer into his jacket pocket, hoping to avoid being harassed for an open container, as the lady cop came out of the car with her pistol pointed directly at him, the woman yelling for him to show her his hands.

Rudy did as he had been ordered and removed his hands from his pockets, his right hand still grasping the can of beer. The lady cop fired two shots, and one of them tore through the M of the arched *Maravilla* tattoo on his stomach. He dropped his beer as he fell to the ground, clutching his jacket against the burning pain and crying out, asking why she had shot him.

It was in the ambulance on the way to White Memorial when Rudy reflected on his Catholic upbringing. He pictured the mural of Our Lady of Guadalupe amid other symbols of Latino culture, the canvas a wall against which he had stood until the gunshot dropped him to the cool concrete sidewalk now stained a crimson red. The bumps in the road felt like hammer strikes against his abdomen, but he focused on the image of Guadalupe and silently said a prayer he hadn't said in more than a decade: *Lord Jesus Christ, Son of God, have mercy on me, a sinner...*

The next time Rudy came to know Christ, he was coming to terms with the third step at a court-ordered AA meeting which took place in a nondescript windowless room with a worn tiled floor and plastic chairs, two folding tables at the back holding urns of coffee and stacks of Styrofoam cups, a podium at the front. He was contemplating this idea of turning over his will and his life to the care of God—*as he understood Him*—and reflecting on the meandering path of his adult life thus far. It had been fifteen years since he was shot and did a nickel for being in possession of a stolen firearm, in spite of his protests that the gun he had possessed at the time wasn't his. While doing his time, first at the county and then at several state pens once he was convicted: Chino, Avenal, and Delano, Rudy held jobs and attended religious services and avoided the politics of gangs to the extent that he could. After all, he represented a neighborhood, and certain things were expected of him because of it, so he carefully negotiated those obstacles and did his time as well as time could be done by a *vato* from East L.A.

But he left Jesus behind along with his bed roll and toothbrush when he returned to the old neighborhood a *veterano*, a *vato* who had been to the pen. He strutted with a little more confidence and would lock eyes with youngsters until they turned away, posturing for the other OGs in the hood. Three months later, he walked into Angel's once more, this time actually intending to commit an armed robbery when he purposefully pulled a gun from his jacket while standing at the register. It had only taken a six-pack of beer, a few huffs of paint, and Mikey's prodding for him to decide that revenge against the Koreans was in order. This time, it was Rudy who got off two shots, striking the man in the store who had grabbed his own pistol rather than emptying the till as he had been ordered to do. Rudy couldn't believe it, being forced to shoot a man when he only wanted retribution for the gunshot he had received and the time he had served thanks to Mrs. Yang, or whatever her name was, her and the lady deputy who put a hole in his gut.

Two days later, the same lady cop who had shot him five years earlier woke him at seven o'clock with the muzzle of *her* pistol pointed at his face. The Mexican cop with the steely brown eyes stood over him as he lay naked in Vero's bed, a thin sheet barely covering his lower body, children crying in an adjacent room. Frozen with fear, he stared at the muzzle of her gun, likely the same one he had seen before, the one that appeared regularly in his mind, slow motion replays of balls of fire and a cloud of smoke and a searing pain enveloping his body as he fell to the ground with a can of beer in his hand.

There were others crowded into the cluttered room, five or six men, presumably detectives from East L.A. station. Like the woman cop, each was dressed in jeans and green jackets with sheriff's insignia on the fronts and backs, gun belts around their waists. Rudy couldn't take his eyes off the beautiful cop who had tried to kill him once before, and he waited for the last flash of light he would ever see.

But the flash never came.

The lady cop holstered her gun and turned away as two male cops grabbed Rudy, flipped him onto his bullet-scarred stomach with the tattoo that looked like a spot of melted wax and then the word, *aravilla*. The cops handcuffed him, and someone told Vero to put his pants on him. Rudy went to jail bare-chested and trying his best to keep a pair of baggy chinos from falling off his narrow hips.

In court, the Latina cop had held his gaze while testifying that Rudy had been identified by the victim and a witness as being the one to shoot the store owner while attempting to rob him, and yes, she admitted, during a contentious cross-examination, it was in fact she who had shot the defendant five years earlier outside of the very store he now stood accused of robbing. It was irrelevant, the judge declared, and the jury apparently agreed.

Rudy got a dime plus a second strike for that one, so when he was paroled nine years later, he left Mikey and *Maravilla* behind, and he moved Vero and her three children—one of whom was his own—to La Mirada. It was a different world than East L.A. though only a half-hour drive down the Santa Ana freeway. He found work through an outreach program where former gangbangers spent time in the neighborhoods and at the schools and parks and social services offices talking to at-risk youth. He would tell them about being shot, about his time in the pen, how his first stint had been easier than the last when he leveled up and split his time at the maximum-security institutions of Corcoran and Pelican Bay, and that the only thing that got him through was his program that included God and sobriety and a separation from the life of gangs in which he had been raised.

He shared these same testaments at his weekly AA meeting in the city of Norwalk, where Rudy was popular among his peers. He was a handsome convict with an easy smile and the tongue of a practiced politician who was comfortable at the podium speaking of his trials and tribulations, his daily struggles, his past sins, and his ongoing efforts to make amends for them.

And it was during one such revelation that, as he scanned the room, careful to make eye contact with each attendee, his mind went blank and his speech suddenly halted as his eyes met the familiar gaze of a woman watching him from the back. She lowered her head and raised a Styrofoam cup in front of her face, and for the remainder of his talk she remained hidden behind her coffee and a purposefully draped lock of hair.

But Rudy had known her at first glance—there was no mistake about it. He could never forget those almond-shaped hazel eyes, the eyes of an outlaw befittingly set on a particularly formidable lady cop.

1

DETECTIVE JOSEFINA SANCHEZ WHIRLED INTO THE COURTROOM, PUSHING through the swinging door with her backside, an overstuffed brown expanding folder tucked beneath one arm, a briefcase dangling from the opposite hand. Written across the top left flap of the folder was *Murder, 187 P.C.,* and beneath it were the names of the victim, Trinidad Flores, and the suspect—now the defendant—Fernando Belmontes. All were neatly printed in black felt marker along with an L.A. County sheriff's file number and the coroner's case number. The folder comprised reports, notes, typewritten statements, and envelopes containing crime scene photographs—everything she might need during the trial. She glanced at the clock on the wall as she made her way to the prosecution table and saw she was fifteen minutes late. Not bad, considering.

Josie had been called to testify yesterday afternoon, but hadn't been excused from the witness stand by the court's final recess of the day. She didn't expect her testimony this morning to take long, but you never knew. In any event, she had planned to arrive early and go over yesterday's testimony with the prosecutor, Justin McKnight, who had glanced back at her as she came through the door and then turned back to the table where he now sat rocking in his chair and tapping his pen on a yellow legal pad before him. Was he irritated at her for being late? She didn't know. She did know that nearly everyone else in the courtroom was looking at her as she now pushed through the swinging half doors that separated the spectators from the business side of the courtroom, namely the judge, his clerk, the bailiff, a jury box, and two tables for the attorneys. Thankfully, the jury box sat empty. You always wanted the jurors to regard you warmly, and scurrying in late could leave any one of them with the wrong impression.

Department 103 was one of infamy, host of one of the most appalling trials of all time. Situated on the ninth floor of the Los Angeles County Superior Courthouse at 210 West Temple Street in downtown Los Angeles, the large chamber was finished in light-colored wood-paneled walls which were accented by dark wood trim that matched the counsel tables and the benches where the spectators sat. Today, a smattering of spectators was comfortably spread out, with plenty of room for others. This was no O.J. crowd, no reporters and none of the lottery winners or others who had paid for their seats in this very chamber a quarter of a century ago. Josie's case stood in stark contrast to that fiasco—just a regular murder trial with nothing famous about it. One man had killed another outside a barroom in East Los Angeles, and few people other than Josie, her partner Dickie, and a handful of the victim's family even cared.

Josie bent down and whispered in the deputy district attorney's ear as she set her file on the counsel table and placed her briefcase on an empty chair. "Sorry I'm late. Rollover accident on the I-5."

She looked up to see the judge focused on his clerk. "Bring in the jury." Then he dropped his chin and looked over a pair of specs that hung at the end of his nose, conveying irritation as he met Josie's gaze. "Detective, you may return to the witness stand, mindful that you are still under oath," he said, gesturing toward the seat in case she had somehow forgotten where it was.

As she made her way to the witness stand, Josie felt her temperature rise, a not-so-unusual physiological response to the spotlight being cast on her. From childhood, she would squirm and perspire as she anticipated having to stand before her peers, and her fear of audiences hadn't subsided. Even briefing cases in front of her colleagues at the bureau caused her anxiety. But testifying was usually different for her. She was always well-prepared for her testimony, and she looked forward to fielding questions from the attorneys. For whatever reason, the number of specta-

The Program

tors or even cameras in the courtroom didn't matter—this was a phenomenon she hadn't quite figured out. But today, suddenly, she flushed under the watchful eye of the scholarly, black-robed African American at the bench, the presiding magistrate who had replaced the disgraced Judge Ito not long after a killer walked free through the very doors Sanchez had crashed through moments before. She took her seat and adjusted the microphone, placed her expandable case file folder on the floor next to her seat, then nudged it a bit out of the way with the toe of her chestnut knee-high Dolce Vita boot. As the jurors settled into their seats, she adjusted her sienna floral Armani knockoff, smoothing the ruffled midi dress and assuring it dropped over her knees and met the top of her boots. With a stoic gaze set on the back of the courtroom, she took slow, deep breaths to calm herself after her frenzied entry. What she needed most was a few slow-pitch questions to allow her time to settle, but that wasn't to be, and she knew it. Her testimony would resume this morning with defense counsel coming at her after a night of preparing to damage her credibility with the jurors.

Just as Josie relaxed, she felt an itch on her leg beneath the top of her right boot. She calmly reached down to scratch it when a terrible thought entered her mind. Suddenly she was no longer calm and collected as she recalled a crime scene with maggots crawling all over the floor while she and her partner examined a bloated and rotted corpse. She had worn these same boots that day, and hours later, while interviewing a suspect at the station, she had a similar sensation and convinced herself that one or more of the maggots had made its way up her leg and into her boot. The more she had tried to ignore it, the worse the sensation had become, and Josie could see in her mind the tiny white larva crawling out of her boot and up her leg and... Her partner had brought the heat to the suspect, the interview having moved into interrogation territory, and any disruption of the flow would have destroyed their best—and likely their *only*—opportunity to get a confession. So she had willed herself to hold it together, to stay composed, to accept that she only had an itch, and there was no way maggots were in her boot or on her leg. Now she just needed to reaffirm that to herself. *No maggots. No maggots...*

The judge was asking counsel if they were prepared to proceed, and Josie began counting breaths again but lost track as her thoughts were consumed with the itch on her leg—she should have thrown the fucking boots away. She had paid just under four hundred dollars, so there hadn't been much chance of her doing that. She could hear her mother saying, *Ustedes son unos desperdiciados.* No *tienen* idea *lo que es* to have no money *para comprar comida.* No *tienen* idea no *tener* money for clothes. *Ustedes piensan que el dinero* grows on trees? A declaration of her disapproval stated in her eclectic mix of Spanish and English—*Spanglish*—and accentuated by head shaking and tongue clicking, perhaps picking at the lint on her own frayed and threadbare thirty-year-old sweater to drive home the point.

"Is the witness ready?" His Honor's voice thundered through the near-empty chamber.

Josie snapped out of her reverie and met the magistrate's eyes. His brows were up, expectantly. Had he asked her something else? What did she miss? She nodded—though somewhat hesitantly—and said, "Yes, Your Honor. I'm ready."

The judge was a former detective himself, though one from a previous generation of cops and an era different than anything Josie knew. It was widely known that the Honorable Charles A. Jackson—the A for Alfred, but his former colleagues had changed it to "Action"—had been a storied homicide cop himself, the only black member of LAPD's infamous hat squad. The nickname came during the fifties when LAPD was a formidable force of serious practitioners of law enforcement, no-nonsense *men* who saw to it at all costs that justice was swift and that the City of Angels remained untarnished, as far as anyone in the suburbs would know. The squad's landmark case had been the Black Dahlia murder, which remains unsolved seventy years later, though it was some considerable time after it happened when Action Jackson donned a fedora himself. Some said he was the last of the hat squad, but Josie knew better; her beloved sheriff's homicide bureau had a hat squad of its own, namely her partner, Dickie Jones. He had broken her in on *the floor*, handling scores of murders in the few years they were together on Team 2. Now they were both assigned to Unsolved Homicides where she was not only burdened with a dozen unsolved cases of her own, cases she brought from *the floor* to Unsolveds, but hundreds of other cases that had cooled off while in the hands of other bulldogs currently or previously assigned to the bureau. Some were now as cold as ice.

The Honorable Action Jackson told the defense to proceed, punctuating his soft-spoken words with a wave of his meaty hand as he leaned back in his tall leather chair and turned his attention to the witness box. Josie proffered a slight closed-mouth smile, then turned her gaze toward the defendant's counselor who stepped to his podium and said, "Good morning, Detective Sanchez."

2

Dickie's iPhone lit up in its cradle on the dash, the display indicating an unknown caller ringing through. He lowered the volume on his AM radio where he monitored traffic reports every ten minutes—*on the ones,* 11 past the hour, 21 past the hour, et cetera—pushed the button to answer the call and aimed his chin at a microphone tucked into the headliner. "Jones," he said flatly.

"Hey dummy, where's your partner this morning?" It was Davey Lopes, one of the senior members of the Unsolveds unit. Dickie pictured him sitting at his desk with his feet propped up, a cup of coffee steaming next to him, his mischievous eyes fixed on the pair of miniature flags that stood in a coffee mug at the edge of his desk: Old Glory and a scarlet flag featuring an eagle, globe and anchor, and a banner beneath the insignia bearing the words *United States Marine Corps.*

"Good morning to you, too, asshole. My partner's in trial this week, what's up?"

"Stover's looking for her, said some dude's trying to beef her for stalking him."

Dickie chuckled. What most men would give to have Josie stalking them. Who in hell would beef her for that? He said, "What'd the captain say? He tell you anything about who this asshole is?"

"Just that the dude's a convict, someone she put away and is now on his ass again. Anyway, just thought I'd give you a heads up. You comin' in today, or what?"

Dickie had no idea what the beef could be about, but he'd send Josie a text the next time traffic bottled up on the southbound I-5 and he came to a stop, let her know the skipper was on the warpath. It was the least a partner could do. He said, "I'm on my way in now, if it's any of your business."

"Good," Lopes said, "get your ass in here. I need you to roll with me out to Pico."

Dickie knew he meant Pico Rivera, a city south and east of downtown L.A. which contracts with the sheriff's department for law enforcement services, but he wasn't certain if Lopes was talking about going somewhere in the city, or to the sheriff's station, aptly named Pico Rivera station. He said, "What's up in Pico?"

"Your mother's ankles. Now hurry up, get your ass in here."

Lopes hung up and Dickie grinned as he turned his radio back up, thinking, *You asshole, Lopes,* then focused on the tail end of another traffic report.

Traffic slowed, so he shot Josie a text:

> Some dude beefed you for riding his ass.

While waiting for a reply, he thought about any cases Josie might be working where a suspect or person of interest could have felt the pressures of an old sore being reopened. That was exactly what it must've felt like to have thought you'd gotten away with murder, only to have a couple of homicide cops knock on your door again ten or twenty years later. That type of surprise contact could sometimes be enough to crack a case wide open, the proverbial floodgates of guilt giving way to the relief of repentance. Dickie thrived on such occurrences. It was the thing he had come to enjoy most about working unsolved cases, showing up on the steps of people who thought they had gotten away with something, thought that the cops had stopped trying. All too often, that was the case—they *had* stopped trying. You could only reopen so many unsolved cases every year, which meant hundreds of them never got a second look. Which made clearing cold cases that much more rewarding.

Perhaps that's what he'd be doing later with Lopes, opening an old wound to see what happened. It was always entertaining to watch the Marine captain-turned-homicide cop put the screws to a guy, especially if that guy was a gangster. Lopes was merciless when it came to gang-bangers, and he had a gift for breaking them.

Dickie saw that Josie was typing a response.

> JOSIE
> ...

Or was she?

> ...

Finally, short and to the point:

> WTF?

> IDK... just what Lopes said. Captain was looking for you.

There were more dots, but then they stopped, and no text appeared to replace them. Traffic was moving again, so Dickie placed his phone back in its cradle and got lost in his thoughts as he crept along in the number one lane, crowding the median to have a better look at what he was up against in this morning's commute. He was thinking about the allegation of Josie stalking someone, and it took him back to the case in which she had been kidnapped and held in the mountains by a game warden named Jacob Spencer. But it hadn't been obvious that it was Spencer who had done it, and it took a year of Josie gnawing on that bone like a true bulldog would before enough evidence was gathered to charge him. Some might have said she stalked him, too, but isn't that what a good detective did? Spencer had hung himself just before the trial started, and Josie had been alone with him in lockup shortly before it happened. Dickie sometimes imagined things that he would keep to himself when pondering to what lengths Josie might go to put a bad man away.

> **JOSIE**
> Can you get a drink after work tonight? We need to talk.

Great, he thought. Whatever it was that the captain had on his plate, Josie must've known it was coming. With traffic now moving along, he opted to hold off on replying just yet. He'd contemplate the whole thing for a while and also find out what the wife had planned for the evening before committing to drinks with Josie. Besides, it wasn't as if they couldn't step outside the office later and discuss whatever they needed to talk about, Dickie knowing it was most likely related to this beef Lopes had told him about.

He had to admit that he was more than a little curious, eager to find out who had lodged a complaint and what it was about. After all, there were few cases that Josie had worked without him, which meant there was a fair chance he would at least know something about it. But nothing came to him at the moment, so he wondered if it were even about a homicide case. Maybe it was something personal, a domestic situation. Maybe Josie was stalking an annoying neighbor, or a hot UPS driver or, God forbid, some hose jockey she met at the gym. It always struck him as odd how little he knew about her personal life.

3

JOSIE FINISHED HER TESTIMONY AND REMAINED IN THE COURTROOM IN THE role of an investigating officer, taking her seat next to McKnight. It was impromptu, not something previously planned or discussed, but a fairly common practice in homicide cases nonetheless. Though the murder of Trinidad Flores was not a complex one, and it was unlikely that the prosecutor would benefit from her remaining at his side, Josie had another agenda. There was something she needed to find out, a so-far unresolved personal mystery, one on which McKnight could perhaps shed some light.

She and McKnight had recently spent an evening preparing for the trial. Afterward, they had gone for drinks, and for the first time in her life, Josie couldn't remember everything that *may* have happened. In fact, she couldn't remember much of it at all. She hadn't had that much to drink—that, she did know—so she should have been able to clearly recall the events of the entire night. But she couldn't.

They had been alone in his office, a small private room on the seventeenth floor of the criminal courts building with a view of the hall of justice across the street, going over her testimony for the trial. It had been a bit overdone, she knew, given the simplicity of the case: two men argued in a bar, they took it outside, and one fatally stabbed the other. Nonetheless, there she had sat late into the evening, confined to a room deco-

The Program

rated with certificates and awards and photographs memorializing McKnight's days on the campus of Chapman University and the Fowler School of Law, as well as on its football turf. Josie had pondered that evening what position he might have played, since he was of only average height and had the build of a runner. Maybe he had been a kicker, or he played safety, a position where speed was more important than size. She had resisted asking so as not to stoke his ego or step onto the slippery slope of mixing business with pleasure. Not that any of her thoughts about him—that evening or in the days and nights that followed—necessarily delved into the pleasurable, or at least not all of them had. Though she would admit, if only to herself, that it had been difficult to suppress the memory of frat boy standing up from behind his desk and plunging a hand deep into the front and then back of his slacks under the guise of tucking in his dress shirt. There was something to be said for narrow hips and a flat stomach on a thirty-something man who spends the bulk of his days behind a desk or in a courtroom.

Following the unabashed adjustments of his wardrobe, McKnight had glanced at his watch and announced that there was time to catch the last of the USC game at Brandy's, a local sports bar with good food and drinks and a big-screen television outside for patio dwellers, which McKnight had suggested would be perfect that evening. She had been caught off guard and couldn't come up with a plausible reason to refuse, so instead she had said, "You don't have anyone expecting you home soon?" She cringed after she said it, thinking she may as have just asked if he planned to take her to bed after. To her actual question, though, he had replied, "Just Chappy, but I'll call my neighbor and have her let him out for me," explaining that Chappy was his Chinese crested, a breed of dog with which Josie was unfamiliar. She had said, "Chinese what?" picturing some type of pug.

Chappy. He had named his toy dog after his preppy school, this intellectual prosecutor who was quick on his feet and probably even faster with his hands, given the speed at which he had shoved one of them deep into the crotch of his slacks right in front of her that night. And what was with the neighbor? *She* would come over and take care of the dog... Josie wagered that this slutty girl-next-door took care of more than just the dog on his lap. And what straight men owned lap dogs anyway? Or was the young lawyer gay? She had pondered that for a moment and then decided it couldn't hurt to have a drink with the man.

So she had gone with him to this Brandy's joint, leaving her car at the courthouse and riding in his BMW because he had told her parking would be at a premium at the pub. She remembered being wedged between McKnight and another thirty-something professional who had shed his tie and worn an open collar, and whose dark eyes contrasted with his overdone toothy smile. Mr. Smiley had greeted her—how could he not; they were exchanging body heat through summer threads, each turned toward their own dates but likely thinking of the stranger beside them whose physical touch was incidental, although not necessarily unwelcome. Certainly not for him, Josie knew.

When McKnight went to the restroom, Smiley made his play, his elbow *accidentally* finding its way beneath the back of her arm and brushing across the side of Josie's breast. They each turned the quarter-turn it took to look into the other's eyes, and Smiley apologized profusely, assured her he hadn't meant to cop a feel—in so many words—and offered to buy her a drink. Of course Josie declined, and her eyes met those of the stranger's companion, a bottle-blonde with heavy makeup and tired eyes that told Josie the bitch was loaded—on what, she had no idea. Droopy forced a smile, as if she were resigned to whatever would or would not happen. Josie turned away from them both, taking the opportunity to scoot her stool a few inches away from Smiley to avoid further contact. She had been hit on by couples before, and she knew how that felt. Smiley and Droopy were looking for a threesome, or maybe even a foursome. Either way, they were looking in the wrong direction.

Josie remembered Mc-what's-his-face returning and having to stand as Josie had left no room for him at the bar in her effort to separate herself from the perverts. As McKnight stood behind her, Josie rotated on her stool for a more intimate setting with him, a subtle message to her neighbors that she was only interested in her date. But was she? Was it even a date? She didn't know. What she did know, though, was that her back was to the bar, and her drink behind her, out of her view. She knew better than to take her eyes off of a drink when out at bars, yet she had somehow managed to overlook that precaution as she focused on ending any interaction with Smiley. At some point, McKnight reached over her to get her drink, and then his, from the bar. With a simple nod, he had suggested they move to a nearby table. Had he noticed something about Smiley as well? She followed him across the patio, where they slid into a more private setting for two as another couple left it.

Josie had no recollection of anything beyond that moment until she awoke the next morning in a king-size bed with satin sheets and a naked dog staring at her. Thankfully, the hairless crested was the only one in the buff. Josie was somewhat relieved to see she was wearing her panties and an oversized T-shirt advertising a CrossFit gym she had never heard of, which had caused her to wonder where she was. She hoped she was with the deputy district attorney with whom she had gone out for drinks. But why did she have no recollection of getting there?

As it turned out, she had accurately assessed that much of the mystery. Shortly after she had awoken, McKnight appeared with coffee in hand. He had demonstrated sincere concern for her well-being, mentioning the condition she had been in by the time they left the pub, that there was no way she could have driven home. He told her she had really been out of it, and she wasn't even able to tell him where she lived so he could drive her there. As he had fussed with her pillows, encouraging her to sit up and have some coffee, he told her he had even thought to look for an ID in her purse so that he could get her home, but the sight of a pistol therein had deterred him from further intrusion.

Josie had ended the pillow talk when a sudden wave of nausea washed over her. She tossed off the covers and pushed past her lawyer host and rushed to the bathroom to throw up, but she found herself mostly dry heaving. That answered the one question she had awakened with: how much had she drunk? Very little, she surmised. It didn't happen often—and not for a very long time—but Josie knew what throwing up after overindulging looked like.

That had brought up the next question, one upon which she deliberated extensively while composing herself to the extent she could behind the closed bathroom door, and with which she still wrestled: could she have blacked out if she hadn't consumed much alcohol? Josie had never experienced any such loss of consciousness and memory, even when she had drunk to excess. Drinking with cops tested the limits of one's ability to handle their alcohol, and Josie—no different from her peers—had become a serious practitioner of consumption. With cops, it began as camaraderie, and oftentimes, for many, morphed into an unacknowledged necessary coping mechanism. So how had she found herself in such an awkward, inexplicable situation?

The lawyer, with his perfect hospitality, had left her with a new toothbrush, clean linens, a piece of dry toast and a soft drink for her upset stomach to replace the untouched coffee. An hour later, he dropped her off at her car, the charcoal-gray Dodge Charger one of a half dozen sedans speckling the vast flat of pavement behind the idle courthouse on a tranquil Saturday morning. She had spent the remainder of that day curled in her bed battling extreme bouts of nausea and unrelenting muscle aches. It had occurred to her that perhaps she had a case of influenza, and later that evening—when she was physically able—she scoured the internet to see if any such combination of the flu and alcohol could result in memory loss. It didn't seem to be the case.

McKnight, who had provided her with his business card early in their association, complete with his personal cell phone number, had since avoided any contact that hadn't been directly linked to their business relationship. Josie had even texted him two or three times to ask if she should bring his T-shirt to his office or mail it to his home. But he hadn't bothered to reply.

The evasive action on McKnight's part had only strengthened her suspicion about him and that regrettable Friday night. Josie had decided she would confront him, and now that her testimony on the one case she had with him was finished, she was compelled to do so without further delay. She would accompany him to his office during the lunch break, close the door behind her, and get to the point. *Why are you avoiding me? What happened that night, Mr. McKnight? I want the truth.* Or maybe the direct approach: *Did you slip me a roofie, you lawyerly son of a bitch?*

4

DICKIE AND LOPES INCHED ALONG THE ALWAYS-CONGESTED SIDE STREETS of Monterey Park, destined for Pico Rivera. It was a straight shot from the office, south on Garfield and across Washington. The two street names conjured images in Dickie's head: a cat and a general, the latter of course being a founding father of our great nation, and our first president. With the dismantling of statues, the rewriting of American history, and the hatred of America's founding principles, Dickie wondered if Washington Boulevard would someday be renamed. It wouldn't surprise him. Maybe they'd change it to BLM Boulevard or ANTIFA Avenue. The world was shifting rapidly, and Dickie didn't like it. He agonized about the future of his beloved country and the way of life that normal working-class Americans enjoyed. His son, now a year old and beginning to walk, would experience a very different world than Dickie had, and the thought of that depressed him.

Lopes said, "What're you over there contemplating, Dickie? Worried about your partner?"

He'd been staring off through his window, watching the world around him, seeing the changes and feeling the tension. Everyone seemed angry, beady eyes the only glimpse you'd ever see of anyone now, everyone masked against the China virus. That's what he called it in spite of the backlash he would occasionally get from others for doing so. If there was one thing you could count on Dickie not to be, it was politically correct. There was more to all of this—the virus, the masks, the spread of radicalism across the nation—and he felt something bad was coming. He knew to trust his gut on these things, because you didn't survive twenty-five years as a cop in L.A. without good instinct.

"Maybe a little. She'll be okay, I'm sure. Whatever it is, it can't be worse than whacking a dude in lockup," Dickie said, and gave a little chuckle to imply he was kidding.

Their eyes met for a brief moment before Lopes turned his attention back to the road. Dickie watched him carefully, looking for any kind of a tell. Neither Lopes nor Josie had ever again brought up the incident that occurred in the court lockup during the trial of Jacob Spencer. The case had just begun when the game warden was found hanging in the courtroom holding cell. Josie had been back to see him shortly before it happened, a very unusual situation that caused some to speculate about what had pushed Spencer to the point of suicide. There were other unanswered questions: Why had he been allowed to keep his belt? The bailiff couldn't recall whether or not he had removed it before placing Spencer in his cell, though that was the procedure. Of course, he had used the belt to hang himself, so this was an important detail. Also, why had Josie been alone with him? There weren't many reasons a detective would have to talk to a defendant once a trial had started, and it was inappropriate to do so without his attorney being present. And what about the bailiff? Why wouldn't he have been with her during that time? But Dickie mostly wondered about the camera in the corner. It was said there was no recording, but was that actually the case? Or had Lopes, who had been the primary investigator of the inmate death, taken some type of action to destroy or conceal it for Josie's sake? Dickie didn't think Lopes would do that if there had been a crime committed—say, murder, for example—but perhaps Josie had done some other thing that aided or encouraged Spencer to take his own life. Would Lopes have cleaned her up on something like that? They were good friends, and Lopes had, at one time, been interested in her romantically. But what single cop—and half the married ones, for that matter—hadn't?

As Dickie continued to study the hardened veteran cop behind the

The Program

wheel, he wondered why he had thrown the comment out there at Lopes. It was chickenshit of him to do so, and he knew it. Completely out of bounds and out of character, truthfully. He had tried to play it off as a joke, but it had been an obvious attempt to get a reaction. And Lopes hadn't given him one.

Dickie turned his gaze back to the passing scenery on his side of the car, regretting that he had said it. Holding his gaze on two winos who appeared to be arguing at the side of a liquor store, Dickie said, "That was a shitty thing for me to have said about my partner."

A moment passed before Lopes responded. "Yeah, it was."

Dickie turned his attention back to Lopes as they came to a stop in a line of cars waiting to turn left. Lopes met his gaze and said, "She didn't do anything that you and I wouldn't have done, and you need to put that whole thing behind you and never bring it up again."

Dickie considered it briefly. "It's not my nature to let things go when there are unanswered questions. You know that about me. You're no different. None of us are. That's why we do what we do, and why we're good at it."

The green arrow appeared and set them back in motion, Lopes now focused on the traffic as they headed east on Washington. He kept his eyes straight ahead and spoke flatly. "There's nothing else to know, no unanswered questions. Spencer hung himself with his belt, and Josie had nothing to do with it. Now drop it, would ya?"

"What about the video?" Dickie snapped, immediately regretting it.

Lopes glanced over. "There was no video, Dickie. Now fucking drop it."

JOSIE LEFT THE COURTHOUSE FEELING WEAK AND PATHETIC, ANGRY WITH herself for not handling McKnight better when he blew her off. He had told her that he had other plans, that he had agreed to have lunch with a colleague, so he didn't have time to chat with her in his office—not even for a few minutes. They had been standing in the hallway just outside of the courtroom, each with arms full of files and surrounded by the flow of people leaving for lunch as well. She had considered calling him out then and there, but she knew better than to make a scene in the hallway outside a courtroom. You never knew when jurors were near, and when they were, their eyes and ears were always wide open.

Pulling out of the parking lot behind the courthouse, Josie's thoughts shifted to what might await her at the office. Someone had beefed her, or so Dickie had informed her through a text message that she had read on one of the breaks, and the captain had gone into Unsolveds this morning looking for her. Should she sneak in and try to avoid him, or go straight to his office and find out what was going on? She couldn't think of anything she had done that might warrant a legitimate complaint being filed against her. Most of the cases she was working on involved intensive case file review and resubmitting evidence in cases where technological advances might help identify a suspect. DNA had been solving decades-old cases for years, and every unsolved unit in the country had teams of investigators going through cold cases looking for evidence that could be re-examined at the lab.

Josie had recently reviewed the unsolved murder of a fourteen-year-old boy who had been killed by a single gunshot that originated from the distant rifle of a concealed shooter. The scope had been discovered in the sniper's hide, apparently knocked off the rifle during the shooter's hasty escape. It was the only physical evidence in the case, and it had been submitted for fingerprints during the initial investigation, but none were found. And although DNA was a thing at the time of that murder, back at the turn of the century, the investigators hadn't considered also submitting the scope to check it for DNA evidence. Back then, it was usually blood, some type of bodily fluid, or hair that would be considered for DNA testing. But the advancement of technology now allowed scientists to analyze smaller and smaller biological samples to develop a DNA profile, and it had been discovered that even skin cells left behind on an object could provide a source of DNA. It occurred to Josie that the recovered rifle scope in the young teen's murder might just have such "touch DNA" evidence—a skin cell, an eyelash, dried remnants from droplets of sweat —and as she had said to her partner, it was worth a shot. She had winked to emphasize the pun, and Dickie had just rolled his eyes. She hadn't yet contacted any persons of interest in that case, as she was still awaiting results from the crime lab.

There were other cold cases she was reviewing, but none she could recall that had resulted in any contact where a complaint might have been made.

Josie was driving uncharacteristically slowly toward the office, utilizing surface streets rather than the freeway to give herself more time to think about it. Since early childhood, she had experienced ulcer-like stomach pangs when trouble loomed. Unfortunately, she seemed to find herself in precarious situations more often than most others, in her view. Yes, she had a mischievous streak, and oftentimes she had brushed aside caution for the thrill of the moment, like the time she and a girlfriend stole her parents' car and drove it to school when she was thirteen.

She still suffered with guilt over an adolescent crime that she hadn't given much thought to until she sought to become a deputy sheriff. When she had applied to the department and was given a background packet to complete, there had been a question about any crimes she might have committed, whether or not said wrongdoings had been detected, attributed to her, or even reported. This had caused Josie great angst as she fretted about the fake ID she had obtained at age eighteen and had used quite regularly until she turned twenty-one. It wasn't even a cheap, counterfeit ID; rather, it was a real one, issued by the DMV based on a real birth certificate she had obtained for just that purpose. How else would a girl who loved to dance get into clubs every weekend? Maria Luna had been her weekend alias for three years, and she well knew when she obtained it that she was committing a crime. She didn't know then that it was a felony, but she realized it shortly after becoming a cop. Josie hadn't thought it necessary to mention the ID in her background paperwork, so for months she had agonized about the impending polygraph examination, which she somehow managed to pass. More than a decade later, she still worried that her past would catch up to her, and each time she was summoned to see the captain, she would wonder if it had. She would think about that damn ID with her flirtatious little eighteen-year-old smile and the mischievous eyes to match, and she knew that someday it would all catch up to her. She would be relieved of her badge and gun and issued a new set of stainless-steel bracelets. Or would they use her own? At times like this, it would occur to her that she needed to dig out that old relic and destroy it. Get rid of the evidence. Jesus, how many people had she sent to prison because they weren't smart enough to get rid of evidence?

But today's trouble had nothing to do with her past transgressions. This was job-related, obviously. Someone had beefed her about something she had done, though she had no idea who that was or what it could have been about. Either way, she told herself—now sipping ice water from a turquoise Yeti tumbler with her MAC Coffee & Cigs lipstick smudges on the straw, unable to quench her sudden thirst—that whatever this was, it had nothing to do with past indiscretions.

Or did it?

She thought about the Coffee & Cigs-shaded DNA she had left on her straw, and it brought her back to the rifle scope and her hope that a DNA profile might come back from the lab on the sniper case. To solve the murder of a fourteen-year-old boy would bring her great satisfaction. The fact that the kid had been killed by a cold-blooded, chickenshit son of a bitch hiding in the bushes on the other side of a parking lot and behind a fence, motivated her even more. Whatever issue the captain had on his desk at the time, she had the Rusty Potter case as her ace in the hole. *I'm on the brink of breaking it open, taking down a child-murdering sniper!*

Josie made a mental note to check in with the crime lab on the Potter case as she turned into the parking lot. She blew out a long breath she hadn't realized she'd been holding, and thought, *here we go.*

5

Josie keyed the back door open and started for her desk while scanning the office to see which allies and enemies were about this morning. Not that she had many enemies, but there were those she didn't trust, and others who made her skin crawl. The former included a host of other female investigators who Josie knew talked behind everyone's back, even one another's, like gossiping old ladies at bingo or the hair salon. The latter—those who made her skin crawl—were a few of her male counterparts whose primary focuses were her girl parts rather than their cases. Some of each were present, along with other investigators for whom Josie had no feelings one way or the other. Not that she was dismissive of others, but she lived her life with the principle that everyone was free to be themselves, to live however they chose to as long as those choices didn't adversely affect others.

She set her purse, briefcase, and poor boy folder on her chair and glanced down the hallway toward the captain's office. From her desk in Unsolveds she could see the doorway to his office, but she couldn't see inside. The door was open and the light was on, but then again it almost always was—that was no indicator as to whether or not the skipper was at the helm.

About a third, or possibly fewer, of the investigators assigned to the bureau were in the office, which also was not uncommon, given the complex scheduling that divided the eighty-some investigators into six teams that were rotated through the on-call and barrel duties. Josie didn't miss being in the rotation for murders and receiving the middle-of-the-night callouts, though she did long for the immediacy of a fresh crime scene and the hunt for a killer. It was far different viewing photographs of scenes from long ago and pursuing suspects who didn't even realize someone still cared, than it was to take a case from the start.

Her desk phone rang as she rose out of her chair, and she gave it a sideways glance. Josie ignored it and started for the skipper's office. Because in spite of her trepidation about the topic du jour, she knew her stomach wouldn't settle until she faced whatever trouble she might now be in.

Captain Stover glanced up from his computer screen as she gave the door a light courtesy tap and stepped into his office. He leaned back in his chair and, with a nod of his head, silently directed her to take a seat in one of the two chairs that sat at the front of his desk. But before the captain's signal, Josie had already started for the one on the right. It was the seat she preferred, but she wasn't sure why. She pondered this briefly and realized that every other time she'd met with the captain—other than when she first came to the bureau and was given the cursory *Welcome to Homicide and don't fuck up* speech—she had been accompanied by her partner, Dickie. He always took the seat to the left, and now, for the first time, she wondered why. With Dickie, it was likely a matter of a tactical advantage —he was hardwired that way. Josie looked around the office as if she had never seen it before, wondering what advantage the other seat might offer. She moved over—a last minute change from the right seat to the left—and Stover frowned, likely contemplating her actions. As she settled into Dickie's preferred chair, she looked around from this new vantage point, searching for some revelation the way one might explore Buddhism—with a medley of foreboding, curiosity, and hope. All she could figure was that Dickie preferred this position because his back would be slightly less to the door than it would be from the seat to the right, and that might have been his only reasoning. She was a little disheartened.

Josie's thoughts faded as the captain's voice boomed in her ear and the familiar name he spoke reverberated in her head: "…Rudy Prada…"

The Program

Her gaze was fixed on the man before her, but she only saw the scene outside of a liquor store in East L.A., the *cholo* wrapped in a heavy jacket on a cool day, a call she received about a man with a gun, a single ray of sunlight glistening off the object in his hand as he removed it from his pocket and faced her. She had drawn her weapon instinctually, and *BAM!*

She was jolted from the reverie by the captain's sudden fist on his desk. He said, "Have you heard a thing I said?"

Josie nodded, now noticing the captain's gold pen set at the corner of his desk, the corner closer to Dickie's seat where she suddenly felt slightly more secure during this otherwise very uncomfortable moment. She wondered if Dickie had ever considered the pens as potential weapons. She pictured him leaping across the table and jabbing one of the two writing instruments and makeshift weapons into the captain's neck after finally losing all his marbles—something she and others sometimes feared Dickie might someday do, and then she considered that perhaps she had watched too many Italian mafia movies, thinking even Dickie wasn't that insane.

Stover was saying, "I'm asking you about Prada, the gangbanger you shot way back when. You remember him, right?"

She nodded, still feeling distant. A near out-of-body experience. Now she felt the itch in her boot again. The maggots. Always the fucking maggots when the pressure was on. Maybe there was something more to that phenomenon—she'd have to explore that with a shrink, something she'd been thinking she might need to do sooner rather than later. She and Dickie could go together.

"What I want to know is what reason you could possibly have to be in contact with him again. Did his name come up in a case you're working on? Please tell me his name came up on an unsolved you and Jones picked up."

She grabbed one of the two pens from the captain's desk, picturing Prada. Seeing Dickie for a moment too, the pen a weapon in the hands of a detective pushed too far. But then she saw Prada again, the handsome ex-con behind the podium during the meeting, and it occurred to her that this was what it was about—Prada must've thought she was on his ass again. Maybe a guilty conscience, or just plain paranoia. No problem then. If Prada and the meeting were why she was here, Josie knew she had done nothing wrong. Her only concern at all now would be how to negotiate the whole AA meeting conversation that would necessarily follow. How might she deal with that? First, anonymous meant anonymous, right? She didn't have to tell him a thing. She *shouldn't* tell him a thing about her looking into the program, because it was very personal. And meant to be anonymous. If she were to tell anyone anything about that, she'd have to explain the blackout that led her there.

He was saying, "Do you have a file you can show me that would justify you tracking this man down?" but slowing his speech, his brow furrowed as he stared at his gold pen in her hand, coming away from its holder, now disappearing beneath the surface of the desk, Josie bending forward in her chair.

She shoved the pen down her boot and stabbed at the itch that seemed to crawl along the side of her calf. Josie raised her eyes and looked at the frowning captain through a lock of hair falling on her face as he said, "... though I would hope you'd be smarter than to take the lead on a case involving a guy you once tried to kill. Especially since it was a questionable shooting as I recall."

Josie sat up at the edge of her seat and stared at the captain a long moment, still holding his pen that she'd used to scratch her leg, the pen now clenched in her fist, pointing at him. "Questionable?" she said. "A man with a gun who tried to rob a liquor store?"

"Didn't he only have a beer?"

"No. I mean, yes, it was a beer he pulled from his pocket. But he did have a gun."

"The point is," the captain continued, and Josie's gaze drifted to the wall behind him, a canvas of self-congratulatory awards and portraits of his various menial accomplishments. The only two captains she had ever served under who were real cops—*by any real cop's standards*—had been at her last assignment, Gangs. One, Jerry Townsend, a former SWAT deputy who had been shot twice while pulling a mortally wounded partner to safety during an SLA-style shootout in Watts, had been her greatest mentor when she was a young detective, and some might say had become her rabbi—someone who looked out for an underling for the remainder of his or her days. She very much missed Jerry, a man gone before his time. His office had been adorned with sports memorabilia on the walls and pictures of his family on his desk, nothing to boast his accomplishments, of which there were many. The other captain she had respected greatly had been Ernie Guzman, a man who had grown up poor in the barrios of Los Angeles, served in the army during Vietnam, and had chipped away at college during his early years as a deputy sheriff, eventually earning a master's degree from the University of Southern California. On his office wall hung portraits of the department executives: the sheriff, his undersheriff and two assistant sheriffs, and nothing else. Similarly, his desktop held a few family photographs and a glass beer stein with the Dodgers logo holding an assortment of pens and highlighters. Josie had worked in this predominantly male environment long enough now to easily recognize the attempts of some to mask their inadequacies as nothing short of dick measuring.

Her thoughts, though, remained on the last words she had registered, the captain asking if there was some justification for her being in contact with Rudy Prada. She would have to come up with something that would satisfy him—she wasn't about to tell him the truth. Couldn't she just say she went to a meeting and there he was? The skipper wouldn't buy that. *What sort of meeting?* he'd demand. And that took everything full circle to the whole anonymous thing. Because that was all she needed, rumors starting that Josie had a drinking problem—even if half the people at the bureau probably did.

So the best thing would be to put a case on Prada, pick some random unsolved case with Mexican gangs and say she got a tip. After all, the dude *is* a gangster, right? Okay, maybe a former gangster. But a tiger doesn't change its stripes, right?

What she needed to do, Josie was now thinking as the captain continued prattling on about citizen complaints and something else, was to find an unsolved murder involving the members of *Maravilla*. She knew from her time working gangs in East Los Angeles that there were numerous murders attributed to them, just as there were many murders attributed to the various gangs everywhere. All she would have to do is find one unsolved case where *Maravilla* had been suspected to be involved, and then come up with a theory that Prada might have information about it. Easy-peasy. She could go as far as to call him a suspect, but that would be crossing a line Josie never wanted to cross. It was one thing to lean on the gangsters because they were dirty or because they had information on other cases, but another thing altogether to brand someone a killer, if they weren't. Sure, Prada had been a thug, and yes, he had shot at least one person Josie knew of for sure. But then again, she had shot Prada once herself, and she had shot a few others, but that didn't make her a murderer. There was a big gray area in life on the streets—from both sides of the law.

So that was it. She'd tell the captain that yes, she was working a case, and Prada might be a key to solving it. He'll want some details, maybe even a case number to throw on the citizen complaint before he files it away, but she would need some time to find a case. An afternoon, maybe. Or if she could put the captain off until the morning, she could stay as late as she needed in order to find a good East L.A. murder to reopen, to come up to speed on the facts, and to create some nexus to Rudy Prada.

She glanced at her watch as Stover finished with a last attempt for clarification on the matter, saying, "...if you have a good reason to be putting pressure on this guy, you better state your case now. We can no longer kiss off complaints just because we're Homicide. The commander gets a copy of every single beef and he expects them to be resolved one way or the other before he sees them."

As she was about to mention that yes, she was working a case, and she'd bring him up to speed on it tomorrow or the next day at the latest, but right now—she would glance at her watch again—she was needed back in court, which of course was a lie. That would be the perfect way to stall the skipper and give her the breathing room she needed.

She met the captain's expectant gaze just as the captain's secretary appeared in the doorway, the tactically advantaged position of Dickie's seat allowing Josie to pick her up immediately in her peripheral vision. She offered a smile and said, "Hi, Kathy."

Kathy didn't smile back. Shifting her uneasy gaze toward the captain, she said, "Sir, there's been a deputy-involved shooting in Pico Rivera."

6

Stover regarded his secretary for a long moment. In the brief silence, Josie's mind kicked into high gear and her body temperature rose —she felt the warmth rise from her stomach through her throat and into her face as she reflected on a couple of text messages she had received from Lopes that morning. He had asked where she was, was she coming into the office today, did she want to go to Pico with him for some follow-up on a case. During a recess when the jury was out of the courtroom and the judge had gone back to his chambers, and her predator prosecutor had busied himself conversing with defense counsel—the defendant no longer at the table, back in lockup for some alone time—she had scrolled through her texts and saw that Dickie had warned her about the captain and this complaint she now had to deal with. Her mother had also texted wanting to know if she could pick up drinking water on the way home. Josie had thought, *Yes, water and tequila, honey*—her mother one of several people in her life currently pushing her over the edge. As for the text from Lopes asking if she was coming into the office and did she want to roll with him out to Pico, she had simply replied that she was in court. He had said fine, she could buy him a drink later, and since she wasn't available, he'd get Dickie to go with him. She could see the two of them in her mind's eye, two big guys crammed into Lopes's Ford Taurus in their shirt sleeves and ties, Dickie with his fedora, the two of them talking sex and murder while sipping coffee they took with them from the office in Styrofoam cups, neither of them the type to stop for a cup at Starbucks or any other trendy coffee joint. Then she saw them coming to a sudden halt, the way it always happened: one minute you're shooting the shit and the next minute you're tossing your cup of coffee out the window and bailing out of the car while your pistol's breaking leather and your pucker factor's hitting eight, nine, ten—and the shoot/don't shoot factors are processed in an instant. A decision is made that can never be reversed, and that will have a ripple effect that changes the lives of many, far more than most people would ever consider. But she couldn't see what happened next, and she hoped it was because she had the wrong picture, that it wasn't Dickie and Lopes busting caps in Pico, just a coincidence that they had gone out there. More likely, it had been a patrol deputy, maybe a pair of them, stopping a gangster who goes for a gat while trying to get away, pulls the piece from his pocket and they put him down before he can get a shot off at them—that was a best-case scenario. She could see that one all the way through, so maybe—she hoped—that's what had happened out in Pico Rivera. And that's what she held on to while she waited for the captain to ask what had happened or for his secretary to realize from his intent stare that he wanted more information—*Jesus, don't keep us in suspense, lady.*

Stover finally said, "Well..." and she still waited for another long moment, clearly troubled by something she knew and everyone else in the room was waiting to hear. Josie was about to grab one of Stover's pens again. Finally, the secretary said, "A deputy's been shot."

Josie pushed out of her chair and said, "I'm rolling," and before either the captain or his secretary could speak another word, she was down the hall and angling toward her desk at the pace of seniors who may have been runners in their youth but have taken to power walking because their knees have failed their sinewy bodies, yet the need for movement still drove them to the sidewalks and paseos every morning in shorts and white sneakers with white socks. Josie grabbed her keys, a radio, and her attaché case—as almost an afterthought—and hurried toward the back door, a wave of adrenaline nearly muting the sounds around her: chatter, laughter, the ringing of phones, someone saying, "Josie, what's up?"

That question hung in her mind as she tore out of the parking lot imagining the worst of all possibilities—a cop had been killed. But if that wasn't bad enough, it might have been someone she knew. Someone she worked with. Someone she loved.

Josie swiped her phone and glanced at the screen to unlock it, thumbed the button to assure the smart device that she wasn't driving, while screeching around a corner and then gunning the motor of her county-issued Dodge Charger and racing up the onramp of the Pomona Freeway heading east. The surface street route was shorter, but she'd be there much faster pushing a hundred on the interstate whenever the conditions allowed it. She flipped a switch to activate both the flashing blue and amber lights on the rear deck—what Dickie always called the *excuse me* lights—and a solid red that was situated against the top of the windshield by the rearview mirror, each completely undetectable on the unmarked car when not in use.

As she merged onto the freeway, she tried calling her partner, but he didn't answer. Now she wished she hadn't called, the lack of response another reason to worry and to dwell on the possibilities. Traffic on the freeway headed east was light, as she had assumed it would be, so Josie moved across the lanes of traffic to the number one and settled in at about 90 mph. She knew she'd take Rosemead south, but it occurred to her she didn't know where in Pico the deputy-involved shooting had taken place. Josie called her office and spoke with Miguel at the front desk, and she asked that he text her the address. She placed her phone on the magnet affixed to the air vent and adjusted it so she would see the message pop up on her screen, and she let out a heavy breath. "Dear God, don't let it be those two knuckleheads."

7

Rudy Prada had a busy day ahead of him, but felt better having the priority of the day behind him, lodging the complaint against the lady cop. He couldn't get his mind off her, which is to say he would see her in his meeting at the back of the room, and then the scene would change and he would see her crouched between the open door and the interior of the black and white cop car, the barrel of her handgun pointed at him. He would inevitably see the flash of light and remember the searing pain, and he would involuntarily reach for the scarred tissue on his abdomen. The last frame of this particular horror show would include the morning she stood over his naked body in bed, pointing her gun at him again, Rudy sure the crazy lady cop was going to pull the trigger on him *again*, yet he somehow remained mesmerized by her piercing brown-eyed gaze. And, as twisted as it would sound if he were to ever tell anyone about it—Mikey, perhaps, or Bobby Young, his sponsor in the program, though he couldn't imagine ever telling either one of them these bizarre and intimate thoughts —that his very real recollection of these terribly traumatic events would evolve into a sexual fantasy: he and the lady cop alone in his bed, the other cops waiting elsewhere in the small house in East L.A. with Vero and the kids. She holsters her gun and leans in for a kiss, her silky brown hair covering his face as her pouty lips lightly touch his own, their tongues

The Program

gently flicking together, and her warm, moist breath engulfing him. She slowly lowers herself onto him while he helps her out of her jacket with the badge on its chest, and her gun belt next, freeing the two of them of the only two things that stood between them, physically and perhaps metaphorically too.

Now he felt guilty about making the complaint, and he wondered what the process would be for him to take it back—what did they call that, retracing?... reneging? He had a business card they gave him with a form; hopefully it would have information about how to undo the complaint. After all, maybe she had come to the meeting for another reason. He realized his reaction had been somewhat hasty, but Jesus, she was the last person he ever expected to cross paths with again once he had moved out of the hood and straightened out his life, to the degree he was able.

Although now that he considered it, maybe God had put her back in his life for a reason. After all, there were several steps of his program that required him to make amends for the things he'd done that had harmed others, and to admit these things to God and at least one person. He had told Vero, but she didn't seem to grasp the gravity of this act, simply saying, "I've done worse shit than that, baby." Saying, "Why you telling me now, baby?" Saying, "Lookit, I don't want to know about all the hoochie mamas you hooked up with back in the day, and if you did any of that homo shit in the joint, you keep that bullshit to yourself."

The lady cop—this Detective Sanchez—she would be good at listening, Rudy reasoned as he cruised down Whittier Boulevard, his next stop the parole office, where he looked forward to showing his progress in the way a child brings home a good report card. Rudy thought of it this way and cringed at what a punk he was being with this newfound need to fit into society as a fully reformed convict and budding responsible citizen. The lady cop, same thing. He wanted to show her he wasn't a bad guy anymore. But why? Why did he care what she thought, this woman who had shot him, terrorized him, sent him to prison twice?

It was the program.

This time, for some reason, he was serious about changing his way of life, even though it was clear he didn't quite have it all worked out as to how he would go about doing this, and to what extent. He wondered if Vero would even be part of his new life, and maybe that was one reason he sought the lady cop's approval. Rudy had been in various court-ordered programs half a dozen times, yet never before had he actually had a desire to change who he was and how he behaved. He'd show up to get his card signed verifying that he was there, and then it was back to the hood with his homies and his bitches and his smoke and his forty ouncers. But not anymore. Not now. He was determined.

He wheeled into the parking lot of the parole office and scanned the *vatos* loitering outside to make sure there were no potential conflicts before getting out of his hoop. Maybe that was part of it; he was tired of living the outlaw life, tired of looking over his shoulder. He set his shades on the dash and looked into the mirror as he ran a plastic comb through his hair and then his thick black mustache before going inside. And for an instant, he wondered if even the 'stache could remain, a symbol of the veteran *vato*, potentially an attractant of law enforcement. That was the other part of it all: he'd need to learn to draw no attention, to fit in, to actually blend with all of these boring-ass people who now surrounded him.

Mr. Langston's assistant handed him a cup and escorted him to the restroom for the urine sample, then he took a seat in the lobby and waited. Fifteen minutes later he was bragging to his parole officer about his leadership role in the program, how he was now sponsoring someone new, a young *vato* from San Pedro who seemed like a tough case, but Rudy could see the potential in him—he could see some of himself in the young man, in fact. Rudy showed Mr. Langston his new driver's license with a smile to match the photo on the card, and said, "I ain't even illegal on the road no more."

Next stop was the DMV, where he was going to see about getting Vero's car registered. He knew there were going to be fees attached from it having been expired for so long and from collecting a few parking tickets over the years, but this would be the final step in becoming legit. He would be a gainfully employed, tax-paying, licensed driver rolling in a ride with straight papers and even an insurance card. He almost couldn't wait to get stopped by the cops again just to show them he was legal. But not by the sheriff, he thought. Never by the sheriff. Maybe the highway patrol or even the LAPD, but he didn't want to get jammed by East L.A. or the sheriffs in Norwalk or even the ones out in Pico Rivera where his cousin Frankie Rosas lived and where Rudy was headed after the DMV to kill time before his meeting this evening. Frankie had called him earlier and asked if he could swing by the pad, saying he had something he needed a hand with. What the hell, Rudy thought... it's not like he wanted to go back to his pad and deal with Vero and her shit all afternoon.

Josie came upon two sheriff's radio cars blocking the street her mapping program directed her to turn on to get to the address Miguel had texted her. She pulled to a stop, and a uniformed female deputy approached Josie's vehicle while her three male counterparts watched from where they stood leaning against the hood of one of the radio cars that held Styrofoam cups of coffee and a cardboard tray. Josie rolled her window down and showed the deputy her badge, saying, "Sheriff's Homicide," the magical phrase that granted unchallenged entry into any crime scene in the county, and sometimes beyond. The deputy nodded and stepped back, motioning for her to continue on her way. The male deputies each turned to watch her go, and it made Josie wonder if they were stricken by the car—let's face it, the charcoal gray Dodge Charger turned heads on its own—or if they were just typical male deputies ogling a woman. Then there were always the few whose expressions and tones would leave the impression they silently questioned the qualifications of a female cop who had made it to the big leagues, and that always caused Josie to hold her head a little higher and strut into the crime scene as if she owned it, praying to be challenged. But this time she didn't give much thought to any of it as she went around the blockade through a narrow opening along the curb and continued toward a large cluster of radio cars and fire trucks and an ambulance at the other end of the block, emergency personnel moving about with urgency.

Josie gunned her Charger once clear of the radio cars and braked hard a moment later when she arrived at the scene of the shooting. Her eyes scanned the crowd and the vehicles scattered about, looking for either Dickie or Lopes's car. As she closed her door behind her, she spotted Lopes's Taurus at the front of the cluster with both doors left open. She moved quickly toward the scene through the maze of vehicles and various personnel until she reached the yellow tape where another uniformed deputy stood with a clipboard—the gatekeeper of the scene. She reached for the sign-in sheet and repeated the passphrase, "Sheriff's Homicide." Then she asked the deputy what happened.

A deputy was shot during a traffic stop, and the suspect was outstanding, she was told.

"A traffic stop," Josie confirmed. "So this was a uniformed deputy who was shot?"

The gatekeeper told her yes, a deputy from Pico Rivera. He was transported to Whittier Presbyterian and is reported to be stable. "He took a round to the shoulder."

Josie finished signing in and again scanned the action in search of her partners. She still didn't see them. She said, "Any idea where the two homicide detectives that belong in that Taurus up there might be?"

The gatekeeper glanced toward the Taurus and said, "I was told that the one with the hat went to the hospital with our deputy. The other one was knocking on doors a little while ago." He turned and pointed toward a house that looked like all the others except that the lawn was dead and several cars were parked where grass should be grown, as the driveway overflowed with others. "Last time I saw him, he was knocking on that front door and announcing himself as the cops. Good luck with that."

Josie knew what the deputy meant just by the appearance of the home, an eyesore in an otherwise tranquil neighborhood where mostly second and third generation Americans showed pride in their slices of the dream. If there were any assholes on the block, *that* house was where you'd find them. No doubt the local deputies were quite familiar with its occupants. She said, "Gangsters living there? Or some other variety of vermin?"

"It's a whole family of gangsters, from the grandma down to the last bambino that popped out of one of the hoodrat daughters last month. They ought to set the place on fire."

Rudy turned onto Frankie's street and saw a roadblock up ahead, two cop cars with a bunch of deputies standing around waiting to harass someone. He veered toward the curb and flipped a U—he didn't have time for all that. He'd try coming in from the other direction to see what was

The Program

up. If he couldn't get in at all, he'd shoot Frankie a text, let him know what happened, blow it off until another day. Sometimes it was best to get out of town when something was going down with the cops. Especially the sheriffs.

He got back on the main boulevard—Rosemead—and had started to work his way around to the other side of the neighborhood when he saw Frankie jogging across the four lanes of traffic and looking back over his shoulder. Rudy pulled across the road and into the parking lot of Smith Park, where Frankie had settled into a fast walk. He pulled alongside him and said, "What's up, Frankie? You runnin' from the cops?" and laughed.

But Frankie didn't laugh back. "Gimme a ride," he said as he went around the hood of the car and came up on the passenger door.

"Dude, the cops have your street blocked off. I was just fucking with you though. Are you really on the run? You aren't strapped, are you? I ain't about going back to the joint with a gun beef, eh."

"Nah, man, I ain't strapped. Come on, just go, *primo*," Frankie said, sliding down in the seat with his head on a swivel. "Get me away from here and I'll tell you what's up, *ese*."

Rudy drove through the parking lot and went out the other side and started south on Rosemead. Pico was too hot for his liking today, and now with this fool he just picked up, who knew how much heat was coming his way. He thought about just how straight he was at the time and reflected on the speeches he gave to youngsters about being particular as to who you hung out with, not letting your homies pull you down, and knowing to walk away when shit's about to jump off. That's the only way you're going to stay alive and stay free. Now here he was in the middle of some type of shit he felt in his gut he should've avoided. He said, "So are the cops looking for you or not, Frankie?"

Frankie seemed to relax as they distanced themselves from his neighborhood. He took a black handkerchief from his rear pocket, the hankie folded and tied in the fashion of a bandana but would always be found hanging from his back pocket, never worn on his head. He used it to wipe the sweat from his face and neck, saying, "Lookit, homie, I ain't gonna say they're *looking for me*, looking for me, but I ain't gonna say they ain't, neither. I mean, how should I know what the hacks are doing back there? I just know I want no part of it."

"But what happened, Frankie?"

He shrugged. "I don't even know, *ese*. Just some shit jumped off and it was all *blam, blam, blam,* and I had to go—know what I mean? I don't want to get wrapped up in any of that bullshit. Anyway, let's go kick it at your place, eh? How's Vero, homie?"

8

Lopes came out of the backyard from the side of the house just as Josie started up the dilapidated steps to the front porch, her pistol drawn and held alongside her leg.

"Hey, what are you doing out here, *chica*?"

She turned to face him. "Looking for you and my partner. What happened? Are you guys involved in this?"

Tossing his head, Lopes beckoned her off the porch and started toward his car. Josie followed, securing her pistol in the pancake holster on her hip, saying, "Davey… LOPES! Can you please just answer me that. Are you guys involved in the shooting?"

He stopped walking and turned to face her, one eye squinting against the sunlight, a slight grin that could be interpreted as a smirk, an answer to her question. He said, "Who, me and your dad? No, we weren't involved in anything. Just happened to be in the neighborhood when some shit jumped off. We're funny that way."

Her dad. She knew he meant her partner, Dickie. Deputies from Firestone always called their training officers their dads.

Josie was now standing in front of him, her arms folded across her chest. "Yeah, you're fucking hysterical that way. How's the deputy?"

Lopes turned again—another nod to pull her along—and walked the last few feet to his car. He reached inside and grabbed his sunglasses and a pack of Marlboro Lights from the dash, closing the door as he came out. The passenger door still stood open, indicating to Josie that Dickie had exited the car in a hurry. They probably both had. Lopes had his shades on now and he lit a smoke, taking a long drag to get it going and then blowing the smoke over his shoulder, away from Josie. "He's fine. Took a round to the shoulder and that's it. Probably be off for six months and they'll give him a medal for bravery or some shit when he comes back, some line-of-duty heroic crap. The way they give out that bling now, me and your dad would look like Mexican generals." He leaned against the car and said, "Anyway, what's up? Why'd they roll you out here?"

Josie took his cigarette from him and had a hit. She coughed while blowing the smoke out and said, "Thanks. Now I need a whiskey to wash it down. When did you start smoking again?"

"I didn't," Lopes said, tossing the pack back onto his dash. "Since when do you smoke?"

"I don't. I think the stress of the job is getting to me. I was in with the captain when he got notified of a deputy-involved shooting out here, and I knew you and Dickie were here—"

"Keeping tabs on us, uh?"

"—and all I could think was, Dear God, please don't add anything else to my plate right now. Anyway, I rolled, in part, to get out of the captain's office. You know, that complaint business he's on the warpath about, reading me the Riot Act while I'm trying to figure out how to get ahead of this thing."

"What's the beef about?" Lopes said, then called out to a deputy who was walking past with a roll of yellow tape, "Hey, string it all the way across the alley to the rear of that house. Looks like our shooter went over the back fence."

The deputy nodded as Josie said, "It's a long story. Way more involved than I care to discuss at a crime scene. Want to get a drink with me and Dickie after work? I'm thinking of going to Corina's and getting smashed."

"He's going out? He never goes out anymore. And who even goes to Corina's anymore? Carillo? Alvarez? Your idiot captain?"

"Wait," she said, "Stover goes there?"

The Program

Lopes shrugged. "He used to. But then he had that little fender bender in his county hoop and I think he's on double-secret probation. He was doinkin' one of the waitresses."

Jesus, male cops, she thought. "Thanks for the heads up. I'll scan the parking lot for the captain's ride before going in. But to answer your question, lots of the OGs on the floor still go up there once in a while. None of the new kids do."

Lopes pushed off the fender and patted his pockets before glancing at his cigarettes on the dash. He reached in for them while Josie continued, saying, "Anyway, Dickie didn't say he was going, but I'm going to talk him into it. I need to tell him about some stuff going on, and to be honest," she said, Lopes now looking at her through his shades as he lit another smoke, "I wouldn't mind bouncing this stuff off you, too."

He handed her one of the two burning cigarettes. "This about the beef the captain got, or something else?"

She said, "Something else. Well, both. It all ties together, sort of."

Lopes chuckled. "Okay, convince *me* to go drinking," he said and rolled his eyes. "Look, I'm going to head over to Whittier Pres to see if Dickie is done getting a statement from the deputy that got shot, then we're getting back to work. Someone from the bureau should be out here to handle this pretty soon, I would think. You mind staying until a team gets here, make sure everything goes smoothly?"

"That's why I'm here, Davey, to make sure everything goes smoothly. It's what I do," she said, and now it was Josie rolling her eyes. She puffed at the cigarette, coughed, and tossed it toward the gutter.

DICKIE HAD HIS NOTEBOOK OPEN ON THE COUNTERTOP OF THE NURSES' station in the emergency room, his fedora pushed up off his forehead and his tie loosened at the collar, his after-hours look long before the end of his day. Sometimes he'd show up at the office in the morning in similar fashion—his never-made-it-home look even though he rarely stayed out all night any longer unless the overtime clock was running. Working Unsolveds made that a rare occurrence, and he was thankful for it. Now if he could only get his baby to start sleeping through the night, he'd be set.

With Emily and him each working full time, getting up with the baby had both of them running on fumes, it seemed. They shared the task, though to be honest, not equally. She slept lighter than he, or perhaps it was a mother thing where she was more in tune to the slightest sound coming over the baby monitor in the middle of the night. Either way—whether she was first to wake or he was, and whether it was Emily who got up with the baby or he—neither of them had slept through more than just a handful of nights in the year since the blue-eyed, blond-haired, beaming little saint they named Angelo had been born. The result was that Dickie could have been the model for a burned-out-headed-to-rehab detective bobblehead.

Lopes angled toward him as two glass sliders closed automatically behind him, the swoosh accented by his wingtips clicking against the gleaming tile floor. "What's his status?" he asked, tossing his own notebook onto the countertop next to Dickie's as he arrived at his side.

"He's stable," Dickie said. "I was able to get a statement from him, and making some notes from his chart. We're done here, and good to go. Did you still want to go knock on that door, follow up on your case?"

"Probably head back to the scene, let 'em know what we found out here and see if they need anything else. Did he name the shooter?"

Dickie shook his head. "Male Hispanic, sixteen to twenty, typical gang attire: baggie jean shorts and a white T-shirt four sizes too big. Raiders hat and dark shades."

"That's it, uh?"

Dickie gave a slight nod as he collected his notebook and pen and pushed the file toward the other side of the counter where a seasoned nurse sat behind a computer, blue light reflecting off her eyeglasses. With a glance he knew she had twenty years in scrubs—likely all of it in the ER. There was little difference in the battle-worn eyes of an emergency room nurse and those of cops; trauma and death take their toll without prejudice. "Thank you, ma'am," Dickie said to get her attention, letting her know he had finished with the file.

"You're welcome, Detective," she replied without making eye contact, palming the file while still focused on the computer monitor before her.

They turned and started down the hall, shoulder to shoulder, two big guys with oversized necks wearing marked-down name-brand suits and silk ties. Sometimes Dickie thought they looked more like mafia hitmen than cops. The glass doors slid open and the smells of antiseptics and the sounds of phones and hushed intercom announcements faded as they moved toward Lopes's Taurus which was parked in a spot reserved for police near the Emergency Room entrance. A pair of EMTs was two spots over, placing an empty gurney into the back of an ambulance, a small man and a woman—neither of them tipping the scales at more than a buck fifty. Dickie looked over the top of the car as he and Lopes were on opposite sides now, each removing their suit jackets and hanging them in the back seat. He said, "I always worry that when I go man-down, I'll get two females that can't lift my fat ass into the ambulance. Ya know?"

"That's what you worry about?"

"I mean, that and other things," Dickie said. They lowered themselves into the sedan, and Dickie removed his hat and swiped at the sweat on his forehead with the palm of his hand, the inside of the car stifling under the midday sun.

Lopes started the car and fiddled with the air conditioner, asking, "Like what?"

Dickie shrugged. "I don't know, Davey, different things. Heart attacks, cancer, shark attacks—"

Lopes looked at him, a grin stretching across his face. "Shark attacks."

"Yeah, you know, Great Whites."

"Because you spend so much time in the ocean."

"I'm just saying. I don't want to be eaten by a shark. I also don't want to have a heart attack, and—oh yeah—I don't want to drown. That's got to be the worst way to go."

Lopes shook his head as he backed out of the spot, pulled the shifter into drive, and wheeled through the parking lot. He said, "Are you still seeing that shrink?"

9

Rudy parked across the street from his home, a casita situated behind the three bedroom, two bath home where Vero's grandparents lived in harmony with three chihuahuas named Nacho, Pablo, and Taco—though Rudy never knew which was which—and various family members at different times, usually downtrodden, out of work, or fresh out of the joint types. It was the pesky ankle biters that forced them all to park outside because the entire property was fenced with four-foot chain link. There was a gate to the walkway that remained secured with a padlock, and a rolling gate across the driveway on which a twenty-five-year-old four-door Nissan Sentra with faded paint and furry seat covers usually sat, though not this afternoon. Even though there was plenty of room for other vehicles to park on the driveway, Don Pepe, the old man, forbade anyone else from using it. He worried that the dogs would get out if less attentive guests and residents parked in the driveway, opening and closing the big gate for access. After all, when he and his wife of fifty-six years, Doña Chepa, came and went—and they *always* came and went together—so went Nacho, Pablo, and Taco, loaded in the Sentra with full run of the front and back seats and the rear deck, so there was never any concern about the gate and their safety. When they left, the gate remained open, but still all were forbidden from using Don Pepe's driveway, even for a

The Program

moment. So even though that was how Rudy found the property this afternoon when he arrived with his *primo*, Frankie Rosas, the gate open and the Sentra gone, he wheeled into a spot across the street, his front tire smacking against the curb.

Frankie pointed at the empty driveway and said, "Why not pull up and get off over there, *ese*?"

They were both stepping out of Vero's car but Frankie was leaning back inside when Rudy said, "The old man will have a fit, eh"—and he saw Frankie slide a pistol under the front seat—"what the fuck are you doing with that, man? You said you weren't strapped!"

"Look, *ese*, you was all uptight. I didn't want you to panic. If we got jammed by the cops, I woulda taken the fall for the gat, *primo*, don't you worry about that. I wouldn't put that on you, man."

Rudy shook his head. "Get it out of my car, man."

Frankie started to reach under the seat and Rudy said, "No, wait. You can't bring it in the house. See, man, just look how your stupid shit puts me in a jam, *ese*. Why the fuck did I have to see you back there? Man, I been clean, straight, doing my program and avoiding all this type of drama, eh. I don't need this shit, man."

Frankie stood outside the passenger's door of the car in his gangster apparel: baggie jean shorts and an oversized white T-shirt, a Raiders cap pulled down low on his head. He was looking at Rudy through dark plastic shades, waiting. The distant sound of bass thumping caused Rudy to look up and down the street, very cognizant that he wasn't from this neighborhood, that although he was now older and trying to live clean and do right by his ol' lady, he would still be viewed as a *vato* by the local gangsters, and perhaps be challenged, jumped, or rolled on. Especially when he had a young fool like Frankie riding with him. Rudy said, "Okay, leave the strap under the seat, but you're calling a homeboy to come pick you up. I ain't taking you anywheres else, *ese*. You're trouble, man, still fucking around with all that shit, and I don't have time for it."

They closed the doors and started across the street, the two side by side now. Rudy slapped his cousin on the side of his head. The force knocked him off balance and he stumbled a step or two away. Frankie held his hand up to shield himself from another blow, if it were to come. Rudy said, "I ought to give you a beatdown, you little motherfucker."

Inside, Vero sat deep in the cushions of a worn couch, her legs folded sideways beneath her, the TV showing music videos but the volume was down. She had a cigarette in her hand that hovered over an overflowing ashtray balanced on the arm of the couch. A sandwich-size plastic Ziploc bag, a lighter, a package of Zig-Zag rolling papers, and a 24 oz. can of Budweiser sat on the coffee table next to her, the bag showing only remnants of the ounce of weed she'd bought two days before. She squinted through a cloud of smoke that hung in the air as Rudy and Frankie came in, leaving the door open behind them. She said, "Where you been, eh? And close the fucking door, goddamnit, letting all the bugs in with you." Her gaze shifted from Rudy to Frankie and she let loose a little chuckle. "What's up, Frankie boy?"

Rudy ignored her and walked through the small living area and into the bathroom, the sounds of chatter fading behind him, his girl asking Frankie what's up Rudy's ass, why'd he come home all pissed off. Rudy thought, *Yeah, why would I be pissed off?* His lazy-ass ol' lady was wearing a hole in the couch rather than cleaning the place up and maybe doing something with herself, and his idiot cousin had brought his heater into Rudy's ride while he was doing his best to stay straight, trying to stay out of the slam and out of *that* life. How could he possibly be pissed off the second he came home?

He took his time in the bathroom contemplating his future. Could he really stay straight while associating with these fools? Can you stay out of the life while your people are up to their necks in it? Maybe he should blow the whole show. Let Vero stay there in a drunken and loaded stupor, kick it with other losers and hook up with dopers and gangsters, maybe get a dude in the joint she can visit on Saturdays. Rudy just wanted to get away at this point, get a fresh start somewhere far away with normal people, dudes that stayed straight like his new friends in the program, and women who did something other than lay around the house all day, drunk. The professional types, he thought.

Like the receptionist at the parole office.

Or the lady cop.

Rudy jolted from his reverie at the sound of a car in the driveway. The front bathroom was situated near the front entry and facing the street, and with the window open, as usual, he would be able to hear the sounds of

The Program

footsteps on the concrete or the jingle of keys. In this case, it was the sound of a tired motor clanging and clattering off, a car door squeaking open, a groan, and then the old man yelling, "Taco, *venga acá. Pinche perro.*" Doña Chepa said, "*La puerta! La puerta!*" Rudy pictured a familiar scene, one of the tiny dogs bolting from the car before Don Pepe could get back to close the gate. He always insisted on his wife staying in the car with the dogs until he could walk back and pull the driveway gate shut behind them, and inevitably, one of the little chihuahuas would escape—usually Taco. Fortunately, Taco's primary ambition was to run to the house next door and fence-fight the dog that lived there, some type of shepherd that would chomp him in one bite if not for the fence, a Taco snack before dinner. Don Pepe's voice faded as he continued a string of commands interspersed with both Spanish and English expletives. Rudy stepped back into the living room to see Frankie and Vero sparking a joint, low-riders full of gangsters bouncing on the muted TV. Rudy needed to get to a meeting.

It was in Norwalk. On his way, Rudy passed the civic center and looked over at the throngs of people walking across the courtyard to and from the parking structure, some in suits and dresses while the *cholos* dressed in starched khakis and oversized pressed button ups, standard *hood* or courthouse attire. The homegirls were there too, and Rudy wondered if they had come from family court, or had they been in the criminal courts building catching their homeboy's hearing. It was hard to say by the way they were dressed, many similar to the one that caught his eye, a heavyset *chola* wearing pajama bottoms and an L.A. Dodgers hoodie, big hoop earrings just to show the court she had made an effort to honor the "business attire" portion of the subpoena. A cigarette dangled from lips painted black, the smoke drifting past her dark, oversized sunglasses and engulfing her head of greasy hair pulled back into a careless bun. A woman, maybe a lady cop or an attorney, passed by the *chola*, her *actual* business attire setting her apart from the many others outside, shapely legs in moderate heels.

A sheriff's patrol car sat at the driveway Rudy was about to pass, and he thought about how nice it was to be clean, to have no worries, to end up with no regrets... The gun! Shit, it was under the seat. Frankie's gun. Suddenly he felt his heartbeat pulsating in his head, and his palms became clammy and damp. He gripped the wheel as if it might fall off if he let loose of it. He kept his eyes straight ahead as he passed, praying the cop inside would pay him no mind. He watched his mirror and the cop turned out behind him, and a moment later he was right on Rudy's tail. He checked his speed: thirty-two. Was it a twenty-five zone through here or thirty-five? He eased off of the accelerator and watched as the needle slowly dropped. Surely he wouldn't get pulled over for just a couple miles-per-hour over the limit, would he? His tags were clear, his license straight, and he even had insurance. He was even wearing his seatbelt! But the gun...

The red and blue lights came on behind him, bright strobes even on a sunny afternoon. Rudy's instinct was to run, lead the cops on a chase and toss the goddamn gun the first chance he got, maybe on a corner where the cops wouldn't see it flying out the window. Eventually pull over and take his beating—there was no doubt the sheriffs would kick your ass if you ran from them—and go to jail for evading, not that big a deal. Maybe for assault on an officer, too. They usually tossed that in there to justify kicking your ass, but the courts must be hip to it because they never gave you any time for it.

A blast from the siren told Rudy it was time to decide. And truthfully, this was perhaps the defining moment in the rest of his life. He wanted to be straight, and he was trying hard to walk the line, but maybe it just couldn't work for a guy like him, a man who'd done hard time and whose past had branded him for life. You can wear long sleeves and button your collar to hide the ink, but these fucking cops knew *who* you were with merely a glance as you putted down the road in the family sedan on your way to your program. And to say so—to tell the officer you're straight, on your way to your program, and that you'd left *the life* behind you—every cop has heard that a thousand times from a thousand *vatos*. Most of whom were lying—they were gangsters for life just going through the motions to keep their parole officers off their backs.

Rudy pictured the piece under his seat, a heater with who knew how many bodies tied to it, the way a cheap gun made its way from one gangster to another. Not to mention what just happened out in Pico, Frankie on the move and seemingly somehow involved with the shit that went down with the cops. Jesus, Rudy thought, what if that gun under his seat had been used to shoot a cop? They'd kill him—the cops, that is. And if he pulled over and gave it up, they'd only beat him, and Frankie's homeboys or someone putting in work for *La Eme* would kill him in the joint. Everyone hated a rat.

The siren went on, but this time not just a toot—the sheriff behind Rudy was essentially saying pull the fuck over, *now!*—in a way that only a cop can, like the way they knock on your door and you know it's not a neighbor or Jehovah's witness.

Rudy took a deep breath, and made a decision that would change his life.

10

AFTER LOPES AND DICKIE LEFT THE HOSPITAL, THEY DROVE BACK TO THE scene of the deputy-involved shooting to find out who would be handling the case and give them the information Dickie had gleaned from his interview of the victim deputy and by speaking with medical staff. Lopes wheeled them around the radio car barricade at the end of the street with a nod of his head—Lopes didn't even bother to flash his badge, which essentially removed any doubt as to *who* he was. He pulled up behind a long line of sedans and parked. The firetrucks and ambulances were gone, and the dozen or so radio cars that had raced to the scene of a "deputy down" broadcast had mostly disappeared, the deputies now back to whatever duties they had abandoned in order to help a fellow cop. Now the administrators were here: Pico Rivera station's captain, Internal Affairs Bureau brass and investigators, members of the Force Training unit, Captain Stover from Homicide and a handful of his detectives—the only people there in ties who could still be considered cops. Dickie opened the back door of Lopes's car and retrieved his jacket, saying, "Better suit up so the house fairies stay happy."

Lopes had already reached for his jacket too, and he caught Dickie's eye over the top of the car. "They should be happy we're fucking sober.

The Program

Speaking of that, did your partner hit you up about having a cocktail up at Corina's Steakhouse after work today?"

"Josie?"

"No, your mother. Yes, dipshit, Josie. She's all stressed out about this beef or maybe something else, I don't know. Anyway, if your old lady will give you a hall pass, it might be good to see what's shaking. That girl doesn't rattle easily."

Dickie nodded to draw Lopes's attention to Josie approaching from behind him, a notebook and pencil in her hand, her designer sunglasses pushed up in her hair.

"What's the word from the hospital?" she asked, now settling in beside Lopes but looking across the car at her partner.

Dickie said, "The deputy is stable, basically laying around telling war stories and eating up the sympathy from the nurses. Gave us a description of the shooter: typical cholo, sixteen to twenty, baggie shorts, white T-shirt, Raiders ball cap, and dark shades."

Josie lowered her sunglasses over her eyes and left her hand there to shield the glare, the afternoon sun reflecting off the windshield. "We've got him named."

Lopes cocked his head. "Yeah, how'd you do that?"

"Neighbor," she said, looking over her shoulder for a moment and coming back. "Two houses north of the scene, an elderly man dropped the name but said he didn't see anything and won't come to court."

"That's helpful," Dickie said.

"Who's the asshole?" Lopes asked.

"Frankie Rosas. His grandmother owns the house," she said, a nod in the direction of the dilapidated home where the concentration of activity took place behind them, "and the neighbor saw Frankie and two other boys walk past his home right before it happened. He had gone out to get his mail and was back at his front door when he heard the shots. He turned and saw Frankie running through the yard toward the back. The other two were nowhere to be seen by then."

"And this Frankie kid matches that description?" Dickie asked.

She nodded. "My understanding. I asked Carter from gangs to get us a six-pack put together, go see if our deputy can ID him."

Lopes said, "Who's got the handle on this?"

"Floyd and Mongo. Their whole team's out here and there's not much else we can do now, really. I was going to wait for Carter to come back out with the photos, then head over to the hospital to get the ID so we can put him in the system and get it out county wide. Probably statewide and down at the border too."

"Okay," Lopes said. "If you don't need anything else from me and your dad here, I think we'll head back to the office."

Josie looked at Dickie and said, "You have time for a beer tonight?"

He considered it for a long moment as images of Emily and Angelo came to him, the two engaged in their own routines, Angelo likely taking his afternoon nap, Emily at the office behind an orderly desk reviewing a file, or maybe she was at the courthouse filing a motion or arguing against one before one of the federal magistrates. Either way, she'd be leaving a little before five as she always did, home by six, and after dinner she'd give Angelo a bath and play with him or read to him for the short hour or so before his bedtime. Dickie hated missing any of it. He had started coming into the office early, seven or so, and leaving by three to beat the traffic and have more time with his son in the afternoon and evening. The nanny, Rosalva, would usually stay around until six, regardless, helping with laundry and dinner and often joining them for the evening meal. She'd become family to them both, a first generation American whose husband was deceased, and the children were grown and living their own busy lives. In fact, Rosalva's daughter worked at the federal courthouse as a clerk to Judge Perl, and Rosalva used to spend several days a week observing proceedings just to have something to do. That was how Emily had come to know her. Now she was part of Dickie and Emily's budding family, and a blessing to say the least.

With the thought of the three of them making do without Dickie for one evening, he said yes to the drinks. He was curious about the issues that were plaguing Josie, and the truth was he was long overdue for a night out with his partners. He had walked around to their side of the car during this contemplation, and now he stood facing Josie. "Are you buying, Sergeant?"

Josie smiled and said, "Sure, it's the least I could do for my partner."

Lopes said, "Jesus, you two… I hope this night doesn't end up in some romantic tryst, at least not between you two."

The Program

Josie sidled up next to Dickie and put her arm through his, leaning into him. She said, "Dickie's completely harmless. I already stuck my tongue down his throat once and he panicked, said I was out of his league, and then he went out and arrested a lady fed just to get his balance back. Like Floyd has always said, Dickie doesn't even like fun."

Dickie held back a grin while recalling that afternoon just a year or so ago, the CHP officer death that led them to a couple of dirty cops, including the Assistant Special Agent in Charge of the ATF's Los Angeles field office. It had been a bizarre day, complete with a biker barroom shootout, and the arrest of ASAC Donner. Josie was mad as hell at Dickie for trying to leave her out of part of the case, and they were in the midst of a fight when it happened. She had spun around to face him—he had thought maybe she was going to slug him—and she planted a wet one on his mouth. She told him that she loved him—as a partner, she had clarified—and then the next second she was all business. Proving in Dickie's mind yet another Floydism: *They're all crazy.*

"Yeah, well, try that on me," Lopes told her, "and it'll turn out a little different. Hell, we'd probably end up on a beach in Mexico, drunk, naked, and broke."

Josie shook her head and smiled. "I'd play for the other team first."

"Now that makes sense," Lopes said, shaking his finger at her. "I should've known you were a switch-hitter."

She flipped him off and started back toward the crime scene.

Lopes and Dickie stood for a moment to watch her walk away. Lopes said, "Come on, Dickie, let's hit the road. We've got police shit to do."

JOSIE WALKED AWAY, PICTURING HER TWO FAVORITE PARTNERS DRIVING OFF with grins on their faces, the two of them no doubt talking shit about her, but in the way that two brothers might tease her on the way to school and then fight anyone else who picked on her once there. She ducked under a strand of yellow tape and paused as she quickly scanned the personnel scattered about, trying to spot Floyd to let him know she was heading out. Her thoughts about Dickie and Lopes and the whereabouts of Floyd vanished as a call came in on her cell. The display showed an unknown caller, and Josie knew that it could have been coming in from their front desk. *What now*, she wondered, hoping it didn't have anything to do with the complaint by Prada. She glanced around the scene and realized the captain had been there just a short time before and wouldn't likely be back at the office already if he had gone back at all. Suddenly she felt irritated again, the thought of being beefed by Rudy Prada, of all people. How did a gangster convict get up the nerve to file a complaint on a deputy who had locked him away twice and even shot him on their first encounter? She was starting to wish that he hadn't survived being shot, and thinking maybe she should have shot him again when she took him down for armed robbery. And why was he even out of prison already?

She said hello and recognized Miguel's voice saying, "Josie, there's a Norwalk unit asking if you'd be available for a 911B, or at least a phone call."

Josie frowned into the phone, wondering why a Norwalk patrol deputy would want to meet with her. She didn't have any Norwalk cases going, and it had been years since she had. "What's up? Did they say?"

"He said to tell you it's concerning Rudy Prada."

11

Rudy Prada sat on the curb taking in the activity around him: motorists gawking as they crept through the congestion caused by the traffic stop that led to his detention. Pedestrians walking behind him on the sidewalk, whispering among themselves, speculating as to what he might have done. A few had commented on "the harassment" by the cops, and at least one *vato* boldly questioned where Rudy was from—the dumb son-of-a-bitch issuing the standard gangster challenge with a deputy right there in earshot. But the cop remained preoccupied on his cell phone, and he didn't hear the challenge nor the complaints about police harassment. The fit young deputy in his tailored tan and green uniform and polished boots finished up his conversation telling someone on the other end of the call, "Tell her it's concerning Rudy Prada."

Rudy pictured the lady cop he couldn't seem to avoid, and whom lately he seemed to think about far too often. In his program he learned about honesty and faith and surrendering to a higher power, but he didn't necessarily think that meant ratting himself out to the cops. So thus far, he had opted for his right to remain silent about the gun the cop found beneath the seat of his car. The program also embraced the concepts of forgiveness—*acts of forgiveness*, as it is written—and this is where Rudy found himself conflicted. Bobby Young, Rudy's sponsor, had told him to make a list of the people he had harmed before recovery, and to go to them and admit his transgressions. To some degree, he had. He had started a list, and he had written down his mom and Mikey and Vero and even the chino from the liquor store he had shot during the robbery. He'd asked for his mom's forgiveness for all of the pain he put her through with the gangs and drugs and stints in various jails and prisons, and of course his mother had forgiven him. She always had, but now she seemed more hopeful about his future. Soon he would tell Mikey about using him as a scapegoat whenever Vero caught him with a gun in his coat or found some hoochie's phone number left in a pocket. Maybe he'd go as far as to tell him about what he had done with Mikey's little sister—several times, actually, when both were young, he in high school and she still in junior high. He looked back on those days with mixed emotions of fondness and guilt. With Vero he'd have to be careful—that amends thing would need to be carefully negotiated with his ol' lady, his child's mother. He definitely wouldn't tell her about Mikey's little sister. Even though it had happened before he knew Vero, she would probably say he was sick, a child molester or some nonsense—regardless that she had probably started fooling around at a similarly young age. And as far as other women—hoodrats, strippers, and even the occasional hooker—nothing good could come from confessing those things to her. As far as his crimes, Vero already knew about most of them, certainly those that had resulted in his arrest. Rudy didn't see any reason to rat himself out to Vero about things that could still come back on him. Everyone knew what could happen when a woman knew things that could send you to the joint—then they owned you.

And Rudy didn't want to be owned by Vero. In fact, he wasn't even sure how long he'd be able to continue living with her, being a part of her life. He could see that they were headed in different directions—she on the same path to nowhere she'd always walked, and he with a whole new outlook on life, thanks to the program he'd finally taken to heart.

Rudy thought about the lady cop with the powerful eyes and thought maybe it would be good to tell her he would never have shot the store-owner had he and Mikey not been high. Let her see this side of him. Let her see how much he'd changed since those days back in East L.A. For some reason he couldn't quite understand, he needed her to know this about him. Maybe he saw *her* as the higher power, a lady cop with a gun

The Program

—one who wasn't afraid to use it. And if he did tell her these things, he could tell her he was sorry about all of it, even the part about putting her in that bad situation that led to their first encounter. Maybe she would even apologize for shooting him. He could forgive her for it, too. In his mind he could see her confiding in him that she, too, had many regrets, and although it hadn't been the same thing—she hadn't done the things she had done to him because of addiction—maybe she had the need to make amends with others for different reasons. Or was it because of addiction? Maybe *that* was why she had come to the meeting the other night, he now considered. If she hadn't been there to arrest him or to stalk him—which really hadn't made any sense to him, anyway—maybe she was there because she needed help. Rudy imagined being her sponsor. Man, how this *higher authority* thing could work in mysterious ways.

"As luck would have it," the cop said while sliding his cell phone into his pocket, "Detective Sergeant Sanchez just happens to be about ten minutes away, and she's headed directly here."

Rudy didn't respond. He lowered his head between his knees and stared at an army of black ants marching along the seam where the asphalt of the road met the concrete footing of the curb and gutter beneath his legs. They were busy creatures, organized and skilled in their ways and undeterred by the giant forces around them. It was a simpler life, he thought, one without gangs and addictions and cops and prisons—or was he wrong about that? For a moment he wished he could shrink to their size and march off with them before she arrived, but that was the old way of thinking he needed to change. There would be no more running away from his troubles; he would meet all challenges head on and face the consequences. With that mindset, he would be more likely to avoid trouble in the first place. Before, he would commit crimes or behave badly after briefly considering the possibilities of getting away with things or being caught. He never thought he'd get caught—he was too slick and cool for that!—so there had been nothing really to deter him. Now he knew to take ownership of his behavior, and that was how he could stay clean and live with the consequences of any mistakes he might make.

But the situation in which he now found himself didn't seem fair. He hadn't done anything wrong, but he was jammed up nonetheless and facing a serious dilemma: rat out his cousin for the gun or take the rap for something he didn't do and be sent back to prison. Who even knew what crimes were on that gun, anyway? Rudy knew of one, for sure.

He needed to think about how this conversation with the lady cop would go, what he might say to her as he explained how it was just his bad luck that the cop found a gun in his car. He would beg her to give him a break, just this once. Tell her how he was trying so hard to go straight.

Otherwise, it would be his third strike and Rudy would never be free to walk the streets again. His final fate now lay in the hands of the lady cop, and how he managed to handle the situation. He said a silent prayer asking for wisdom, guidance, and a lot of luck. And then he watched the marching ants below him, and waited.

On the way to Norwalk, Josie called Dickie and said, "That little asshole from East L.A. who I shot and then busted for robbery a few years after, and who I've literally put in prison twice, myself, and who had the balls to file a complaint against me for stalking him, just got picked up in Norwalk with a gun."

"Well it appears your day is looking up, partner."

"No, it's not. The little shit is asking to see me, and I'm on my way there now. What am I supposed to do with that? Why would he want to speak with me? What could he possibly have to say to me? And how's that going to play out with a complaint sitting on the captain's desk?"

"You can't go. It's that simple, Josie. Blow it off and head back to the office or go to the bar or whatever it is you need to do to keep you from making this worse."

"How's it going to be worse?"

Dickie didn't answer right away.

She said, "You there?"

"Yeah, I'm thinking."

"I bet I know what he's up to," Josie said. "He's going to try to negotiate a gun arrest for the complaint against me. He must think I'll lose my job over the complaint or something, as if he could get out of a gun beef and avoid prison. Looking at a third strike, he'd better know where Hoffa's buried if he thinks he's getting a break."

The Program

There was another moment of silence and Josie could hear the sounds of car doors closing, Lopes saying something in the background. Finally, Dickie said, "We're at the office. You should come in, meet us here."

"I'm pulling up on them now," she said, glancing over her shoulder as she merged into the left lane, prepared to turn in where she saw the patrol car on a traffic stop, offset from the vehicle the deputy had stopped. Traffic was backed up as two lanes merged into one and everyone slowed to see the action.

Dickie was saying, "Josie..."

A man sat on the curb between the radio car and the vehicle that had been stopped. His hands were cuffed behind his back and his head rested on his knees as if he were taking a nap or saying a prayer. Josie thought, *You don't have a prayer now, buddy*, as she whipped a U-turn and came in behind the radio car, blue and amber lights now flashing on the rear deck of her Charger.

"Gotta go, partner," she said, and disconnected.

DICKIE SET HIS PHONE ON HIS DESK, PLOPPED INTO HIS CHAIR AND SAT back in it as he looked over at Lopes, who was waiting expectantly. He was about to tell him how hard-headed his partner could be at times, or that she was driving him crazy, or that she was out of control and about to get herself into even deeper shit with the captain. He took a breath and let it out slowly, but before he could start telling Lopes about his partner's shortcomings, Captain Stover appeared in the doorway of their office.

"Where's your partner, Jones?"

Like most cops, before anything else, Dickie was a trained observer. Nothing was ignored and everything at least registered a thought, if only to be recalled and analyzed later. He immediately noted the captain had his suit jacket over his arm and a briefcase in his hand. Dickie glanced at his watch, wondering if it was actually the end of the day already—that would be end of the day for an admin guy, not a detective—or was the captain just returning from something else, an executive meeting or a martini lunch. Then he recalled Stover had been out at the scene in Pico, and he considered that he might have just returned from that. Without lying, he said, "Last we saw her, she was still out at the deputy-involved shooting in Pico, boss. Didn't you see her there? She was helping out Floyd and his partner with the scene. Anything I can pass along to her?"

Stover shot a glance toward Lopes and came back to Dickie, his face a mask of skepticism. "No, I'll finish up with her in the morning. Try to keep her out of trouble, would you?"

Dickie leaned back a little farther and plopped a wingtip-encased foot onto his desk. "You bet, skipper."

The captain shook his head, said, "I'm asking you to keep someone out of trouble. How stupid am I?" He pointed his finger at Dickie. "Don't say a thing."

Dickie didn't respond and the captain disappeared.

Lopes said, "The amazing part is you didn't answer him."

"I'm maturing."

12

The Norwalk deputy, a no-nonsense type whose uniform appearance would pass an academy inspection—which was no small feat for a cop working the streets—turned to greet Josie as she approached, a slight breeze blowing her jacket open to display her badge and gun. Not that the deputy wouldn't know who she was otherwise. Even if he hadn't called for her to come over, he would recognize her at first glance as a detective, and likely be smart enough to put her at Homicide. She definitely wasn't an executive, and nobody had ever accused her of being from Internal Affairs or working Forgery Fraud. Josie had always been a street cop, and all real cops had a different aura than those who just got their tickets punched and moved onward and upward.

"You've crossed paths with one of my longtime favorite crooks." Josie smiled and held out a business card for the deputy. "Josie Sanchez. Thanks for calling."

The deputy took the card. "Tracy Jennings, and you're welcome."

Tracy. She liked that name for a man, and suddenly she took in the fit shape that wore the uniform so proudly. He likely worked out regularly and had outdoor interests, things that, like being a street cop, demanded a level of physical fitness in order to be done with any seriousness at all. Things like mountain biking, hiking, maybe surfing. For all she knew, he jumped out of planes or off cliffs with a pair of wings during his off time. It always amazed her how cops seemed to be constantly chasing an adrenaline rush, as if being a cop in L.A. didn't provide enough excitement in one's life. But he also seemed to be a bit of the serious type. He hadn't smiled back at her, and she hadn't caught him checking her out, something to which Josie was no stranger. She glanced at his hand and saw there was no wedding band. No jewelry of any sort, other than a bulky watch with all sorts of gadgets, another indication of his being a sports enthusiast. The absence of a ring meant nothing. Most street cops wouldn't wear rings for a number of reasons, primarily officer safety. Cops generally preferred that the people with whom they interacted didn't know anything about them personally, especially anything about their families or even the existence of one. There were also concerns that a ring could get caught on a chain link fence when climbing over, or it could get hung up on any number of other things during an altercation. On the other hand, so to speak, some cops preferred to appear *available* when they happened upon a pleasant and friendly encounter—something all cops experienced at some point in their careers, some more so than others. Some constantly. Some hunted those encounters the way others looked for bad guys or fresh coffee.

He said, "I found a gun beneath the front seat, but he claims it isn't his. The car is registered to him and Veronica Garcia. He said it isn't her gun, either. When I asked him a few other questions, he said he needed to talk to you. I figured he's your informant, so I made the call to your office."

Josie shook her head. "Hardly an informant. I shot him once, put him away twice, but I've never had a casual conversation with the man in my life."

"You're serious?"

"About shooting him?" she clarified.

He nodded.

She said, "Serious as a bullet in the gut."

That comment turned the corners of his mouth up slightly, maybe the best she would get from him.

He said, "What do you want me to do with him?"

"Have you run the gun?"

"Yes, ma'am. No record on file."

She nodded, turning her attention toward Prada who sat hunkered

The Program

down on the curb. He glanced up as if he could feel her stare, but then averted his eyes downward again. Josie had always been amazed at the power of focus. In the same way you could stare at a fellow student in a classroom two seats up and a row over from where you sat until they turned to see you watching them, you had to be careful about directing too much focus on a bad guy, especially if you were undercover and doing surveillance, or off-duty and trying to mind your own business. There was some type of energy in the universe that some people had—and certainly most cops had it—that you had to be aware of and treat like a weapon or the delicate gift that it was.

Josie looked away from Prada and scanned her surroundings again, something she did routinely as all cops would, and she let out a breath slowly and felt her muscles relax and her tension ease. She turned to the deputy and said, "I'll talk to him, but not here. Can you take him to the station for me, and I'll meet you guys there? I am quite curious about a couple of things, why he would drop my name being one of them."

The deputy nodded. "Yes, ma'am. What would you like me to do with his car?"

Rudy Prada looked over and spoke up. "Officer Sanchez, could you please give me a break and not impound my car? I just finished getting straight with everything, the registration, my license... I'm trying so hard, and I don't have the money right now to get it out of impound. I promise you I'll be straight when we talk—on my kids, ma'am."

"That's Sergeant Sanchez, Prada."

"Yes, ma'am."

Josie turned back to the deputy. "Tracy, can you put his car in the parking lot and lock it up?"

"You bet," he said. "I'll do it right now if you'll watch him and my radio car for a minute." He nodded in the direction behind her. "I can put it right there for a couple hours. If he goes to jail, he'll have to get someone to come get it, or it will be impounded."

She said thank you just as Rudy also called out, "Thank you, Deputy. Thank you, Sergeant Sanchez."

Deputy Jennings drove Rudy's car into the adjacent lot and locked it up, then jogged back to where Josie and Rudy waited in silence, only the sounds of the city between them. He moved with the grace of a colt, effortless strides that allowed him to cover more ground than it appeared. Jennings arrived at his radio car moments later. He helped Rudy to his feet and guided him into the back seat. Josie followed them around the block and into the rear parking lot of Norwalk station. The deputy placed Rudy in a locked interview room and removed his cuffs. Outside in a hallway, he met with Josie and handed her a plastic bag containing Prada's personal belongings: a wallet, a black comb, a keyring with numerous keys, and a bronze coin commemorating his first year of sobriety. There was also a booking slip in the bag, partly completed. Jennings told her to have the jailer let him know if Prada was to be booked, and he'd come back in and take care of everything.

He said, "What do you want me to do with the gun?"

Josie considered it for a moment. "Hold it as evidence for now and preserve it for prints. I'll figure out what to do with it after I talk to him."

"Sounds good, Sergeant."

With that he started for the back door where his radio car waited in the lot. Josie called out to his back. "Thanks, Tracy." He glanced over his shoulder, showing her the slight smile once more before walking out into the bright afternoon, a sliver of sunshine disappearing as the door closed behind him.

Josie turned and looked through the small window on the interview room door and saw Rudy waiting inside, his eyes soft and his brows furrowed, showing apprehension or maybe regret. Dickie's words resounded in her head, *blow it off,* but she shoved him out of her mind and pushed through the door. "What's up, *pendejo*?"

"How am I a *pendejo*? Why's it got to be that way?"

She shook her head and chuckled. "Really, dude? You want me to make you a list?"

"I've been respectful to you, Sergeant Sanchez. I never even sued you for shooting me."

She pulled a chair out and sat across from him. "You filed a complaint on me for showing up at your meeting. What kind of dick move was that? Now my captain and probably everyone else knows I went to AA. So much for fucking *anonymous*."

He folded his hands on the table, looked her in the eyes. "That was a dick move, I ain't gonna lie. But I thought—"

"You thought what, I was actually there for you? Like how would I know you were there? Why would I be looking for you, anyway? Have you killed anyone lately? You know I work Homicide now, not Gangs. So why would I be looking for you?"

"I didn't know you worked Homicide until I called Gangs at East L.A. and asked about you. Now I know, and to be honest, I've reflected back and realized I made a mistake. I was going to call your captain and tell him that."

"Little late, buddy. Now you're going back to prison for ex-con with a gun."

He looked down for a long moment, and when his gaze met hers again his eyes were moist and sincere. "I been doing so good, living my life and doing my program, just doing everything I can every single day—*one day at a time*—to stay straight and to live a meaningful life. I talk to kids at the schools and young gangsters on the streets, and I do my outreach bit and try to help others avoid the mistakes I've made."

"You just made a big one, rolling around with a heater in your ride."

He shook his head. "It ain't mine though, Sanchez. You have to believe me, man. Look, I can't go back to the joint. I'd rather die than go back now. It ain't like it was before when getting locked up was just part of the deal, you'd do your time and hang with your homies. Don't you understand what I'm telling you? I don't have no homies no more. I'm straight. I'm not trying to be in that life anymore, deputy."

"Sergeant."

"Sergeant Sanchez... please find it in your heart to believe what I'm telling you. You were in the meeting. You heard me speak to everyone, openly give my testimony, own my mistakes and shortcomings. If I was just there to keep my parole officer off my ass, would I be up there baring my soul? No, you know I wouldn't. I'd be sitting in the back row with you, drinking coffee. Come on, I know you've got a heart. You didn't even want to shoot me that morning outside the liquor store—I saw it in your eyes after. You hoped I wouldn't die, and I didn't. And I was respectful to you the next time when you came into my home and arrested me for that robbery. I saw something in your eyes that morning too, and it's stayed with me all this time. It's something I can't quite shake. You've had a positive influence on my life, ma'am—whether you know it or not—and I just pray that you'll see fit to give me one chance to prove that I'm a good human being, that I have a life now that's worth salvaging. And I also pray for you, believe it or not. I mean, I just recently started, but I pray for your health and safety, even prosperity. Please, Sergeant, just this one time, can you believe in me? Give me one chance? I beg you."

13

THEY TOOK A SMALL TABLE IN A CORNER ON THE OPPOSITE SIDE OF THE dark and musty room from the jukebox where they could have a conversation without yelling at one another. Josie had insisted on it. She didn't want to compete with the sounds of old country or new pop while telling the boys about Rudy Prada, the complaint, the gun, or the temporary get-out-of-jail free card she issued him just an hour or so ago. Dickie had grumbled about the seating arrangement—he and Lopes had been bellied up to the bar when she arrived, and he glanced at the table behind them with obvious disdain when she suggested the move to them. But there hadn't been three stools together anywhere at the bar top anyway, which was often the case during happy hour at Harpy's, the quaint Monterey Park watering hole popular with local residents and cops who were from the downtown and surrounding area assignments. Though they had talked of going to Corina's, Josie had talked them out of it. The last thing she was willing to do was take a chance of running into the captain there.

The three of them gathered their cocktails and settled in at a table.

Josie began, but she hadn't gotten far before Lopes said, "What? *You're* going to AA?"

She sipped her Tito's and cranberry and set it on the cocktail napkin before her, carefully placing it while deciding how much of this story to tell, and how to tell it. In hindsight, she should've skipped the part about seeing Rudy Prada at the meeting in Norwalk, but then how would she have explained the complaint?

Lopes said to Dickie, "AA is for quitters. We aren't quitters." And the two Neanderthals toasted to their stance against sobriety.

Dickie pointed to her drink. "Is that straight cranberry?"

Josie could feel the pressure building as her two partners had a good time with her predicament, neither of them having a clue that she wasn't in the mood to make light of it at all. Typical men, she thought, so often on completely different wavelengths than the women who had something to say to them. For detectives, sometimes these two weren't much brighter than the flickering fluorescents recessed in the ceiling, and right now they were even less entertaining than the shrieking polyester bimbo at the end of the bar who was apparently warming up for karaoke. Josie took another sip and plopped her glass on the table as if it were a gavel.

"No, it's not straight cranberry, partner. Even if I had actually stopped drinking, I wouldn't be able to deal with the two of you sober. Jesus."

"So you're a double quitter," Lopes observed. "You quit drinking and now you've fallen off the wagon."

"Can you both shut up for a minute and listen to me?"

Dickie and Lopes exchanged glances and Josie waited for their attention. Lopes took a long swig of his beer, looking over the bottle at her with his piercing dark eyes. Dickie, his fedora pushed up high on his forehead—his *I've had a rough day, It's too damn hot for a hat,* or *Don't bother me I'm thinking* configuration—sat tapping his finger on the beer bottle he held in his left hand, his wedding band clinking with the beat of a Johnny Cash classic, the type of song you didn't hear on the radio any longer and wouldn't find on too many jukeboxes either—you certainly wouldn't have heard it playing at Corina's. She let out a breath and began. "You're going to think I've lost my mind but hear me out before you say a thing."

Three rounds of drinks later the trio sat with solemn faces and the dull glazed eyes of mourners. This starkly contrasted with the noisy background of booming voices and laughter drowning out the music and the distant sounds of a cue ball cracking open a fresh rack, billiard balls clacking against one another before plunging into holes and rattling through the return system and falling into the coin-operated ball container.

After a long moment of silence among them, Lopes said, "So that little twerp McKnight slipped you a roofie, uh? I'll kill him."

"I don't know that for certain," she replied, not meeting Lopes's eyes.

"Sounds pretty certain to me," Dickie offered. "I'm with Lopes—we kill him."

"You can't kill a deputy district attorney."

Lopes and Dickie looked at one another and smiled, as if it were a challenge. Two boys showing off for the girl. *Who says we can't jump off that cliff?* She said, "More than likely it was the creep sitting next to me, copping his feels every chance he got. That's who you should kill."

"Okay," Dickie said. Lopes shrugged his approval.

"But honestly, I can't prove anything—that's been the problem! That's why I went to the meeting and why I seriously considered not drinking ever again."

"Not the solution," Lopes said.

"Yeah," Dickie agreed, "you just need to stop dating pussies and perverts."

"He's hardly a pussy," she said.

"Oh, that's right, he played college football. While I was busy serving my country, I might add. But anyway, yeah, I'm sure he's a really tough guy," Lopes said with a smirk.

"Honestly, you guys, he was a gentleman. That's the thing that makes me think it was that grinning asshole that sat next to me, and not McKnight. He didn't touch me—I can assure both of you that he didn't, though I'm not going to explain to you how I know. You're going to just have to trust me. The thing is, I'll never know for sure that he hadn't intended to. You know what I mean?" Josie shook her head and let a long breath seep out as she picked up her glass and rattled the ice, contemplating having another.

Dickie stood and picked up the empties, made his way to the bar. Josie didn't object.

Lopes said, "I'm seriously going to fucking kill him. I've never liked that asshole anyway."

She reached over the table and put her hand on his forearm. "Promise me you won't do or say anything to him. I have to work this out on my own." Josie considered for a very brief moment sharing with him that she wasn't even sure that McKnight was straight. Tell him about the naked dog named Chappy and the meticulously curated décor and fragrant bathroom with fluffy towels and cloths, and a unisex robe for any guests who might stay over. The man was either gay or a very discerning swordsman.

Perhaps, she considered, Smiley had slipped her the roofie, but that didn't mean that McKnight wouldn't have otherwise taken advantage of the situation had the timing been different. Though now she felt some guilt for not only considering him the culprit but telling two of the most A-type cops she'd ever known. These guys wouldn't let it go, and all she could hope now was that she could diffuse the situation to a point where cooler heads would prevail.

Lopes had called out for Dickie to grab some beer nuts or something else to munch on, and now Dickie was back placing another round on the table. Lopes reminded him about the beer nuts and Dickie said, "Jesus, dude… give me a second, would ya? I've only got two hands." A few moments later, he was settled back at the table, and they all had fresh cocktails and two bags of beer nuts to share among them.

As Josie ate a handful of nuts, she realized how hungry she was and that she hadn't eaten anything since breakfast. She said, "We should've gone to Corina's—I'm starving."

Dickie rolled his eyes, apparently fighting back the *I told you so*.

Lopes checked his watch. "We can finish these drinks and go up the street to that taco stand, or drive downtown and the choices are limitless: The Pantry, Cole's, The Perch… Hell, we could go to Tommy's or Burrito King, for all I care. I'm starving too."

"I'm going to bow out and head home after this one, but I do have a few questions before I go," Dickie said, holding Josie's gaze.

She took a sip of her Tito's and cranberry and said, "Shoot."

"All this about McKnight and your waning love life, yet you haven't explained anything about this cholo you shot who's now filed a complaint against you. And now you're going to give him a pass after a Norwalk deputy caught him with a gun. What the hell's that all about?"

Lopes said, "Yeah, cha-cha girl, what's up with that?"

Josie kept her gaze on her glass as she organized her thoughts, trying to figure the best explanation of a complex situation. The heaviness of her partners' contemplations had not escaped her.

The Program

"Here's the thing: I went to the AA meeting because I was devastated about not remembering a night out drinking. The truth is, I had a hard time accepting that someone had been able to drug me. I'm a cop—that's not supposed to happen. It's embarrassing to even think about it, let alone mention it to my partners. But anyway, I'm sitting there, and this dude at the podium talking about his life seemed familiar—"

"Because you shot him a couple times," Dickie said, and smiled.

"—once, actually. But yeah, it dawns on me who this guy is, but it still didn't quite match the dude I remembered. He's grown up now, obviously. He was clean-cut and dressed business casual and mostly well-spoken—he didn't come off as a gangster or cholo or homeboy at all. And I knew the second our eyes met that he recognized me. Can you imagine? I went to the AA in Norwalk because it's far from my home and from the office, and I thought surely, I wouldn't run into anybody I knew. My luck, I swear."

"So he thinks you're stalking him and beefs you," Lopes said.

Josie nodded. "Yeah, but then he's on his way to a meeting and gets stopped by the cops and has a gun beneath his seat. He swears it's not his."

Dickie chuckled. "Of course he does."

She shook her head. "I know, I know... but I believe him. You'd have to get to know the guy to understand, but he's different than most of the dudes who've found God in prison and go to meetings until they're off parole. This guy is serious about it. He told me everything he's done, everything he's doing—working with at-risk kids and speaking at community meetings and meeting with politicians. The guy is honestly trying his best to stay clean, and he seems to be sincere about changing his life."

"But he's got a gun under his seat."

She met Lopes's gaze. "Yeah, he did. And he's giving up his own cousin for it."

"Yeah? He probably knows there ain't no bodies on it."

Josie finished her drink and set it down. "Well, actually, Rudy thinks his cousin might have been the one who shot our deputy this morning out in Pico."

Lopes and Dickie exchanged glances.

She said, "Frankie Rosas. That's his cousin."

A HALF HOUR'S DRIVE DOWN THE SANTA ANA FREEWAY FROM WHERE Josie, Dickie, and Lopes wrapped up their conversation, Rudy Prada packed his bags while Vero paced and stormed in and out of the room, cussing him for leaving, accusing him of cheating, threatening to cut his balls off or shoot him in the back when he walked out the door. She wore black gym shorts that showed her plump legs with bruises and the start of varicose veins, and a dirty wife-beater with no bra, her large sagging breasts jiggling beneath it as she waved her arms about, a cigarette burning between her fingers. Nacho, Pablo, and Taco yapped incessantly outside his bedroom window, the trio of ankle biters joining in the ruckus because they had nothing better to do while Don Pepe and Doña Chepa likely sat in their living room next door with the TV so loud they wouldn't hear any of it. They might not even hear the gunshot when he left, if Vero held true to her word. Rudy didn't doubt that she might.

But this was the final separation from The Life that Rudy knew he needed if he were to stay straight this time, and he had reached the point where he would rather take a chance of being shot on the way out than to end up back in the joint with all the *vatos* and their drugs and violence and prison politics that would also leave him dead, if only in his own mind and soul. As he pushed past her and moved through the living room, Frankie Rosas stood between him and the door.

"What happened to the heater, *ese*?"

Rudy stepped to his left and Frankie mirrored the movement. He took a deep breath and held it for a moment, aware of Vero at his side. Finally, he let the breath out slowly and said, "They didn't find it."

Frankie said, "But they might find it at the impound, right?"

Rudy shrugged.

"And then they'll come back to you and ask you about it, eh?"

"Yeah, maybe," Rudy said. "But I don't know why there was a gun in my girl's car, and that's all there is to it. It ain't like I'm gonna rat you out, *primo*."

Rudy took another step left and Frankie, with his wet eyes and boozy breath, bowed up and ready to fight, moved right to block him again. But before his lead foot found purchase on the stained tile beneath him, Rudy threw a right hook that he knew Frankie never saw coming. It landed on his left temple and dropped him in his tracks, his eyes rolling back in his head.

Vero punched Rudy in the back of his head. "Motherfucker," she screamed, and she started to come in with another fist when Rudy turned, caught her arm with one hand, and backed her against the wall, his fist drawn back, cocked.

"Do it, you motherfucker," she hissed, spittle flying from her plum-colored lips, her dark-painted eyes wide in rage. "Go ahead and hit me, you bitch."

He pushed her away and turned back for the door, stepped over Frankie, and walked out. The trio of chihuahuas followed him to the gate and stayed there barking as Rudy started down the sidewalk, waiting for a gunshot.

14

THE NEXT MORNING, STOVER STUCK HIS HEAD INTO UNSOLVEDS AND SAID, "Sanchez, your boy dropped the complaint. What'd you do, threaten to shoot him again?"

"You know it, boss," she said as she turned from the work on her desk to face him. "It works with *cholos* and bitches and sometimes partners and bosses too." She smiled to take the edge off the last part of her comment.

"Yeah, well, maybe you can try sailing smoothly for a while like your partner," he said with a nod toward Dickie, who hadn't bothered to look up from his computer. "Jones hasn't caused me any grief for nearly a year. It's a personal record for him."

Dickie looked up and smiled.

Josie said, "Our whole goal in life is to solve murders and keep you happy, boss. Thanks for stopping in." She turned back to her computer and saw in her peripheral vision that he had moved on.

Dickie, his eyes back on the computer, his fingers spread over the keyboard as if prepared to launch a torrent of alphabet missiles, said, "I love that guy."

Josie tapped her pen on her desk to draw his attention, and Dickie swiveled his chair to face her. "I've got to get that gun from Norwalk and take it up to the crime lab."

He rocked back in his chair and tipped his hat high on his head. "You think it's going to come back to Pico?"

"I think it has a fair chance. Prada said his cousin didn't say whether or not he was a shooter, but that he was there when some shit went down. Prada didn't ask for details, didn't want any."

"Because he's straight now," Dickie said with a grin.

"He saw his cousin crossing Rosemead toward the park, which would've been away from the direction of the shooting. He was jacked up and needed a ride to get out of there, and he said that some shit had just gone down with the cops and that shots were fired. We know from the witness he was at least there. Whether or not he was the shooter, I don't know. That's what we have to figure out."

"And if he's not?"

"Whatd'ya mean?"

"If Prada's cousin isn't the shooter—or should I say, if that gun doesn't match the bullets from that shooting, what are you going to do with him? He gave you a gun and a story to stay out of jail, and you let him walk before you determined whether or not his cousin was involved, or if his story is even straight. It feels like you're taking some unnecessary chances with this guy, and I'm a little confused about it. You feeling bad about having shot him, or what?"

The last thing Josie needed was for Dickie to question her decision making or her motives. She had become accustomed to his unwavering support in all things, and she needed that now as much as ever—maybe more. Though she did understand where he was coming from, because he didn't know Rudy Prada the way she now knew him, or perhaps the way her gut was guiding her about him. Dickie hadn't sat and talked to the man. Yeah, convicts were full of shit most of the time, but she felt Rudy was sincere in his efforts to stay clean, and she felt that if Dickie sat with him for an hour, he, too, would feel the genuineness of him. It wasn't as if Prada was the first bad boy or convict to go straight and become a productive member of society, though those who did were indeed a rare bunch.

Josie said, "Ride with me to the crime lab, and I'll buy you an early lunch after. Then we'll swing back and get the results—Manny said they could put a rush on the examination—and then go talk to Rudy. Because either way, that's next on the agenda. Either the gun comes back to the

Pico shooting and we brace him for details about the cousin and his whereabouts, or it doesn't, and we find out what's what with the story he told me."

Dickie sat in apparent contemplation for a long moment, his gaze locked on Josie. She gave him a smile and prompted him. "Well?"

"Okay, deal. But I get to pick where we go for lunch."

"Deal."

They were sitting at the end of a long community-style bench inside Philippe's downtown, Dickie enjoying the famous French Dip roast beef sandwich, Josie working on a chicken Caesar salad and reflecting on her interview with Rudy Prada at Norwalk station.

She set her fork down and looked at Dickie. "One of the things Rudy told me was that he was working his way through the steps of his program—"

"AA," Dickie surmised.

She nodded and continued, "Yeah, and he is currently working at making amends for the things he's done that have caused others harm, things he might not have done if he hadn't been using drugs and alcohol."

"Okay."

"Well, he actually said he owed me an apology for what he put me through."

"What he put you through?" Dickie said, his eyebrows raised. Then he chuckled and took a bite of his sandwich.

Josie took another bite and finished chewing it while picking through her salad with a fork. She didn't look up when she spoke. "I thought it was very thoughtful of him. He said he knows it isn't easy on a cop when they have to shoot someone, and he took ownership of his conduct that led to that morning outside the market in East L.A. He told me that he had lied about the gun in his jacket belonging to his friend, Mikey, and he knows that had he not been messing around with gangs and guns, I wouldn't have had to shoot him—I wouldn't have feared for my safety and been in that situation that morning."

She looked up and met Dickie's eyes.

The Program

He said, "Wow."

Josie nodded. "I'm telling you the man is sincere."

"And so you believe he didn't know about the gun under his seat."

She shook her head. "He knew about it. When they arrived at his house after he picked up Frankie in Pico yesterday, Frankie took a gun out of his pants and slid it under the seat. Rudy went off on him about having the gun, but he didn't want him bringing it into his house, so he told him to leave it in the car. He had forgotten it was there when he left for his meeting later in the afternoon. He said we'll get Frankie Rosas's prints off it, but we won't get his because he never touched it."

Dickie pushed a food basket containing only crumbs and an empty wrapper away from him and pulled his iced tea closer, surrounding it with his hand but leaving it there on the table. He glanced to his left as three ladies joined the table with soft drinks in their hands, and said flatly to Josie, "I guess we'll know soon enough."

Josie had only eaten half her salad, but she was done, and she could tell that her partner was itching to get out now that the lunch crowd had descended onto Phillippe's en masse. She pushed away from the table and said, "I guess we will."

VERO HAD PROBABLY HELPED FRANKIE TO HIS FEET AFTER RUDY LEFT THE house with his worldly possessions slung over his shoulder in a duffle bag he'd *borrowed* from Don Pepe. They had likely spent the rest of the evening sitting on the couch drinking their cheap liquor and beer, and smoking weed while talking shit about Rudy, saying he'd turned into a punk, maybe saying he'd turned rat. Surmising how the car got impounded but he didn't go to jail, and what reason would the cops have had to tow their car, anyway? Hadn't Rudy told her he'd just gotten it registered? And that his license was straight now too? Rudy could hear the conversation and picture the two of them in a haze of smoke for the rest of the night, a music video marathon on TV, or maybe they had put on a movie, something like *End of Watch* where *vatos* shoot it out with the cops and some *homies* they all knew from the streets had debut-acting parts in it. It was getting easier and easier for *cholos* to make a living without selling dope, thanks to Hollywood.

Now, late the next morning, Rudy pictured them crashed on the couch or maybe in his bed, his cousin and his girl now a thing with him out of the picture. Sleeping late and starting over sometime after noon, a "morning" beer and leftover beans and a few fried *huevos* with corn tortillas. Rudy was hungry now himself. He would check out of the motel and grab something to eat while he tried to figure out his next move. There were no more *homies* to rely on, places he could just show up and crash for a while —couch-surfing and bumming around—so he had to come up with another plan. There was Bobby Young, his sponsor in the program who he knew would always be there for him, but to what extent? Would he —*could he*—help Rudy with a place to stay and some wheels? It was worth a shot. Give him a call and tell him what's up and see if he offered any help. Or wait and catch a meeting later and hope Bobby was there. Or text him and say, Hey brother, I've landed on some hard times and I'm hurting—let him know he'd be at a meeting this afternoon if Bobby could be there for him. Or some shit like that.

Or call the lady cop. Officer Sanchez. *Sergeant Sanchez*, actually. Detective?

Josie.

How about that? Get on a first name basis with her. Earn her trust and gain her friendship, see what happens—anything was possible. When Frankie's prints came back on that gun and his didn't, she would know she could trust him. Maybe he would give her some other cases, drop some names on a few murders he knew about from back in the day, as long as she kept his name out of it. Didn't she work the cold cases now? Yes, she did. Rudy recalled her saying so, and he remembered staring at her card that said something about Homicide Bureau and cold cases or unsolved cases or something like that. Truthfully, he'd paid more attention to the name: Josefina Sanchez. *Josie*.

Rudy checked out of the motel and walked to a nearby Denny's where he ordered the breakfast special, a Value Slam for five bucks. The days of getting a Grand Slam for around that price were gone, apparently. When he finished eating, he texted his sponsor and waited for a reply. Soon the dishes were cleared, and his check waited on the edge of the table. But

Rudy had nowhere to go, so he sat drinking coffee for another hour and waited.

Bobby Young still hadn't responded to his text two hours later when Rudy used the restroom and departed, his duffle slung over his back. It occurred to him that he was now homeless, and he saw it differently than he ever had before—it didn't seem so disgraceful any longer. He thought about shelter and transportation and decided his first priority was to get to a meeting. He could go to several of them today, actually. That would resolve the shelter issue, give him somewhere cool to hang out, and there was always plenty of coffee for the attendees. Sometimes cookies or donuts. Surely someone, at some point, would offer him a place to stay until he could get back on his feet.

15

Rudy answered the phone sounding short of breath, and that caused Josie to picture him in a variety of situations: finishing a workout; having a nooner with Vero; running from the cops. She revisited the workout scene in her mind, seeing it as the likely scenario, Rudy being in good shape, not overdone like some convicts who'd spend all their time on the weight pile and develop huge arms and chests but their legs could be sued for lack of support. No, Rudy was built more like a fighter, lean and defined and quick on his feet—the type who would be graceful shuffling in the ring while weaving and bobbing and throwing quick jabs and powerful crosses. She had no idea if Rudy had ever boxed, though she imagined he probably had. If not, he had probably been a good street fighter when he was young in East L.A. and running with the gang. Boxing was a popular sport in many Hispanic neighborhoods, and almost every downtrodden community boasted at least one gym where the thuds of heavy bags and the buckitta-buckitta backitta-backitta of speed bags and the sounds of sharp breaths and grunts and groans and shuffling feet hung in dense, pungent air.

"Are you running from the cops, Rudy?"

He chuckled. "No ma'am. I just jogged across Imperial Highway dodging traffic with a fifty-pound duffle on my back. People drive like fools out here, you know it?"

She pictured Imperial Highway, a main thoroughfare through Norwalk and about twenty other cities, the forty-mile expressway stretching through three counties from the city of Orange to Vista Del Mar on the coast of the Pacific Ocean. Pedestrians took their lives into their own hands when they chose to dart across the four lanes of steady traffic rather than using the crosswalks and waiting for a signal that all was clear. Sometimes even then they were putting themselves at risk among L.A.'s aggressive commuters. You surely didn't step off a curb until the driver turning right met your eyes.

"Where're you headed?"

"Huh?"

Josie said, "Right now, where are you going? My partner and I need to hook up with you for a few minutes, talk about some things."

"Oh, gotcha. Um, I don't really have any plans till I go to the Alano after a while."

Josie knew that by "Alano" he was referring to the AA meeting where she had seen him for the first time in a decade, the previous time having been at his sentencing for the robbery. She knew that some of the attendees called it the 502 club, which had puzzled her at first, as "502" was the sheriff's radio code for drunk driving. It turned out the nickname was purely coincidental, though fitting. She couldn't help but think that some deputy, at some point, had been involved in the program and instrumental in its naming. She said, "Okay, where will you be until then? We can head your way now."

"I got nowhere to go, Sergeant. In fact, I got nowhere to be—I'm out of the house."

"What happened?"

She heard him make a sucking sound that she had grown to detest, a street thing that some gangsters used in a manner of saying "fuck you" without saying it. Back in the days when respect was demanded of these hoodlums, the sucking of one's teeth could put the pearly whites in immediate peril. Though for many, this became more of a habit, a way to show disgust with any particular situation, and Josie didn't think he meant any disrespect to her. He said, "I had to check out, you know? Get away from the drama and the bullshit. Me and the ol' lady was fighting about the car being impounded—"

"Wait, they impounded your car?"

"Yeah, or at least I assume they did. It was gone from where the cop parked it when I walked back over there after you let me go."

"Oh shit," Josie said. "I'll check into that. I'm sorry, they weren't supposed to do that."

"Nah, it's cool, but that put me in a jam, 'cause I had to explain that the cops took my car, and I made up some shit about being pulled over for something minor and the paperwork didn't match their computer."

Josie could hear the traffic in the background as she pictured the scene by the courthouse where they parked his car. She thought about all the visiting criminals in and out of that building, and the crowd that had watched Rudy get hauled off by the cop. Had someone watched the cop park Rudy's car and ripped it off after they had all gone?

Rudy was saying, "...and so of course Frankie was asking about the gun, and he acted like he didn't believe me when I said the cops didn't find it. That's when the two of them acted like they were trying to put a rat jacket on me, so I bailed before shit got bad."

Josie pictured Rudy's girlfriend as she might appear now, a decade since she had last seen her. *Vero*. Veronica something or other, as Josie recalled. A fairly typical homegirl from the neighborhood, small and cute with overdone makeup and big hair back when she and Rudy were young. Josie wondered if now Vero was plump from childbirth and booze and a typical diet of starches and carbs. Still wearing big hair and face paint and body-hugging wife-beaters without a bra, just a larger size. She said, "Where are you going to stay now?"

"I don't know," he said, and let that hang there for a minute. "That's something I have to figure out, eh? I'm tryin' to stay out of the life so that sort of limits my options, you know?" He let out a nervous chuckle and added, "You have any suggestions?"

"Do *I* have any suggestions?"

"Yeah, like can you hook me up with something, witness protection or whatnot?"

Josie let the question hang between them for a beat. "Rudy, you're not a witness."

The Program

"I tole you that the gat in my car was Frankie's, and that he had something to do with that shit in Pico, eh? Don't that make me a witness?"

"Well, we need to talk about that gun and your cousin. Where can we meet? Should we just meet at the Alano?"

Now it was Rudy who allowed for a moment of silence on the phone. She figured he was thinking about the appearance of him meeting with the cops at a place where he now found comfort and confidence, not to mention new friends. It was probably not the best suggestion, she realized.

He said, "Look, I know Frankie had something to do with that cop being shot, and now you got the gun, and I'm your witness that it was Frankie's and that he was running away from where that shit went down. There's other stuff I could give you also. I'm down on my luck and willing to do some shit I've never considered doing before if you can just help me out. I'm kinda desperate now."

She looked over to see Dickie glancing back and forth from the road to her as they crept through traffic coming into the East L.A. interchange. She mouthed the word "Norwalk" so he'd know not to take the Pomona Freeway toward the office, but to continue south on the Long Beach Freeway instead. They would pick up the I-5 South from there and could be in Norwalk in half an hour as long as there were no traffic disasters to negotiate, which would actually be amazing in the L.A. basin. Josie said into the phone, "Are you anywhere near the sheriff's station?"

"I'm right by the civic," he said.

She knew he meant the civic center, directly next door to Norwalk Sheriff's station. Somewhere near where he had been stopped with the gun in Vero's car, and where Josie had gone to meet him and Deputy Jennings. She said, "Go to the sheriff's station and tell them in the lobby that you're there to meet with Homicide, and that we're on our way. Don't talk to anyone else about that gun."

He made a sucking sound again and said, "Okay, see you there."

Josie pictured herself slapping him upside his head when she saw him, knocking the suck right out of him. Twice in one conversation, she couldn't help but question if it was intentional disrespect. She didn't think so, but it was one of those things that bugged her badly enough that she couldn't let it go unaddressed.

She disconnected and began checking emails on her phone, saying to

Dickie in the otherwise silent car, "Homeboy's going to shit when we drop the news on him."

THEY FOUND RUDY WAITING PATIENTLY IN THE LOBBY OF NORWALK station, seated on a wooden bench with his duffle at his feet. He wore his black L.A. Dodgers ball cap low, and large plastic sunglasses covered his eyes. Josie assumed this was done in the interest of remaining incognito, Rudy preparing himself for the witness protection program, apparently. She didn't have the heart to tell him that what you saw in the movies or heard on the streets about changing identities and living high on the government dole simply wasn't so. In L.A. County, at least, about the most they could do for a witness in danger was to move them. The witness relocation fund would allow for basic moving expenses and first and last payments on a reasonably-priced rental. The feds might provide a monthly stipend to their more infamous mobsters-turned-witness stoolies, but in L.A. the best you could hope for was a relocation from East L.A. to El Monte, or Compton to Pomona—one gang-infested, crime-ridden community to another.

When he didn't look up as they approached, Josie realized he must have dozed off. It always amazed her how comfortable crooks could be in the arms of the law. Arrest someone and they'd be asleep on the bench in the booking cage before you finished your paperwork. Bring in a witness to a mass murder, women and children slaughtered before them, and they'd lay their heads on the desk like first graders and be out for the count until the investigator barged in and scraped a metal chair across the linoleum floor. She stood in front of him, contemplating just how to arouse Rudy without startling him when Dickie kicked the duffle bag at his feet, sending a loud thud through the quiet lobby and knocking the bag against Rudy's legs.

He woke with a start and said, "The fuck," then seemed to recognize his visitors. He sat up straight and pushed the bill of his hat up from his face, pulled his sunglasses off and stuffed them in the pocket of his oversized plaid button-up short-sleeve shirt. "Oh, sorry," he offered, "I must've dozed off. Didn't sleep too good last night, ya know?"

The Program

Dickie said, "Let's go," and turned on his heel. Never one for beating around the bush with these guys.

Josie waited for Rudy to stand up and gather his belongings, then the two of them followed her partner to the interior lobby door that would lead them down the hallway to an interview room. She said, "Where did you say you were staying now?"

"Well, that's the thing," he said, pausing at the door to answer her. "I ain't got nowhere to go. Last night I popped for a room at some fleabag up the way, a place full of hookers and junkies and roaches. I ain't going back there though, even if it means sleeping in the park or finding a shelter. What did you find out about that gun? My cousin's prints were all over it, right?"

She gestured for him to continue on. "Let's get in a room and we'll talk about it."

The three of them filed into a small room with a table and four plastic chairs, a configuration found in just about every interview room throughout the county. The chairs squeaked against the floor as the three of them settled into their seats, the sounds amplified against the barren walls. Dickie began flipping through some papers in a file folder as Josie got right to it.

"Rudy, we have a serious problem with this gun they took out of your car."

"A problem?" he said, leaning in with his brows crowded together. "Whatd'ya mean? What kind of problem? I already tole you everything, and it was the truth. Frankie had the gun with him when I picked him up over there in Pico, and the fool left it in my car. Anything he did with that gun isn't on me, eh."

Josie leaned back and looked at Dickie, a signal for him to take it from there. He had already assumed the role of bad cop when he kicked Rudy out of his slumber. It was a role he played quite comfortably and with certain expertise, so she would let him break the news to Prada while she watched closely for any expression or reaction that would betray knowledge or guilt.

Dickie pulled a single paper from the file and appeared to be scanning the contents of it while Josie and Rudy waited silently, Rudy intense and on edge. Josie involuntarily revisited the sensation of maggots crawling in her boot, though today she wore slip-on flats from Cucu Fashion with Bombas liners beneath straight leg slacks so snug she didn't think a maggot could nuzzle its way up her leg. Besides, she hadn't been at a crime scene with maggots for more than a year now—thank God!

Rudy's eyes flicked from the paper Dickie held in his hands to meet Josie's gaze, but only for an instant. The deadpan eyes showed concern, and Josie forgot about the sensation on her leg as she focused on the former outlaw across the table from her. In a moment, she knew, the room would be filled with tension, and it would be her job to accurately read Prada's responses to what he was about to hear.

Dickie placed the paper on the table and shoved it toward Rudy. "Your gun has nothing to do with the Pico shooting, Mr. Prada—"

"It's not *my* gun, I tole you!"

"—but it has a far more troubling history, my friend."

Prada leaned back and let out a breath, looked from Dickie to Josie and back. He repeated himself, nearly mumbling the words this time: "It's not my gun."

"Your gun was used in a robbery-murder, Mr. Prada."

"Not my gun!"

Dickie sat back in his chair and let out a heavy breath, studying Prada for a long moment, no doubt looking for any tell that he knew what might be coming. Josie waited patiently, measuring every subtle change of expression, every involuntary movement the way a professional poker player watches an opponent who just pushed all his chips toward the middle of the table.

Dickie said, "Mr. Prada, we're talking about the murder of a city councilman. You're in deep shit this time, my friend."

"On the bright side," Josie added, "your issue about where to stay has just been resolved."

16

Dickie and Josie sat at one end of a long table in the quiet confines of the Homicide Bureau's conference room. Across from them, Lopes, with his tie loosened and sleeves turned up, leaned back in a tall leather chair and drummed a pen on its arm while staring at the ceiling, muted taps accentuating the silence. Josie watched him for a moment and thought about the night the two of them ended up at her place after hitting a couple bars at the end of their day. He had slept on a chaise next to the pool, though she was certain he had had other hopes and plans for the arrangement. Truthfully, so had Josie; however, she had learned to resist the advances of drunken colleagues and the urges of a single woman, especially when alcohol was involved. The risk-reward ratio was just too high, and office romances were plagued with rumor, drama, and jealousy. Sure, the men would high-five one another, but at least one female colleague would get word of it and talk incessantly to the other girls about what a slut she was or what a pig he was. Women were their own worst enemies when it came to some equalities.

Floyd sat next to Lopes, a contrast in his Brooks Brothers sharkskin suit, fixated on his phone. Having his alone time. Uninterested. Bored. Maybe wondering why Josie insisted he join them in the conference room for a meeting but hadn't provided any details about the subject matter. He didn't know the captain had approved bringing him into Unsolveds to assist with this investigation as a special assignment, a break from the on-call schedule and handling new cases. Until he realized that, he'd likely feel mostly inconvenienced by having to attend this meeting. However, when he learned there was overtime involved, he'd be all in for the effort —a real team player. Josie planned to partner him with Lopes, and it would be the four of them—Lopes and Floyd, she and Dickie—who would run with this case until it was resolved one way or the other. Once and for all, perhaps. Floyd glanced up from his phone as if he felt Josie thinking of him. She broke eye contact first, and he returned to reading emails or scrolling through Facebook or watching Bruce Lee videos or whatever it was he had been so focused on—it wasn't as if he'd been playing Wordle or Scrabble to pass the time.

Dickie hovered over a murder book composed seventeen years prior by two investigators who were no longer with the department—both had since retired and one was now deceased. He was flipping pages and jotting notes into a new notebook he had just started, one that now bore the same file number and victim's name as the case he sat reviewing. Dickie with his fedora pushed up high on his forehead, all work and no play.

Josie had reviewed only the case summary and had decided to wait to see what the consensus would be before diving into the files—wait to see what the captain would have to say about this new information they had developed through the crime lab. Would he give them free rein to reinvestigate the case, or would he tell them to allow the district attorney to direct their efforts? After all, the case had already been adjudicated, a man convicted and doing time on a case where the murder weapon had never been recovered. But now it had. Did that change anything? That's what she really wanted to know. Guns were passed around through gangs and beyond, and sometimes a gun with bodies on it would be found on someone who had nothing to do with the killing. Sometimes the person caught with the iron wouldn't even be affiliated with the actual killer or that person's gang. It was said a gun never bounced twice in the ghetto. Toss one from a window when the cops were chasing you and the piece would be re-homed before its barrel cooled. Josie felt confident that was the case with Prada and this hot-potato gun that was found beneath his seat. *Frankie's gun*, allegedly. She didn't see how either of them could

The Program

have been involved in the killing of the councilman, Frankie being too young at the time, probably twelve or thirteen, and Rudy, just a couple years older, not the type. Or was he? She tried to recall his rap sheet before she had first encountered Prada outside the liquor store in East L.A., but the details weren't clear to her. She did recall he had priors then, but to what extent she wasn't sure. His and Frankie's backgrounds would be thoroughly investigated though, with a focus on the year a city councilman took two to the chest and a coup de grâce to the melon. An execution for sure, but why? She glanced at Dickie, whose nose was still in the files, and thought that he'd probably have a few thoughts on the matter by the time this meeting got started. Knowing Dickie, he might have the thing solved.

If they were given the green light to run with the case—that is to say that if after they determined whether the recovered gun changed anything in the People's case against the one who had been convicted of killing the councilman—then Josie would commit to the sizable task of reviewing all the files. It would be something she'd do in the evenings or during a weekend at home—a bottle of wine and a lot of true crime reading. A binge of sorts. It never worked for her to try reading large volumes of files at the office where distractions were numerous and persistent. For now, she'd rely on Dickie's assessment from his review and hear out the captain once the meeting got started. Dickie would have a few pages of notes by then, the man having not looked up from the murder book since they'd left the off-site Homicide library with the dusty file box in hand.

Right now, Josie focused on *her* defense. The captain would undoubtedly come down on her when he learned that she had allowed Prada to be released after the gun was found beneath his seat. She could hear him saying, What did you do, let him walk on a gun charge if he'd drop the complaint against you? Or, How do you give a parolee gangster a pass on a gun? Maybe both. Maybe he'd also give her that steely stare he could hold in silence for a long moment, his way of telling you he thought you were an idiot without actually having to say it. Josie would have to explain to the man that Prada was providing information on some other cases now and that they believed him when he said that the gun wasn't his. She still believed him, for some reason. Josie felt he had told her the truth about Frankie and how he happened upon him in Pico Rivera and gave him a ride back to Norwalk. The traffic stop in Norwalk that led them all to where they were now was only bad luck for Rudy, and a potential can of worms for the rest of them—especially the district attorney's office. The captain would roll his eyes, let her know how much smarter he was than she, and Josie would let him think so and not get drawn into a fight the way her partner, Dickie, might. There was nothing to gain in the little pissing contests so many of her male colleagues would mindlessly enter into.

As far as Rudy walking out of jail that first day he was caught with the gun, it was now a moot point; she and her partner had booked Prada into Norwalk for being a convicted felon in possession of a firearm. *There*. That part had been resolved. He wasn't on the lam now that the gun had come back red hot with a high-profile murder attached to it. Josie could only imagine the meltdown the captain would have had, had they not been able to find Rudy and take him into custody. After all, it would be he who had to answer to the sheriff and the press, not her or Dickie. So, no harm, no foul—right? Everything was all sorted out, and given the fiasco this had been, at least now she felt they were on solid ground. She only hoped the captain would see it the same way.

Josie took a deep breath and let it out slowly as the sounds of dress shoes clicking against the tile floor in the hallway outside signaled the approach of her captain, and at least one other person. A moment later, the door flung open and Stover stepped in, Lieutenant Neely from Internal Affairs right behind him.

PRADA LAY ON A THIN PLASTIC-COVERED MATTRESS THAT SMELLED LIKE dirty socks and vomit, and was situated on a steel-framed bunk that hung suspended from a cinderblock wall in the dingy confines of the Norwalk jail. His booking package had been completed: the booking slip filled out and signed, photographs taken, a medical questionnaire completed, and his fingerprints had been scanned into a machine that reminded him of a photocopier. He had watched as the jailer manipulated one finger and then the next onto the glass, the image of his prints displayed on the screen before them. He remembered the first few times he had been busted it was the cop who arrested him that rolled his prints. First, the deputy would squirt a blob of black ink from a tube onto a plate of glass that was bolted to the bench, and then he would use a roller to spread a thin layer of that ink across the glass. He'd grab your arm, jostle it around until he had your hand just so, and then roll your fingers, one at a time, onto the glass to cover the tips in ink, before rolling your prints onto the card. The cop would yank you around and push and pull your arm, then yell at you to fucking relax as if it were your fault that the result of his efforts looked like black blobs and he had to do it over. This method with the computer seemed neater, cleaner, and simplified, and the jailer had been at ease with the whole process—Rudy had had no concerns about getting his ass kicked for fucking up the cop's print card.

He wore a wristband bearing his name and a booking number which would be his jail identification for all things while he remained as a guest of the sheriff. He'd have the number memorized by tomorrow, and the sound of his name accompanied by the last three digits of his L.A. County jail number would become his identity: *Prada, seven-four-zero*. It could be months before they shipped him back to prison on a parole violation, and that was only *if* they dropped the gun charge. Otherwise, he could be there for a year or longer fighting a new case, and that would be miserable. The county jail was far worse than prison for a man who knew the system and wasn't afraid of the Big House. Doing time with fools at the county who didn't know how to jail brought too much drama, and the cops there were too intense, not laid back like many of the hacks in the joint.

He wished he could stay there at the Norwalk jail, maybe work as a trustee. He'd bring that up to Sanchez when she came back to talk about the gun. Anything to keep from going to county jail. He would need to keep her and her asshole partner happy if he expected any favors from them, and he would do that by providing them information, even though it went against the code of the street. This would change his life. He'd never be able to go back to his neighborhood, and he'd have to be careful about running into people who knew him wherever he went. And as far as the stint he was about to serve, he'd have to do his time in solitary or at a low-level joint with the homos and snitches—people he fucking hated doing time with. But at least he wouldn't get shanked in the chow hall or out on the yard or, God forbid, while naked in the shower. At least in a low-level pen he'd be respected and left alone, for the most part. Maybe he could get a job in the wood shop or library, get paid a couple bucks a week while passing time.

Rudy needed a cigarette, and he longed for the days when smoking in jail was not only permissible, but you could buy cigarettes at the "store." Or you could take them from the white boys—at least from some of them. The drunk drivers and child molesters. Not the bikers or peckerwoods who had been to the joint. He'd have no problem getting cigarettes once he was back in the pen, cigarettes and tattoo guns and cell phones and anything else he wanted, truthfully. Prison was like that. Get caught with a cell phone in the county, on the other hand, the sheriff would disappear your ass after his goons gave you a good beating. Yeah, if you had to do time, prison trumped county jail all day long.

A siren wailed and the sounds of screeching tires conjured images of sheriff's squad cars tearing out of the station parking lot, racing to a call. Rudy had witnessed the scene many times growing up in East L.A. where the cops liked getting down as much as the *vatos* did. You learned to stay clear of their paths whether you were walking or driving or at the party they had come to disburse. Rudy turned onto his side and closed his eyes, thinking about those days in the barrio, his newfound troubles with the cops, and this whole idea of turning rat—the idea of which kept him from sleep.

17

JOSIE AND DICKIE LINGERED IN THE CONFERENCE ROOM, EACH AVOIDING eye contact until everyone had left and sounds of their voices no longer echoed in the hallways, the brass having been tucked back into their holes. Josie felt the lingering tension, her partner fuming beneath his fedora that another *pogue* from Internal Affairs had weaseled her way into the bureau. They, Josie and Dickie, would be reporting directly to her on this case and all others, the admin lieutenant being the one who oversaw Unsolveds. Lopes and Floyd hadn't seemed bothered by the revelation, but Lopes never worried about the brass anyway. He avoided them for the most part, doing his job and never informing any of them about what he was doing or what he had done. Never seeking permission nor approval, nor accolades for a job well done. He truly didn't give a shit. He didn't do the job for any other reason than that he thoroughly enjoyed the thrill of the chase, and he thrived on putting killers away. Who knew why Floyd seemed uninterested in the whole affair. He could've been plotting to overthrow the sheriff, or he might have just had something scheduled and needed the meeting to end so he could get the hell out of there. Possibly a haircut. Maybe a manicure. With Floyd, it could've been anything from taking his daughter out for an ice cream to going to the dojo for a session of sword fighting.

Unlike Floyd, Dickie was no mystery, wearing his emotions on his sleeve. He was as predictable as gunfire on New Year's Eve when it came to what he might be thinking, what he planned to do, and how he felt about any particular situation. Josie could tell he was pissed that Neely from IA was his new boss. He'd be further pissed that the captain had instructed them to run everything they did with this case by her *before* it was done. And he would also be none too happy that Stover had told them to work closely with the district attorney's office as well, and to seek and follow their guidance throughout the investigation. Dickie didn't always play well with others, especially when *others* were lawyers or feds.

Dickie rapped his knuckle against the tabletop twice and stood up from his chair as if he had had his say in the matter, though he had said nothing at all.

Josie said, "We're not going to chat?"

He didn't look over at her; rather, he kept his gaze on the file folder before him for a long moment, as if willing the secrets of the case to be revealed. He said, "I wasn't about to say anything during the meeting, and I'm not going to repeat this to anyone other than you. Not yet, anyway. Not until we put some of these pieces together. But—"

It was as if he had lost his train of thought or blacked out, coming to an abrupt stop and still locked on the file before him.

She said, "But what, partner?"

After a long moment passed, he finally looked Josie in her eyes. "I don't like the setup here. Something feels off."

"You don't like that Neely came over."

"No, I don't," he said. "But mostly I don't like the timing of it."

Josie stood up from her chair now as well and began gathering her belongings, preparing to leave that windowless room of gloom. "Like what, you think she's still working for the dark side while being assigned to Homicide?"

"You never know."

"You're being paranoid."

Dickie tucked the case file under his arm and pushed his chair to the table, paused for a moment and met her gaze once more. "You haven't read the file yet. I can tell you a couple of things that might change your mind about that."

"Okay, tell me."

Dickie pulled his chair back out and plopped into it, nodded a suggestion for Josie to do the same. He said, "Was Victor Robles still at the bureau when you got here?"

Josie shook her head, slowly, thinking no, but trying to put a face to the name. "I don't think so."

Dickie waited, giving her time.

She sat down on the edge of her seat, propped her hands on her knees. "No, the more I think of it, I'm pretty sure he wasn't here. The name is somewhat familiar, but I don't think I know him. Was he involved in this case somehow?"

"Yeah, he was one of the primary investigators. When I saw his name on the murder book, I had a feeling this was going to be a problem case. Then she comes in—"

"She?"

"Your new lieutenant, Brenda Neely. Formerly known as Brenda Parks, Brenda Martinez, and Brenda Robles. I think Neely is her maiden, and she's finally done going through the department looking for Mister Goodbar."

Josie allowed herself a moment to absorb that information and to contemplate where her partner might be going with all this. Neely had apparently been married to Victor Robles, who was one of the primaries on the councilman murder. What did that mean? A coincidence, or something else? Clearly her partner was thinking of the *something else*. But what could it be? She said, "Okay, so our new lieutenant was married to one of the investigators on the councilman case. Are you going to tell me there's something strange about that, that it's more than just a coincidence?"

Dickie leaned back in his chair, holding her gaze. "Honestly, I don't know. Maybe it is, maybe it isn't. But I don't like that we have to run everything by her as we essentially reinvestigate a case her husband investigated, a case where there might be a problem with the conviction."

"We don't know that yet, that there's any problem with the conviction."

"No, we don't," Dickie conceded.

"Then it seems you might be worried about nothing. Did you not get along with him, or is there more to this bad feeling you have?"

"Who, Vic? I never worked with him, was never even on the same team with him in the few short years we were both here. He was a drunk—I can tell you that. I had the impression he was one of the lazy ones, but other than that—"

"So he was here a while after you got here, but you never worked with him. He drank like everyone else here. And then what, he transferred out? Got fired? Retired?"

Dickie shook his head. "And then he ate his gun."

18

THERE WERE TWO SUBSEQUENT MEETINGS. THE FIRST WAS HELD IN A conference room at the district attorney's office, which comprises the entire seventeenth floor of the criminal justice center at 210 W. Temple Street, Los Angeles; the second took place a half hour after its conclusion in a Chinatown restaurant bar.

The record would show that the former had been orchestrated by Justin McKnight, who was assigned to lead "the review" of criminal complaint LACBA0097832, the People vs. Anthony Lewis Macias. It was attended by McKnight's supervisor, Ashley Levin, and two other deputy district attorneys who would assist him with the case, as well as by sheriff's homicide investigators Josefina Sanchez, Richard Jones, David Lopes, and Matt Tyler, accompanied by their lieutenant, Brenda Neely.

A stenographer had recorded the minutes, the highlights of which included the following:

On the night of August 3, 2005, at approximately 2130 hours, Los Angeles City Councilman Raymond Jose Juarez of Highland Park was shot to death in front of 3417 Pomeroy Street, City Terrace, an unincorporated community in Los Angeles County, generally known as East Los Angeles. This location is residential and located approximately six miles from the victim's home. Mr. Juarez was a 37-year-old Hispanic, married with two children, ages seven and four at the time. His wife, Gabriela Juarez, 33, was a schoolteacher at Highland Park Elementary. According to the case file notes, the homicide report, and transcripts from the trial, Ms. Juarez had no idea what her husband would've been doing at that location.

Mr. Juarez was shot at the open passenger door of his vehicle, which had been parked facing west along the north curb line of Pomeroy. His briefcase sat on the passenger seat, and it was believed he had opened the door to set it there, or to retrieve it. There was a loaded firearm in the briefcase, registered to Mr. Juarez, who had a concealed carry permit issued by the sheriff of Los Angeles County. There was no evidence that the weapon had been fired.

Two expended 9mm cartridge cases were recovered from the scene, and three expended 9mm projectiles were taken from the victim's body during the postmortem examination: one from his head, and two from his thoracic cage. The two gunshots to the chest were determined to have had a slightly downward, slightly right to left, and an approximate 30 degree front-to-back trajectory. The gunshot to his head was back to front, downward, and slightly left to right.

Gunshot residue was detected on the victim's clothing, and stippling was noted around the head wound, indicating that all three shots were fired at close range, and that the headshot was likely the last, almost certainly a coup de grâce.

During a canvass for witnesses, detectives learned that Mr. Juarez was known to employees of the *Carniceria La Maria* located around the corner from where he was killed, on City Terrace Drive. Mr. Juarez had not gone into the market that night, though he was an occasional customer who would stop by to pick up groceries and beer.

There were no security cameras outside the store; however, an interior video camera captured images of an individual who was identified as Anthony Lewis Macias, the defendant. He was dressed in baggy khaki pants and a dark hoodie, attire that could have easily concealed a firearm. He appeared to be nervous, roaming throughout the store with no apparent direction, and continually looking toward the front door. Eventually, he went to the counter and purchased a single cigarette—a common offering unique to ghettos and barrios—and departed. Outside the store he turned to the right toward Pomeroy Street where the murder occurred.

Macias was the only customer to have entered and exited the store in the hour leading up to the murder who also fit a profile of someone who might be involved in criminal activity. He too was known to the store clerk, and that is how he had been quickly identified. He was eighteen at the time of the murder, a resident of City Terrace, and a member of the Maravilla street gang. He had a record of violent criminal activity including armed robbery, and he was on probation at the time.

Investigators and L.A. County Probation officers contacted Macias at his home two days after the murder, and in accordance with the terms of his probation, they conducted a search of his person and the premises. Clothing similar to that he was seen wearing on the night of the murder was seized as evidence. There were dark stains on the left sleeve of a black hoodie sweatshirt, and those stains were later determined to be the victim's blood.

Macias denied any involvement or even knowledge of Juarez's killing. Although no other evidence was found to link him to the murder other than the victim's blood on his sweatshirt and the video that put him near the scene minutes before the murder occurred, a jury convicted him of first-degree murder. He was sentenced to twenty-five years to life. All appeals have been exhausted, and Macias will be eligible for parole next year.

No motive was ever determined, though investigators believed that Macias intended to rob the victim and was met with resistance. That was the theory presented to the jury as well, even though the victim's briefcase containing a pistol remained at the scene, in plain view of the killer.

The murder weapon has now been recovered. A pistol seized from the vehicle of a violent career criminal named Rudy Prada has been positively matched to the firearms evidence found at the scene and taken from the victim's remains. It should be noted that Mr. Prada lived in the general vicinity of the murder at that time, and he, too, was an active member of the Maravilla street gang.

The purpose of this case review is to determine what, if any, part Rudy Prada had in the murder—not to retry the case against Macias, who is still believed to have been the killer. The direction would focus on determining if there was any motive other than robbery, and to establish a nexus between Macias and Prada if one exists, per Deputy District Attorney Justin McKnight.

LOPES SLID INTO THE BACK OF THE BOOTH, A LARGE ROUND TABLE WITH a circular bench seat with a tall back, covered in shiny red vinyl and framed with dark wood. The flame of a candle centered on the table flickered against the moving air as the others slid in on both sides of him: Josie to his right, followed by Dickie, and Floyd to his left. The waiter who had seated them, handed each a menu and asked if anyone wanted a cocktail. Josie said she'd just have water. Lopes ordered a beer. Floyd ordered a beer as well. Dickie said, "I'll have an old fashioned."

Lopes said, "That sounds good. Me too."

"So no beer?" the waiter asked.

"I'll have both," he said.

Floyd said, "Same for me."

Josie said, "You better bring me one too."

They didn't wait for the drinks to come before the discussion began. Lopes said, "That boyfriend of yours is too fucking stupid to know there's about a dozen Maravilla gangs and half of them are rivals of the other half."

"My boyfriend?" Josie said, pointing a dinner knife at him.

Dickie said, "Yeah, what have we decided to do about that? Is killing him still an option, even though we're now working under his direction on this piece-of-shit case?"

"It's always an option, Dickie," said Floyd. Then he looked at Josie. "You're dating McKnight? I thought he was gay."

She turned the knife his direction. "I've had the desire to stab someone the last couple days. Keep it up, Floyd."

"Anyway," Lopes said, "that's first. Find out who those two fools ran with and see if it's even possible they could be in on something together. I'm telling you, the Maravillas have more issues than a busload of drag queens on their way to a wig sale. They're spread all over, a hunnerd different sets, always at war with each other and every other neighborhood in the county."

Dickie grinned. "Okay, yeah, let's see if Macias and Prada are even from compatible gangs, or if they're mortal enemies. That's a good starting point. Then we need to find out if they've ever been arrested together, done time at the same joint, banged the same hoodrats, whatever."

Josie pictured Rudy Prada with his girl, Vero, back in the day, and again she wondered what she'd look like today. It wasn't a pretty picture. Then she saw him as he appeared fifteen years ago, young and mischievous, a good-looking kid but one with something to prove. She pictured him outside the market—first, Angel's, the day she shot him, then outside of the *Carniceria La Maria,* waiting in the shadows for Macias, the two of them going to put in some work. But for who? *La Eme*? Had it been a hit, or was it straight-up robbery? She didn't think Prada was the type to shoot a man in cold blood, to do a hit. But maybe it had been a robbery gone bad. After all, he had shot the Asian clerk at Angel's Market back in the day.

Drinks came and silence fell over the table until the waiter moved on and everyone had taken their first sips of the day. Lopes was back on Maravilla, saying, "There's Gage Maravilla, Ford Maravilla, Marriana Maravilla—"

Floyd took a call on his cell and was saying, "Uh-huh... yep... "

"—Fraser Maravilla, Raskals Maravilla, High Times Maravilla—"

Josie was thinking of the Maravillas he hadn't named yet, wondering if he would get them all. Wondering if he would remember there's a Lopez Maravilla, and thinking maybe she would give him some shit if he forgot *that* one.

Floyd said into his phone, "Tell him I got called out on something, and we'll have to reschedule." Getting off his phone he said, "Fuck Maravilla."

Lopes glanced at him but continued talking to Josie and Dickie again, rattling them off: "Juarez Maravilla, Gage Maravilla... Did I already say Gage?"

Josie nodded. "Yes, but you've missed a few others."

"Okay, Miss Gang Expert. What'd I forget?"

"Well, there's Lopez Maravilla. I thought for sure you'd get that one."

Lopes shook his head. "Dude, whatever."

She said, "El Hoyo Maravilla, Arizona Maravilla, Kern, Lote, Pomeroy…"

Dickie pulled the cherry out of his old fashioned, said, "I think we've got it—there's a shit ton of 'em," and ate it.

Lopes snapped his fingers and pointed at Josie. "That's right, Pomeroy Maravilla. That's their turf off Pomeroy and City Terrace, right there where it went down."

"Jesus, all this Mexican bullshit," Dickie said. "Okay, Lopes, you and Floyd figure the gang shit out. Josie and I will work on backgrounds, see if we can put Macias and Prada together, or Macias and Prada's cousin, Frankie Rosas, together. Meanwhile, we feed Neely and McKnight nothing but the bare minimum." He glanced at his menu. "What's good here?"

Josie reached across him and pointed to a dish. "I like the Kung Pao chicken."

Dickie said, "It's all the fucking same, whether you buy it here or at the donut store in Compton, or a truck stop off the interstate. Chinese is Chinese." He leaned over and pointed at Lopes's menu. "I like the sweet and sour pork."

19

"Excuse me, deputy. Sir."

The deputy assigned as dayshift jailer at Norwalk had one immediate goal in his professional life, and that was to get the hell out of the jail and back on patrol. But he was riding the pine, as they called it, stuck inside at a desk for three months doing his penance. His name was Schauer. Some would consider him an old salt, a guy who hadn't promoted—hadn't ever taken a test nor even inquired about the prospect of it—and who had no desire to be a detective, an instructor, or anything else. He was a cop. Schauer lived to put on his uniform, go "10-8"—in service—and put the car in harm's way, so to speak. To place himself between predators and prey, the sheepdog mentality of proactive cops.

He was the most senior deputy sheriff at Norwalk Station, making the jailer assignment even that much more humiliating and demoralizing. He had just over a month to go until freedom, so he had committed to being on his best behavior. After all, it was his attitude that had put him in jail to begin with, just like half the crooks that came in. In hindsight, telling the scheduling sergeant he wouldn't make a pimple on a cop's ass, and that he, Schauer, had forgotten more about police work than the young sergeant would ever know, had not been a great idea. To say Schauer was outspoken would be an understatement; the man would tell Jesus his zipper was down.

With his eye on the prize, Schauer made a conscious effort to keep a low profile while running the jail as smoothly as possible—which meant, in part, keeping his guests happy. He turned toward the cell from where the inmate had called out, forced a smile that came off more like he'd bitten into a lemon, and said, "Yes, how may I help you, sir?"

The inmate, Prada, *seven four zero*, was seated on his steel-framed bunk, wearing only white boxer shorts in the stuffy and stale concrete cell. Perhaps he was accustomed to the jailers not responding to him, because it wasn't until Schauer stopped and asked how he could help that Prada came off his bed and hurried to the steel-bar gate to address him. "Sir," he started.

Schauer took in the man's tattoos, instinctively. After all, they told a story—all of them did. There had been more than a few gangsters convicted of murder, in part, because they inked their criminal accomplishments on their bodies. He had a tattoo across his stomach that had been fucked up by what Schauer assumed to be a gunshot wound, obviously destroying the M in the word Maravilla. Although Schauer had been assigned to Norwalk station for the last six years, his first patrol assignment had been at East L.A. station where he had spent more than a decade on the streets, and was very familiar with Maravilla. He studied the man before him, trying to see a younger version of him, wondering if they had crossed paths before. There was a familiarity, but he couldn't put his finger on it. Did he know this *veterano*? Had he arrested him? Jacked him up on a street corner or in the park? He probably had done one or the other, maybe both. He said, "What's an East L.A. *vato* doing in Norwalk?"

Prada took hold of the bars the way all inmates did when they stood at the gates of their cells. He answered Schauer's question, saying he and his old lady lived in Norwalk, that yeah, he was from East L.A., but then came to a stop as if he didn't want to elaborate about that. He said, "And I'm clean now too, Deputy. I don't fuck around with the gangs, and I got clean tests and everything—you can ask my parole officer. Also, I'm in a program right over here,"—indicating a general direction of outside the jail with a nod of his head— "and I do an outreach over in La Mirada. Swear on my kids, Deputy, that other life's behind me." After a moment,

Prada said, "You were in East L.A. before, weren't you? I feel like I know you."

Schauer nodded, but that was all the information about himself he was willing to provide. He'd learned a long time before to not get sucked into answering questions, allowing the roles to be reversed and taking a chance of giving up too much information, or allowing an unwanted familiarity between him and anyone on *the other side*. He said, "What do you want, Prada?"

Prada seemed to think about it for a moment, maybe organizing his thoughts. He said, "I have to talk to the woman sergeant at Homicide, Miss Sanchez. I been thinking about some things, and I can give her some more information. I'm working with her on something, and I think she'll want to talk to me. I just need someone to reach out and let her know. Her name's Sanchez. She's a sergeant over there at Homicide, used to work East L.A."

"You already told me that. And yeah, I know her."

Prada reached down and rubbed the scar on his stomach and smiled. "Matter of fact, she did this."

After a moment of looking at the scar, Schauer grinned. "You the dude she shot outside the market on Third Street?"

Prada nodded. "Yeah, I fucked up. We're good though, now. We're cool."

Schauer chuckled. "You're lucky she was a boot back then. She's lit some dudes up since then, didn't stop after putting just one round in 'em. Know what I mean?"

Prada's eyes darkened, probably considering what could have been. "Yes sir, I know what you mean."

"I'll get a message to her, let her know you want to talk to her."

"Thank you, uh, Deputy…"

Schauer turned the right side of his chest toward him and pointed at his name tag. "Schauer, but don't spell it like the place you make love in prison. It's S-C-H-A-U-E-R. German, 'case you were wondering. One-hundred percent peckerwood, Mr. Prada."

"Where are we on the McKnight deal?"

Josie looked over at her partner. Dickie sat beneath a gray straw fedora, a pair of Oakleys hiding his blue eyes. "What do you mean? There is no *deal*."

He glanced at her from behind the wheel, the two of them headed back to the office after a cocktail lunch in Chinatown, nothing new nor unexpected from homicide dicks. "I mean, you said he might've slipped you something, and I thought we were going to figure this out and deal with it. I can't stand to look at him after hearing about that night. It's all I can do to not strangle him with his tie. And now we have to work with this dipshit on the councilman case?"

"I told you guys," she said, "I can't imagine it was McKnight who slipped me something—if that's what happened. I mean, why would a guy like him have to drug a girl to get laid?"

"So what, you think he's hot?"

Josie didn't answer. Instead she said, "Like Floyd says, dude's probably gay anyway. But either way, I know for sure he didn't do anything to me, so we need to just let it drop and move on."

"How do you know that?"

"Partner, you don't want to know how I know that. Trust me. Girl stuff."

Dickie nodded. "Fine, but that doesn't mean he hadn't planned to do something. If that asshole's a predator—if he did this to you, a cop, for Christ's sake—someone needs to fix his little red wagon for him. And I'm just the guy to do it. I hate fucking predators."

"His little red wagon."

"Yeah, so to speak."

Josie recalled that morning she had found herself alone in the prosecutor's bed, and as she had done a thousand times, she revisited every detail the same way she'd comb through a crime scene or statement trying to find any inconsistency, something that didn't add up, anything that could be used against him. She wasn't about to tell her partner this, but she knew she hadn't been raped because Aunt Flo had paid a visit—it had been that time of the month. Her panties and feminine products were all in place as they should have been, undisturbed. But could that have deterred him, or was he a gentleman all along? Had he, as Dickie alluded, planned to have done something but stopped when he discovered that minor inconvenience? Had he molested her in other ways? These were the questions she couldn't answer, thoughts that haunted her, made her stay with it like it was another of her cold cases.

Maybe Lopes was right, they should kill him. Just in case.

But her instinct told her otherwise. In her gut, she didn't see McKnight as the predator, someone who would slip her something. After all, he was a good-looking guy who could get his fair share of girls to bed if that was what he wanted. If he was straight, she was sure he did. Josie thought about the new-in-a-package spare toothbrush and wondered how many he kept on hand. Maybe the dude was a major player, frat boy with his naked poodle or whatever the little creature was. Crested? Is that what he had told her? Poodle, crested—what was the difference anyhow?

Her phone rang, pulling her thoughts from McKnight and perhaps putting an end to the awkward conversation her partner had started.

"Sergeant Sanchez," she said, and in the same moment knew her partner would be rolling his eyes, if only in his own mind. At Homicide, there was technically no rank of sergeant—all investigators were just that, investigators. Some were sergeants, some were deputies. Their salaries were virtually identical, and a sergeant at Homicide had no supervisory roll whatsoever. They were equals in every way, as far as rank was concerned. Dickie would answer his phone with a simple, "Jones." Or at the office, he might say, "L.A. Sheriff's Homicide," and not bother providing his name. And mock her when she picked up in the office, saying, "Los Angeles County Sheriff's Homicide Bureau, Sergeant Sanchez speaking."

A male voice on the other end of the call said, "Sanchez, Schauer here."

Josie knew the voice, and the name was unmistakable—there was only one Schauer she'd ever known in her life. She pictured him driving a black and white in East L.A. where they had first met, she as a patrol trainee, and he as a menacing station icon, the type of deputy nobody could picture in any configuration other than in his tan and green uniform, encased in a black and white as if it were molded around him, part of his being. It was as if he'd been born a thirty-year-old cop with twenty-five years of experience—and that was back then, fifteen years ago. You didn't see him in a suit and tie behind a desk, and you couldn't picture him at a parent-teacher conference. He probably didn't even have a family. Did he own a home, or live in the bunk room? She didn't know. She only knew that Schauer was hard and serious and intimidating to the newly assigned, but she had grown very fond of him the day she had shot a man in East L.A.—Prada, namely. Schauer had been the first unit to arrive after the shooting, and in the way only a veteran cop like him could, took control of the chaotic scene while also somehow managing to calm her and reassure her during those early moments when everything had seemed so surreal, that she was okay, that she had done the right thing. Those were moments every cop prepared for and imagined happening, but those who experienced them were often surprised by how otherworldly the moments before, during, and after a deadly encounter actually felt.

She glanced at Dickie to measure his response as she said, "Hello, Schauer." (She never called him by his first name, Jim, because there had been a Jim in her life and she now hated the name.) "What a pleasant surprise it is to hear from you, though I doubt this is a social call."

"Well, I was going to ask you out, actually, but heard you're playing for the other team now."

She grinned, still watching Dickie, who had only glanced at her once or twice as they maneuvered through L.A. traffic. This "playing for the other side" was something Dickie would tease her about, he and Lopes both, and others who seemed to be enthralled with her personal life, which she tried to keep private. And now she was hearing it from Schauer, that salty old cop with a limp, who couldn't still chase a crook but had enough talent to keep from having to. For that matter, some people would turn themselves in after he'd go by and tell their mothers he was looking for them. What was with these men presuming she was gay? Was it just a fantasy, or normal childlike behavior?

"As flattered as I am that you had wanted to ask me out, we've missed the prom. And truthfully, you might be on to something about me changing teams. Men are driving me nuts."

Dickie glanced over at her and frowned.

Schauer said, "Your boy Prada needs to talk to you."

"What's he want now, any idea?"

The Program

"He said he needs to give you some information. Said he's working with you on a case."

"Yeah, well, we'll see."

"He looked familiar to me, then he told me he's the one you shot outside the market."

Josie allowed that to hang there for a moment as she pondered why Prada would tell people.

Schauer said, "Showed me where you fucked up his tattoo."

"He'll be lucky if I don't come down there and shoot him again. Jesus, this guy."

"Hey," he said, "not in *my* jail you won't! Like your buddy, Prada, I'm on double secret probation and trying to stay clean over here."

20

Josie blew off going to see Prada at Norwalk. Instead, she called Schauer back and asked that he make sure Prada didn't get shipped out over the weekend. Each of the twenty-three sheriff's stations throughout the county had a booking cage and small jail, most often referred to as holding cells. These station jails were regularly emptied and the inmates were transported downtown where they would be processed through the Inmate Reception Center, and then housed at any of the half a dozen large-capacity jails around the county: Twin Towers and Men's Central Jail downtown, Peter J. Pitchess Detention Center and North County Correctional Center in Castaic, nearly an hour's drive north. The last thing she wanted was to drive to Wayside—the former name still used generically to refer to any of the north county facilities located in Castaic—and she didn't want to hassle with going downtown to visit with him at MCJ or Twin Towers. It was far easier to visit inmates when they remained housed at a local station, so oftentimes when a homicide detective was working with someone in custody—especially on a high-profile case—it was not uncommon to request that the inmate wasn't transferred out. However, it could happen in spite of such a request, especially over a weekend when more arrests were made and holding cell space was at a premium. Schauer had assured her that Prada would be held there at Norwalk, and he said he

The Program

would tell him to cool off, that Josie wouldn't be able to see him until next week.

That had allowed her to go with the plan of sliding out of the office early Friday afternoon, not long after their secondary meeting on the Councilman Juarez case that had been disguised as a cocktail luncheon, or perhaps the other way around. She sat on her living room floor with the case file reports, notes, and photographs spread around her on the carpeted floor, a beige leather sofa her backrest. Classic rock played through her earbuds, a barrier between her focus on the case and the potential distraction that was her mother's Netflix sitcom addiction. She had just started *El Cartel 2*, having binged through the 57 episodes that comprised the first season, and she was very much on the edge of her seat as Pepe Cadena "navigated the treacherous waters of warring cartels in Mexico and Colombia while avoiding capture by the DEA and police." That's what Josie read about the show after fielding far too many questions from her mother about what the DEA could or couldn't do in their quest to capture a drug lord. At some point, she had told her, "*Mamá*, it's just a show. *No es la vida real*. And I don't know what the DEA does in the jungles of South America." Then she showed her she was putting in the earbuds and said, "I need to focus on my case now, *Mamá*." Josie thinking her mother was probably pulling for the bad guys in her show. Maybe in life.

As she shifted her thoughts to the case, Josie considered the focus of their reinvestigation as she and the others had discussed in general terms: a city councilman had been shot and killed in East L.A., and a local gang member had been prosecuted for the crime. Now they had the murder weapon, and it was their job to determine if its discovery changed anything as far as Anthony Macias's conviction, and what, if anything, Rudy Prada and/or Frankie Rosas had to do with it. But she wondered if there were more to it, and she reminded herself to remain open to alternative possibilities, should any arise.

She began with the victim. Who was he? What was he doing at that location at that time? Could he have been involved in something that hadn't been revealed? Or was there a woman in the mix, a little something on the side that would draw the councilor into seedy neighborhoods he might have been well advised to avoid?

What motive might someone have had for killing him, if it hadn't been a simple street robbery? The age-old scorned lover? The lover's husband or boyfriend? Maybe the councilman was into dope, and this whole thing was as simple as a street deal gone bad or the attempted ripoff of a customer.

Juarez was 37 at the time of his death, married with two children, a boy and a girl, who would now be grown. Josie pictured them as college students, second-generation Mexican Americans who would know the importance of education in their pursuits of the American dream. She saw the girl as a young woman, a professional in business attire who followed in her father's footsteps, an attractive young lawyer making her way up the steps to city hall, an attaché case in one hand, a Starbucks in the other. Her younger brother likely still on campus, or maybe in the military. Many second- and third-generation Americans took great pride in serving their country. Or maybe they had gone the other direction, one in jail and the other on a street corner, representing. That was the thing, you never knew. Josie had known some great parents who ended up with rotten kids.

Juarez had been serving his second term as a Los Angeles City councilman of District 14, which encompassed downtown, Boyle Heights, Eagle Rock, Garvanza, El Sereno, Glassell Park, Monterey Hills, and Lincoln Heights. He was killed on August 3, 2005 at about 2130 hours—9:30 at night. The location was 3417 Pomeroy Street, City Terrace, a residential county area within the East Los Angeles district. Josie made a note to run a check of that residence and the adjacent homes through the CalGangs database, if for no other reason than to be certain that Prada or Rosas didn't have any affiliation with the location. The genius of the often-criticized gang tracking software—created by a former sheriff's gang investigator—was that with a simple address search, you could potentially discover any gang activity at the location, including any arrests that had been made there, and even any field interviews or crime reports.

Nine thirty wasn't late by most standards, but for a city councilman who had a wife and small children at home, you would hope there had been a good reason for him to be out. Maybe he had had a meeting to attend, or some type of community event. After all, the location where he was killed wasn't far from Lincoln Heights, a part of his district.

Josie made a note:

Establish timeline of victim that evening

She started to turn to the next page in the murder book, and stopped, picked her notepad up again.

Timeline of suspect
Timelines of Prada and Rosas
Timeline of victim's wife (and look into their relationship)

That spurred another thought:

Check insurance policies and payouts

Josie knew you could never go wrong by looking closest to home when investigating murder, especially when the victim did not fall into a high-risk category.

If it *was* a robbery, why wasn't the briefcase taken? And what were the odds that Juarez would park around the corner from the market, on a gang-infested residential street, unless there was no parking out front. Why would he? Would he not recognize the danger of it? Or was he there for another reason?

Check parking restrictions in front of market
Look into possible drug use by victim
Review cell phone records

She had just scratched the surface, and there were already more questions than answers. There was a shootout on the television, Hispanic men blasting at one another from behind cars and around the corners of buildings, flames coming from the barrels of fully automatic rifles as cartridge casings flew through the air. Josie's mom, Esmeralda, had leaned forward in her chair to get a closer look, her eyes wide with excitement, a handkerchief clutched in a frail hand. Queen was playing in Josie's ear, "Another One Bites the Dust," appropriately.

Now Josie was at the scene investigation, a report written by the late homicide detective, Victor Robles. The shootout on TV was over and Josie couldn't help but think what a mess *that* scene would be to investigate: hundreds, if not thousands, of casings all over the ground, projectiles lodged in buildings and cars and in the bodies of at least four *narcos* who lay posed in bloody and torn clothing, their eyes all closed as if death had been peaceful. Josie knew that wouldn't have been the case.

In the report there were measurements and descriptions of the various items of evidence found at the scene. Josie spread crime scene photos around her for reference as she read through the report. Something bothered her. There were two expended casings found, but hadn't someone said during the briefing—maybe Dickie, or McKnight—that the victim had been shot three times? She thumbed to the back of the murder book where she found the coroner's protocol, browsed through it until she came to the part she was interested in at that moment, and made another note:

Three gunshots - one to the head, two to the torso

Close range

Gunshots to the chest – downward, L-R, front-back

Gunshot to the head – back-front, downward, R-L

She said, "Where's the other casing?"

Her mom glanced over, her face a question mark, and then went back to her show.

Josie added to her notepad:

Where was the third casing

And there was something else gnawing at her.

Why the headshot if it was only a robbery?

She could see it now in her mind's eye, the first two gunshots in a direct confrontation, the victim facing his killer. Then he was shot twice in the chest, went down, and—just as depicted in scene photos—he had turned back toward his car, there at the passenger's door, as if trying to get into the car. Maybe he had thought to go for the gun in his briefcase.

He hadn't heard nor seen the final shot.

She said to Dickie, "Did they not find it, or did the killer take it for a souvenir? I mean, I know we don't always find every shell casing, but when a councilman is killed, you'd think they'd get the metal detectors out there and comb through that scene until there was no doubt that it *wasn't* there. Right? I mean, maybe it was kicked into a storm drain by a paramedic, or it got stuck in the tread of his boot and he took it back to his station with him, maybe home. I realize there are plenty of explanations, but it bothers me a bit."

It was Monday morning, and each of them was commuting to the office in that glorious L.A. traffic under an infinite blue sky that made Josie wish she were headed to the beach instead. When was the last time she had enjoyed a day in the sun, the briny smell of the ocean mixed with the orange blossom fragrance of her suntan lotion, the tickly feel of wet sand between her toes as cold water splashed her legs and seagulls cawed above her? Too long ago to remember, truthfully; she needed a vacation. A real one, an unplugged getaway to some tropical location where a dark-skinned cabana boy supplied her with fruity and fresh cocktails throughout the day and night, and fish tacos were abundant.

Dickie's voice through her speakers brought her back to the grind of commuting in L.A. "I wouldn't think too much about it, partner. As you've said, there are many possibilities."

She refocused on those things that had bothered her about the Juarez murder. After a moment, she said, "I'm just wondering—"

But Dickie had already begun. "For all we know, good ol' Vic Robles showed up to the crime scene drunk and kicked it down a storm drain himself. What are you wondering?"

"Well..."

"Yes?"

"I had a thought, so I reviewed the firearms report, just to be clear—"

"About?"

"Well, not all three projectiles recovered from the victim were positively identified through ballistics."

"Like they didn't do it? They didn't compare each one to the other, or what?"

"No, like the projectile recovered from the head was too badly deformed for a ballistics comparison, but it was assumed to be from the same weapon."

Dickie sighed into the phone. "So if I'm following your train of thought, you think there were only two casings found at the scene because there were two different weapons, and one of them didn't eject a casing."

"Right. Like maybe there was another gun, but it was a revolver."

"So, two shooters."

She said, "It's just a thought."

"Macias and somebody else?"

Josie shrugged, alone in her county car, cool air from the vent lifting her hair. "Who knows? Or maybe Macias wasn't even part of it."

Dickie didn't respond to that right away, and Josie pictured him with his squinting eyes, pondering the possibilities. Finally, he said, "Josie, they found the victim's blood on his sweatshirt, remember?"

Now it was her turn to consider things. After a moment, she said, "Yeah, that's right. I don't know, partner, maybe I'm trying too hard to find a flaw in this case."

"But why? It's just another case."

"I don't know. Maybe because now Prada is being pulled into it because of the gun. I don't think he had anything to do with it, partner. What was he, sixteen, seventeen at the time?"

"How old was he when he walked into that market in East L.A. with a gun in his pocket?"

Now her voice was quiet, soft. "Nineteen."

"And what's the youngest killer you've arrested?"

She let a moment pass. "Fourteen."

Dickie didn't say anything. He didn't need to. But Josie did need to say something. She had to explain her gut to her partner so he wouldn't think she was being naïve, or that somehow, she'd been blinded by some emotional connection to Prada. That wasn't the case. Yes, she felt he was sincerely trying to get back on the right track, but she also knew he had a history, and some of that history was bad. But how bad? That was the question. She figured they would have a better idea of that by the end of the week, or sooner. She said, "Okay, partner, I get your point. I guess we'll know more once we get into these backgrounds. Where're you at? I'm about fifteen out from the office."

Dickie said, "I've been sitting here in the parking lot for ten minutes, finishing up a conversation with one of the best homicide detectives I've ever known—certainly the hottest."

Josie blushed and felt an emotion coming over her. God, she loved her partner. Even when she got off track and maybe seemed irrational or sounded silly or looked dumb, he was right there to pick her up, support her, make her smile again. She said, "If you weren't married, I'd give you a giant kiss—right on the smacker. Walk into the office and plant one on you in front of everyone."

He said, "It didn't stop you last time."

21

It had been only five days since they'd learned that Prada's gun —which is how it was referred to by everyone except Josie—had come back to the councilman murder. In that time, Josie and Dickie had arrested Prada, tracked down the original case file at the Homicide library—a file box full of documents and evidence from 2005—and they had each gone through all the reports and photos and evidence. Most of that review had taken place over the last several days, and primarily on their own time over the weekend. At least that had been the case for Josie. They had met with Chappy's master, Justin McKnight, who briefed them on the facts of the court case, and offered them some direction as to how to navigate the potential dust cloud that might arise, should they unveil anything that could overturn Macias's conviction. Lastly, they held a secret meeting of their own, Josie and Dickie, Floyd and Lopes, at which they mapped out a strategy that excluded the one order given by the captain, that Lieutenant Neely be briefed on all developments and kept in the loop on all courses of action, before said actions were taken.

Now here she stood in the doorway of Unsolveds, this appointed overseer of all things related to a nearly two-decades dead councilman, her mere presence a screech against the chalkboard for Josie. Lopes was nearly horizontal behind his desk, leaned back in his chair with both feet propped on the clutter-free environment of his workspace, a phone tucked against his shoulder. Dickie was gone, though Josie knew he must have been somewhere in the office. He had told her he was there before she arrived, and she had seen his car in the lot when she pulled in a short time ago.

Josie continued going through her email, paying no mind to the presence of her lieutenant.

Neely said, "Do you guys have an update for me on the councilman case? Captain is asking."

Lopes said into the phone, "Let me call you back," then hung up and nodded to Josie, essentially telling her, It's all yours, kid.

Josie turned in her chair to face the lieutenant, taking in her wardrobe of the day: an emerald green wrap dress with a black blazer and sling-back pumps on her feet. The woman knew fashion, she'd give her that. But a little overdone, maybe? This was Homicide, not Sheriff's Headquarters where many sought to enhance their careers through office connections and after-hours cocktails, or more. But then again, she also wasn't an investigator. Neely wouldn't have any reason to leave the office, ever. This woman was an admin lieutenant disguised as a fashion model, and Josie wasn't sure if she admired or hated her. She'd have to see.

For now, she'd test her tolerance. Josie said, "I'm sorry, what did you say? I was reading an email."

Neely glanced at Lopes and came back to her, annoyance in her tone. "I *asked* if there were any updates on the councilman's case. The captain has requested that you keep me apprised of your efforts and results. I assume you've put your other cases aside and that you're working solely on it?"

Josie looked over at Lopes, who held a stoic gaze—the cold, unreadable stare of a veteran detective who was quick to bluff, unrelenting in his raising the pot, and never prepared to fold. No help to her at all, and clearly not budging. It was on her alone. She said, "We are mostly in the case review process, not a lot to report just yet."

"I see."

Perhaps she did, but then again maybe she didn't. The woman had never worked Homicide, much less Unsolveds, and the truth of it was, she had never even been a detective. Her so-called detective experience was supervising Internal Affairs cases, which was to say she had none at all. She wouldn't know that an average murder book comprised several hundred or more pages of reports and documents, and that cases such as the councilman's murder could easily require two or three volumes. Then there were the transcripts of various court proceedings: namely a preliminary hearing and then the trial. Perhaps appellate court transcripts as well. These documents could be thousands of pages, easily.

Josie assumed the lieutenant knew none of this, even though she had been married to a homicide detective at one time, for however long that might have lasted. So she likely didn't "see," and Josie had no doubt that another question loomed. She waited, offering nothing. Leaving the ball in the lieutenant's court as she stood now leaning against the doorway, one hose-encased ankle crossed over the other, her arms folded beneath her generously-sized breasts.

After a moment, Neely reset her positioning from laid back to authoritative, standing erect again and firmly on both feet. She said, "Okay then, carry on. I look forward to a report on your progress in the very near future."

She left and Lopes grinned at Josie. "Do we hate her?"

"I'm definitely leaning that way."

THE LADY COP HAD LEFT HIM HANGING. SHE HADN'T COME BACK TO TALK about Frankie and the gun, and she hadn't told Schauer anything about when she might be back, at least according to him. Rudy would ask him a couple times a day until he'd beat him to the punch—the heavy-framed copper lumbering down the corridor doing his jail checks—he'd say, "No, Prada, I haven't heard from her." And Rudy would put his head back on his pillow and stare at the ceiling and ponder his future that wasn't working out the way he had thought it would once he got straight. It may have been good he was locked up, he thought, or else he'd probably be looking to get drunk or high with all the shit he was dealing with.

They were all the same that way, bitches leaving you hanging when you needed them most. He and Mikey had once asked Vero to drive them to score some dope, the connection in a rival gang neighborhood, and they had told her no matter what, don't leave them stranded in that hood. He had told her, "You hear gunshots, you sit there at the wheel until we come out or the coroner arrives." She had said, "Who'd be doing the shooting? You scoring dope or ripping the dude?" She was smart like that—too smart for her own good sometimes. He hadn't bothered to answer her question, only reiterated to her that she'd better be there when they came out. Be there and be ready to split in a hurry. What he hadn't prepared her for was the arrival of cops, this deal going down in the city, Lincoln Heights in LAPD's jurisdiction. And the cops did arrive—*just his luck*—and she broke the first rule of staying put. Vero dropped it into gear and eased away, leaving the boys on their own. She could've at least honked or something, let them know there was a problem. Rudy and Mikey made it out the back but getting home hadn't been a piece of cake. They were chased twice by rival gang members and shot at once, too busy running and dodging bullets to bother shooting back. He should've learned then that you couldn't even rely on your ol' lady—how were you going to rely on a lady cop?

His plan now was to work on this Schauer dude. Prada could tell the guy was a hardcore cop just by the way he carried himself, the way he looked at you when you talked to him, studied you like a human lie detector and always appeared ready to pounce. He wasn't the type you'd be able to bullshit, not here nor on the streets. But he *was* the type who'd get a hard-on to make a big bust, take down a big score or put a killer in jail. A lot of these cops lived for nothing else.

Next time the dude came through on his rounds, Rudy would hit him up, see what might interest him. He'd want to know what Rudy wanted in return, and he'd put it to him simple: I just can't go back to County. He'd ask that Schauer keep him at Norwalk but get him out of the tiny cell. Make him a trustee or something. Tell him he'd put some work in for him, hell, he'd even buy drugs for him when he was back on the streets, help him put some big dope cases together. Or he could drop a dime now and then and let him know who's holding—guns or dope, whatever he wanted. When some *vato* got capped, he'd supply him with the name of the shooter. Everyone on the street always knew anyway; it amazed Rudy sometimes that the cops couldn't figure it out. He could even tell him about some old cases, some of the shit that went down in East L.A. back in the day, if Sanchez didn't care enough to come talk to him. Maybe tell Schauer the story behind that gun Frankie left in his car, quit acting like he didn't know anything about it or the man who got whacked by it.

At this point, Rudy had to take care of himself no matter what that meant as far as his reputation on the street. After a few days of staring at the concrete ceiling, offending himself with his body odor—five days now without the opportunity to shower—and thinking about all the things he'd gotten away with, all the things he still needed to make amends for, he'd come to terms with one thing over all else: he couldn't go back to the joint.

22

Dickie walked in and put his suit jacket and hat on a wooden coat tree that stood next to his desk, pulled his chair out and plopped down into it with a groan. He glanced back and forth from Josie to Lopes as he said, "What'd she want?"

Lopes said, "She was looking for you."

While Josie said, at the same time, "An update. Where were you?"

He likely knew Lopes was being facetious, Josie figured, since he ignored Lopes and said to her, "I saw her headed this way and suddenly needed an emergency cup of joe. But see? This is what I was talking about. She needed an update. As if we suddenly need a lieutenant to monitor our progress on a case. I can't stand that broad, and I don't understand why your captain wants her involved in our cases."

"Case," Lopes said, pushing out of his chair. "Just this one." He stood behind his desk, hands on his hips, his crisp white shirt sleeves turned up at the cuffs, his collar unbuttoned and the Windsor knot on his plaid tie loosened. Everyone always seemed exhausted here, even at the start of the day. He unwrapped a stick of gum and shoved it in his mouth, began chewing around his words. "This one piece of shit that's probably a big nothing. Guns turn up after other cases are adjudicated all the time. Usually doesn't change the outcome of any prosecution."

The Program

Dickie nodded but didn't say anything, clearly still stewing over the whole bit.

"Also," Lopes continued, his eyes now on Dickie, "we no longer refer to our female companions and coworkers as 'broads'—this isn't the fifties, Dickie, as much as you hate to admit it."

Josie grinned. "Dickie's a relic."

"I don't see how 'broads' is so bad," Dickie defended. "These asshole rappers call 'em all kinds of bitches and hoes and nobody says a word about it—not the broads from NOW or anyone else. And that's when they're not rapping about killing cops."

Lopes started in on rappers, naming a few of the more popular ones who he felt should be in prison. One was a former dope-slinging, cap-busting gangster who had become an American icon, performing at the Super Bowl and appearing in beer commercials alongside dudes he would've robbed for their shoes when doing time in the county. That got Dickie started, and he'd be hard to stop, off the subject of the lieutenant for the time being. The two of them solving society's ills in Unsolveds.

Josie had other things on her mind, primarily the list of things to do on the councilman case she'd compiled during her case review over the weekend while her mother had worried about Pepe Cadena and the drug cartels and periodically telling her, "*Mija*, you need a life besides that job. You need to find a good man, get married, raise some kids." Of course, all of this said in a mix of English and Spanish with no discernible reason for the blending of languages. And Josie now thinking she already had kids to take care of, Lopes and Dickie being enough for her as they had somehow moved on to the topic of Stevie Nicks, Dickie telling Lopes—to Lopes's apparent amazement—that Stevie had used the name Sarah Anderson when she checked in at the Betty Ford Center rehab facility in Rancho Mirage, California. Lopes saying, "No shit, how do you know this stuff?" and Josie just wondering how they got from gangster rap to Stevie Nicks, thinking, there must've been a sharp left turn that had something to do with sex.

Her desk phone rang, and she grabbed it. "Los Angeles County Sheriff's Homicide Bureau, Sergeant Sanchez speaking."

She listened to the familiar voice saying, "Sanchez, Schauer here," and watched Lopes and Dickie end their boyhood fantasies conversation to stop and listen in.

To throw them off, she said, "Yes, commander, how may I help you?"

"Are you drinking already?" Schauer said, likely thinking she hadn't heard him correctly when he had identified himself.

"That's a great idea, sir. How may I help you?" she said, staying with the formal tone to keep the boys guessing.

After a moment of silence on the line, Schauer said, "Josie, can you hear me? This is Schauer."

"Yes sir, both of them are here with me now," she said, glancing up to see their reactions. Nothing to read on Lopes but Dickie's brows were bunched together, and his eyes were narrowed at her as if she were the enemy suddenly, her partner about to launch into one of his tirades. She decided to drop the façade and let them off the hook, but Schauer abruptly disconnected.

Josie placed her phone back in its cradle and forced a smile. "It was Schauer down at Norwalk, trying to make me think he was Commander Barnes." She picked the phone back up and dialed Norwalk, said, "Jailer, please," and a moment later, "Schauer, Sanchez here. Did you need something?"

"If you've been taken hostage, say, 'Thank you, Commander,' and give me some type of hint as to where you are. Otherwise, I'll drop a call to Psych Services and see about getting you in for an appointment, find out what the fuck is wrong with you. Now, what will it be, Sergeant?"

Josie forced a chuckle. "Yeah, you got me that time, Schauer. Now what can I do for you? How's my boy holding up down there in your jail?"

She noticed the boys went back to their devices—Lopes on his cell phone now and Dickie looking at his computer—the two of them finished with their conversations about gangster rappers and Stevie Nicks, and no longer interested in her phone conversation.

Schauer was saying, "He wants to work for me."

"Like a trustee?"

"Yeah, something like that. A trustee, an informant..."

"Whatever you're comfortable with," Josie said, "just as long as you hold on to him there. Wait, what's he going to give you information on?"

The Program

"He didn't offer anything specific, just said he could give me dope and other stuff, maybe even murders, once he's back out."

She glanced around the office again and leaned back in her chair. Why would Prada want to be a snitch for Schauer? Why would he turn rat at all? That was the question she needed to ponder, because she didn't really see him as the informant type. Sure, he had told them about the gun he was caught with, but that made sense to her. If the gun righteously belonged to his cousin, Frankie, and if Prada was, as he professed, now straight, clean and sober, and uninvolved with gang life and criminal activity, she could see him doing whatever it took to stay clean and out of prison. But to go beyond that, to become an informant to some other cop, what was in it for him?

"He's working you," Josie said flatly. "Prada is smart, and he can be slick. He's a likable guy and I think he knows it, uses it to get him places —or in this case, to get him out of someplace. You better be careful with how much leeway you give him."

She heard Schauer sigh into the phone, exasperated, or maybe bored. He said, "Sanchez, who are you talking to?"

"I know—"

"I've got more time sliding through intersections in uncontrolled four-wheel locked skids than you put in a radio car. Don't tell me how to handle my informants."

She grinned into the phone, picturing crusty old Schauer in his youth overdriving to a call for assistance and locking up all four to avoid a collision. She had done it herself—every cop in a high-activity area had. You learned to settle down after a year or two on the streets, once you'd rolled code three to dozens of priority calls and been involved in half a dozen or more pursuits. But she couldn't imagine Schauer had overdriven to a call since Christ was a crossing guard. Chances were, he would now take the long route and wait for traffic lights to turn green, having long ago adapted to the unwritten policeman's policy to never beat Rescue to a call. Let the firemen and paramedics start CPR or first aid, stuff gauze into the sucking chest wound of a gunshot gangster. Sure, like all cops, he'd take some chances rolling to a call of a baby not breathing, and yeah, he'd go balls to the wall on a deputy requesting assistance, involved in a fight or shooting. But otherwise, Josie didn't see Schauer getting too worked up over anything other than last call at The Shack, if there were such a thing. The Shack—a dingy bar located in East L.A.'s jurisdiction—seldom respected the two o'clock cutoff for its deputy patrons. Instead, the door would be locked so that no outsiders could happen in, and the beer and liquor flowed until no lawman—or woman—was standing.

"Okay, big guy. Do what you want with Prada as long as you keep him there. My partner and I will likely come see him in the next day or two—I'll give you a heads up before we come."

"I can hardly wait," he said, clicking off without another word.

To the disconnected line, Josie said, "Great... okay... uh-huh... okay, yeah, well good luck with your penis enlargement. Talk soon... uh-huh, yes, fuck you very much. Bye-bye." She smacked her lips near the receiver with an exaggerated *mu-ahh* sound, as if signing off with a big wet kiss.

After hanging up the phone, she looked up to see Dickie and Lopes watching her, each showing anticipation of what might come next, an explanation or maybe a rant. Instead she said, "Which one of you two cheap bastards is buying me lunch today?"

"HOW DO YOU ACCUSE SOMEONE OF SLIPPING YOU A MICKEY, ESPECIALLY A deputy district attorney? I honestly don't think that it was him. The truth of it is, I can't even prove I was drugged. So no, I haven't confronted him yet. I wouldn't know where to start. I had planned to after court last week, but it didn't work out, and now—with McKnight being involved in this councilman ordeal—I'm frankly glad I've kept my mouth shut."

She wheeled into a space on the side of the parking lot where the building offered shade this time of the afternoon. She left the motor running and the air conditioner blowing, and felt her hair lifting from her shoulders. The coolness flowing against her sweat-dampened skin after the short drive from *In-N-Out* to the office, the car not having had time to cool down, was wonderful. She turned toward Dickie, who had his fedora in one hand while wiping a handkerchief across his forehead with the other. Josie continued, "But if you have a clue about how we figure it out, Detective, I'm all ears."

He was fiddling with the vents now, apparently trying to get a more direct airflow. Dickie said, "We can set him up."

Josie snapped back, "That's a little dangerous."

"Yeah, maybe. Let me ask you something. If he didn't do anything to you—if he's not the predator we worry he might be—would you be interested in him, romantically? I mean, you must at least be attracted to him if you went out for drinks."

She narrowed her eyes as she thought about it, but she didn't think her partner could tell, her doe-like browns concealed behind oversized designer knockoffs. Josie wasn't about to wear her *Guccis* at work, take a chance of dropping them onto a leaking corpse or having them crushed by a left hook—not that she anticipated much violence working Unsolveds. But you never knew. After a moment of consideration, she finally answered him. "Maybe."

Dickie chuckled. "Women."

"What? It's a maybe. I mean, yeah, he's attractive—though maybe a bit cocky. Has a promising career. He's fashionable and his condo is *elegantly appointed*," she said, finishing the sentence with the flair of an aristocrat. "I don't know, maybe he's gay. I wondered that, to be honest. Him and his little naked dog, Chappy."

"Okay, well let's find out. What would that hurt?"

She didn't know what it could hurt, but something about the idea of it didn't seem right. She said, "Maybe, but not until we're finished with this councilman thing. I'm not making this any more uncomfortable than it already is. But I would like to know what you've got in mind. Set him up how?"

"Another date, only this time with some watchful eyes protecting you."

"You."

"Yeah, of course. Maybe Lopes and Floyd too."

"He knows all of you. How are you going to be nearby and go undetected?"

Dickie put his hat back on his head and adjusted it the way he always did, down and then up, like there was some special place it sat on his dome, but he couldn't find the sweet spot without going all Helen Keller with it.

He said, "We'll figure something out, don't worry about that."

She turned the car off and popped open her door. "No, perish the thought. Why would I worry about you and Lopes and Floyd cooking up a scheme? Nothing to be concerned with there."

Dickie popped his door too and unfolded himself from the car with a groan. Josie wondered if it was his back again, or his knees. The job had taken its toll on him and it showed. He must've read her thoughts, looking at her over the back of the car as they walked toward the rear door to the office. "I need to get these knees looked at, but I'm not letting them cut on me." He took a last slurp of his Arnold Palmer, tossed the cup in a trash can that sat by the door, and pulled it open and held it for her.

"Thank you," she said, as the cool air of the office rushed over her.

Dickie, right behind her, said, "My pleasure, partner. I have to take good care of you so that you can help carry me across the finish line."

23

"I'm worried he's going to rat us out."

Vero sat with her bare legs propped on a coffee table littered with fast-food wrappers and overflowing ashtrays, empty beer cans and a half bottle of tequila. She considered Frankie's words while holding a flame to the bottom of a glass pipe and sucking in two lungs full of crack vapor, the flame flickering against the breeze from a ceiling fan twirling lazily above her.

He said, "I got to have him taken out, Vero. It's just business."

Vero's head fell back against the wall, the couch cushion supporting her neck. Her cutoff jean shorts were unbuttoned, allowing her belly room to relax, and her boobs sagged beneath a nearly see-through wife-beater, damp with perspiration, dirty and stained. Frankie shook his head as he took it in, wondering how she ever got this bad. Thinking about how pretty she was back when they were young, how everyone, including himself, had lusted over her. Thinking about the nude Polaroids Rudy had shown him back in those days and remembering the few occasions while Rudy was doing time when she got drunk and fell into Frankie's arms, and the two of them ended up in her bed—in Rudy's bed! And thinking about how he now felt, thinking that he wouldn't touch her with the neighbor's dick—not again, anyway. Yeah, he had jumped her after Rudy split last week, but that was like getting laid after doing a number, pulling a job or putting in some work, doing a drive-by in a rival's neighborhood. Frankie always needed sex as he came down from such natural highs, the most exhilarating moments he'd ever experienced. Which is why many of the homies let a hoodrat roll with them when putting in work—so they could get off right after, sometimes before they were even safely back in their own neighborhoods. Sometimes it cost them though, the bitches rolling over on them the first time a cop caught them dirty, holding dope or hooking or cashing phony checks at *el mercado*. And yeah, he had been with her another time or two since Rudy split, but as he stared at her now, he couldn't see how he had stooped so low. Veronica had gone full hoodrat, and she no longer had the looks to entice anyone other than the most desperate *vatos*. Maybe that's why Rudy had checked out, another way to see it that Frankie hadn't considered.

Vero raised her head and met his gaze. She was stoned, her expression stoic and unreadable, seemingly deep in thought, but Frankie had no idea where she was in her head. He had just suggested they kill the father of one of her children, the man she had been with since she was sixteen. Frankie could see evil in her eyes, perhaps anger at his suggestion. But she was too loaded for him to explain himself, to tell her about his homie who was locked up in Norwalk, and who had heard Rudy talking to the hack there, Rudy telling the jailer he had some things to tell him and asking for a private conversation. That was flat out snitching, and Frankie needed Vero to understand this. It wasn't just *his* ass on the line, but hers too. He needed the bitch to sober up for a day so he could explain it all to her and make sure she was good with what needed to be done, and make sure she would be able to keep her mouth shut after.

Vero said, "So fucking kill him, *primo*. The fuck I care?" and she put her head back against the wall and closed her eyes.

Frankie's heart suddenly pounded in his ears, his breath short and rapid the way it would be before a fight, the anticipation of actually doing Rudy leaving him nervous and jittery. He needed something to drink, a beer maybe, or some of the tequila from Vero's bottle. He went into the kitchen and grabbed a Budweiser out of the fridge, popped it and drained half the can with one long pull. Now he felt good, ready to fight… ready to kill.

Ready to fuck. He started back for the living room feeling himself become aroused, thinking, she'll do... thinking, she ain't half bad, really. When he came around the corner, Vero's shorts were on the ground and she was sprawled across the couch with her legs wide open, a smile on her face, a tear streaking black mascara down her cheek. She pulled the bottom of her shirt up to wipe it away, her left tit popping out beneath it, "Rudy" tattooed across it with a rose. She stretched her shirt back over the boob to cover it and most of her flabby stomach, and said, "Come and get it, foo'."

There was no turning back now, he knew. He was hard and ready, and any port in a storm, right? Frankie glanced out the front window and saw it was still light outside, no worry about anyone seeing in. He was careful like that, concerned about his enemies, which were many. You didn't want to be caught slipping, literally caught with your pants down. The front door was closed, and the old man next door was gone with his woman— Frankie had watched the two of them load up with the three yapping dogs a half hour earlier and depart. Her grandparents. Nosy bastards. But with them gone and nobody else around, he had nothing to lose but maybe some self-respect, and his *primo*. But that fucker was living on borrowed time anyway, Frankie coming to terms with the fact that Rudy had to be taken out. He had too much on them to let him walk away if the path he was going down included turning rat. Vero seemed to be on the same page. But how would she feel when she sobered up—if she ever did. Keep that junkie ass loaded and you were probably okay, but if she got to jonesing, needed a fix bad, who knew what kind of shit she would do to score some dope. Then, if she were to get busted, well, nobody squeals like a bitch headed to slam.

Frankie slid into her, Vero with her eyes closed and moaning enough that he knew she wasn't dead or unconscious, but not like she was into what they had going. The bitch probably thinking she was doing him a favor, putting out because that's what she always did—for anyone and nearly everyone. Rudy was always too blind to see it, and he was better than her. Rudy deserved better, and everyone but Rudy knew it. She was an evil bitch that had never been loyal, and Rudy had always loved her like he was her one-and-only, and she his ride-or-die. But he wasn't, and neither was she.

Frankie was finishing, far too soon, but in a way he was glad. He couldn't stand to be there another minute with her. What had she said when he brought up whacking her supposed lifelong love? So fucking kill him, *primo*. The fuck do I care?

Frankie zipped up and grabbed a beer for the road from the fridge, the last one. As he walked back through the living room, Vero was snoring, her disgusting vagina displayed for anyone to see. She should cover herself, for Christ's sake, Frankie thought as he approached the front door. What if her parents came in, or one of the kids dropped by?

His hand on the doorknob, he had a thought—several, actually, clear and crisp, Frankie in his zone again. He knew what he had to do. He set his beer on a table that held a lamp with no shade and sat next to the front door, and he walked back over to her. There he stood, staring at her. Listening to her snore now. Looking at her disgusting fat belly and that nasty snatch. He pulled a .25 auto from his pocket and shot the bitch twice in her face.

Her eyes popped wide open, and they remained that way, two saucers set above a bloody cavity where her nose used to be, and a distorted mouth, open and bloody, teeth missing from the front. Her left arm came up as if she had a question, but then it dropped perpendicular to her body and hung off the edge of the couch. Her last breath rattled from her bloody throat, and she was gone. Frankie thought he saw her spirit seep from her body and vanish through the wall behind her, some wicked shit he'd experienced before, mostly in dreams of other people he'd killed. He didn't think others had the power to hear or see spirits, that you only gained that once the devil knew he could trust you, that you were his for eternity. Frankie never understood the *vatos* who wore crosses or said a prayer at a homie's funeral or professed to be cool with God when they went out and took lives for their hood. That shit was gangster work, and any fool with half a brain knew you couldn't be a gangster and still make it to heaven.

He strolled out of Vero's pad, adrenaline rushing through him as he relived in his mind putting the barrel of a gun inches from her face and pulling the trigger. He was at peace with what he had done because she had betrayed his *primo*, and to be honest, she was basically no use to anyone now, the booze and drugs turning her into a lazy, loudmouthed bitch. She was better off this way. They were all better off this way.

The Program

And if there was one thing Frankie firmly believed in, it was taking care of the hood, protecting the homies. That included from within. The bitch had too much dirt on everyone, and there was no sense in leaving loose ends when there was gangster shit to be done.

24

One benefit to working Unsolveds was that you were no longer on call for murders—you didn't take fresh cases other than during extraordinary times where all hands were required on deck. Which meant you didn't get middle-of-the-night calls very often, and you didn't expect your phone to ring after midnight when you were out having a cocktail or two with your friends.

Lopes said, "Who's calling you now, the pretty boy D.A., McFuckface?"

She shrugged, pushed the button to receive the call, and brought the phone to her ear. Josie covered her other ear with her free hand so she could hear over the noises of the bar, music and talk and laughter, and now Lopes scraping his chair back from the table, likely headed to the boys' room or maybe up to the bar for another round. Josie thought to tell him no more for her, especially no more until she found out who was calling her at this hour, and why. But it was too late; he was on a mission.

"Sergeant Sanchez," she said into the phone.

"Josie, it's Miguel at the office."

"Hi, Miguel."

"Hey, we sent a team out to a murder in La Mirada a little while ago, and they want to talk to you."

The Program

"Who is it?"

"The team? Luna and Wright."

They were both newer detectives assigned to the bureau, and Josie didn't know either of them well. "Okay, interesting. Why do they want to talk to me? You know, never mind—what's a good number for one of them? I'll just call and get you out of the middle."

"Something about your business card being at the scene." He provided Luna's cell number and said, "Hey, can I ask a favor?"

Josie had finished scribbling the number on a cocktail napkin, and Lopes was putting two more drinks on the table, frowning at her note. "Sure," she said.

"If you have to come back by the office tonight, could you pick up some chow? I forgot my lunch at home, and I'm starving. All I've had are two candy bars from the vending machine."

She pictured Miguel with his soft, round physique, a young man who spent too much time in office chairs and likely an equal amount of time on his couch, watching movies or playing video games. She knew he wasn't going to ask her to pick up a salad somewhere. Josie said, "If I have to come by, I'll give you a call. But hopefully that won't happen because I'm nowhere near the office right now, and I need to get home."

"Okay," he said. "Thanks."

She disconnected and reached for the fresh drink, a Tito's and cranberry, and answered the question on Lopes's face. "Luna and Wright caught a case in La Mirada, and they need to talk to me. Apparently, my card was at the scene."

Lopes lowered himself into his chair. "That could be anything. How many people do we give our cards to every month?"

She was punching the number Miguel gave her into her phone, and she didn't look up to answer. "A lot. But not many of them live in La Mirada."

"You think it might have something to do with Prada." It wasn't a question.

Josie nodded, then looked off behind his shoulder and watched two drunks standing near the bar either getting ready to fight or make love, the two fifty-ish men with their foreheads practically touching the way wild animals prepared to fight, these two morons each with one hand on the other's shoulder. Into the phone she said, "Luna, Josie Sanchez here. What's up?"

"Hey, I've got a one eighty-seven down here in La Mirada, and your card was located on the premises. Victim's name is Veronica Garcia—"

"Jesus."

"—adult female, and the resident here at this location. She lives in a back house on her grandparents' property."

"How was she killed?"

"Shot in the face twice with a small-caliber weapon. You know her?"

Josie pictured Vero from the image she still held from many years ago when Vero was an attractive young woman but living the *vida loco*, a lifestyle that ages one quickly or keeps you from aging at all. Now someone had shot her in the face. Any detective would first look at a victim's lover, when the victim was a woman who was murdered in her own home, but Josie knew Prada was locked up. That would eliminate the first obvious suspect. Then she had a terrible thought—was he? Was Prada still locked up? She'd check on that next, just to be certain, even though her instinct told her that he was, and also that he wouldn't murder Vero. She said, "Yeah, I know her. Do you have any suspects?"

"We have nothing yet. She was found by her grandfather. He and her grandmother had been out for the evening and when they got home, the grandfather came back to the house to check on something and saw her sprawled on the couch, obviously dead."

Josie took in a breath. Lopes whispered, "Who got whacked?"

She held up a finger, saying into the phone now, "You've got a Mincey warrant to process the scene, right?"

"No, ma'am," he said, "Grandpa owns the home, and he gave us consent."

Josie rolled her eyes and shook her head, and Lopes shook his head too, knowing where this was going.

She said, "It doesn't matter if he gave you consent. If the killer has legal standing there, you have to have a Mincey. You have to look at Grandpa as nothing more than the landlord, see?" Josie couldn't believe the lack of training some of these new investigators received—or maybe they were just more inclined to take shortcuts. She said, "If the victim had some dude shacked up with her, the courts could rule that he had legal standing, and you lose any evidence from the scene. Even if the dude had only been staying there a few days. You can't take that chance."

"Her old man is locked up, according to the grandfather. That's why we felt we were on solid ground here."

Josie shook her head again—no sense in trying to get this guy to see it. "Is she still there?"

"We just notified the coroner about ten ago that we're ready for them to roll. They have an hour ETA."

Josie glanced at her watch. "I'll be there in twenty minutes."

She disconnected, pushed her fresh drink to the center of the table and stood up. The two drunks at the end of the bar were now arm-in-arm, singing. Didn't mean they wouldn't be exchanging blows later, but she and Lopes wouldn't be around to see it. They had to go. She looked Lopes in his watery eyes and said, "Sober up, Detective—we're going to La Mirada."

THEY HIT JACK IN THE BOX AND GRABBED COFFEES TO GO, AND JOSIE called the Norwalk jailer to confirm Rudy Prada remained in custody. According to the roster, the graveyard shift jailer said around a yawn, he was there. That wasn't good enough for Josie though, not with some of the screw-ups she had witnessed or heard about over the years, especially when it came to trustee inmates, and hadn't Schauer said he was making Prada a trustee? She believed he had. Trustees at a station were given a lot of freedom, and sometimes they'd take full advantage of the lack of supervision. Dickie had told her when he was leaving the station one night, back when he worked Firestone, he had noticed a car blacked out in the alley—this was at about three in the morning. He went around the block and came up on it and caught the station trustee having an unauthorized conjugal visit. It wouldn't take much for Prada to slip out for a few hours if Schauer had, in fact, made him a station trustee, and Norwalk station wasn't far from where he lived with Vero in La Mirada. So Josie asked the female jailer to go physically check the cell, look at his wristband for confirmation, and make damn sure that Prada was there. Reluctantly, she said she would.

As they arrived at the crime scene, Josie took a call from Norwalk station—the jailer confirming Prada was snug in his bunk. No, he had not been made a trustee, and he had not been out of his cell since yesterday morning when they ran showers for the inmates.

They stepped inside and paused at the doorway, the two of them taking in an unpleasant but familiar scene. Lopes said, "Who's going to shoot her in the face? That's a bit of rage, if you ask me. Personal. A scorned lover. Someone that can't stand to look at her. Maybe someone who had just finished having sex with her."

Josie was nodding along, on the same page. After all, there she was with her hoochie out for everyone to see. There were a pair of shorts on the ground, tattered jean shorts that didn't appear to have been washed for some time, but no panties in view. Had the killer taken them? Was this a sexual predator case? They had barely exchanged pleasantries with Luna and his partner when they first came in, and now the two of them were off to the side, each with their eyes glued to their cell phones.

"Did either of you come across her panties?" she asked.

Luna shook his head and his partner said, "No. Nothing out here in the living room."

She thought about it. Had they had sex in the bedroom? No, the shorts were here on the ground. They were removed for the purposes of sex, perhaps quick and maybe even rough—she hadn't bothered to remove her top and get all the way naked.

"Any signs of forced entry?"

"No. Door was found open by the old man in the front house. Doesn't appear it was forced open."

Lopes said, "I'd make sure your coroner's investigator handles this as a sexual assault murder, processes her for hairs and fibers and someone else's DNA down there."

"Yessir," Luna said.

"Where was my card found?" Josie asked.

Luna stepped across the room and Josie followed. He pointed it out, the card sitting on an end table next to an overflowing ashtray. He said, "We left it there where we found it, had the crime lab document it in photos."

"Have them take it and process it for prints, too," she said.

"Yes ma'am."

"Did you get a Mincey yet?"

"Waiting on a signature. Did a quick one after you called and sent it to Judge Lambert over at Norwalk. I mean, he's not at Norwalk now, middle of the night, but the D.A.'s command post got us his number and we emailed it to him. I was just checking my phone to see if he'd returned it."

Lopes said, "The old days, you had to fax it to them or drive to their homes and get it signed. Of course, they never lived nearby—you don't get a lot of murders in a judge's neighborhood. You guys have it too easy now."

Josie didn't pay much attention to the chatter the boys seemed to be having now, Lopes and Luna reminiscing about the good ol' days. She was focusing on details: the tequila bottle, open beer cans, at least two brands of cigarettes in the dirty ashtrays, one on the coffee table near Vero, the other on the end table near Josie's card. Did Prada smoke? She didn't know, but she dismissed the idea of a cigarette butt having his DNA on it, comfortable that he hadn't left the jail. Would Luna and his partner take all the butts? She was confident they would, given that their scene investigation seemed to be on hold, awaiting the Mincey. Once they had it, the crime lab could collect the evidence and the coroner's investigator could come have a look, take some notes, jab the liver for a temperature, and take Vero downtown where she would cool off for a few days until someone dissected her.

"You'll take the cigarette butts?" Josie said, just confirming these two were on the same page.

"Yes, ma'am, we will."

She didn't look back at them, but she could see in her peripheral vision that Luna and Lopes were now standing side by side looking in her direction. She said, "Okay, good. Just checking."

Lopes said in a hushed voice, "Probably a good idea. That and all the booze containers."

Josie stood peering toward the front window. She could see lights inside the front house, but that was about it. She knew though—from having looked into the window as she and Lopes walked up, and having seen the detectives moving about in the living room not far from the victim—that if it weren't dark outside, you would be able to see to the street from this position. Which meant someone from the street could easily see them as they stood there now. So if Vero and her guest were going to have sex, would they have left the window coverings open, as they were now? Or if the killer were going to rape and murder her, would he have left the window coverings open? Or had it been daytime when this happened, evening when it was discovered? She took a long look at Vero but got no answers. The coroner would check for rigor mortis setting in, the extremities stiffening first, usually within four hours. The larger limbs being stiff would indicate she'd been there longer, and of course the liver temperature would more accurately indicate time of death. Josie glanced at her watch: it was nearly two now. She guessed Vero had been dead for six hours or more. She'd see soon enough, if Lopes didn't object to them staying around until the coroner's investigator arrived and conducted his examination. If this was a daytime murder, as she believed it had been, then who would be able to come and go through the front door, past the grandparents' home and in front of neighbors, without anyone taking note or caring? Someone who had been here before, or someone who appeared as all other guests normally did: a gangster, she would assume.

"Were the lights on?" she asked, addressing no one in particular.

Luna seemed to be the lead of the two budding detectives, doing all of the talking. "Yes."

"Did you ask the old man if he had turned them on?"

A brief silence followed. Then, "No ma'am, but we will."

She was still taking everything in, nearly inch by inch, moving almost imperceptibly, her gaze cutting swaths through the crime scene like a farmer mowing his hay: slowly, surely, not leaving any patches or strips of feed standing in the field.

"I'd like to wait for the coroner," she said, her mind's eye seeing Lopes behind her, checking his watch and likely wondering why she was so obsessed with this woman's death—this girlfriend of Rudy Prada. Josie stood still for a moment, arranging her thoughts, and then she turned to face him. "It's all tied together somehow—I can feel it."

Lopes lifted his chin as if telling her to go on, or asking her to explain.

She said, "Prada gets busted with a gun that comes back to the murder of a councilman seventeen years ago. He tells us it's Frankie's gun. We let him walk, at first, which would be cause for concern for Frankie, knowing ex-cons don't walk on gun charges. Then we lock Prada up, and Vero gets killed." Josie looked over at Vero once more, directing the conversation to the evidence at hand. "Maybe someone is starting to panic about everything going down."

"Frankie," Lopes duly noted.

Josie, her gaze lingering on the indecency of the death before her, a haggard woman who was once a little girl that giggled and played and dreamed of a future that surely looked much different than this. The mother of Rudy Prada's child half naked, shot in the face in her own home. She turned back to Lopes and Luna, who quietly watched her. "The question is, what was the motive? Is this revenge, or is it a message?"

"Who would the message be for?" Lopes asked.

"Prada," she said, turning her gaze to meet his now. "Frankie Rosas thinks Rudy is talking. About what though? That's the question. About the gun, obviously, but related to Pico, or something else?"

"The councilman."

She nodded. "That's what I'm wondering."

In the silence that followed she heard a motor idling, and then not, a car door opening, and then the thud of it being shut. The coroner, she presumed. Josie had something to say that needed to be said before anyone outside of their bureau was in the room, so she turned to Luna once more and said, "This might have something to do with the murder of an L.A. city councilman. That theory stays here for now, between just us. Even back at the bureau, let's keep that on the QT until I say otherwise. But my point is, be diligent on this one, gentlemen. No shortcuts."

Luna nodded as a light tap sounded from behind her, a man saying, "Good evening, folks. I've come for your dead."

25

JOSIE WAS ALREADY AWAKE WHEN HER PHONE VIBRATED AGAINST HER nightstand, and she knew instinctively who was calling. She had been lying in bed, trying to get motivated and thinking about how she would explain to her partner everything that had happened last night. Contemplating just how she would show him the way the dots connected in her mind. He had no doubt sensed that she needed to talk to him. Dickie was funny that way. He'd explain it as having ESPN, or women's intuition. When she'd make fun of him for it, he'd tell her she was being rather *mocklatory*. It would make her wonder if he were related to Yogi Berra, who was more famous for his malaprops than his baseball career, mind-boggling statements the press would have their own field days with such as: "It's déjà vu all over again;" "Half the lies they tell about me aren't true;" and, "Pair up in threes."

The last thing she wanted was to answer the phone and have a conversation with her partner before she even had a cup of coffee or brushed her teeth or showered the three hours of sleep from her exhausted body. There was too much to cover about last night, the many thoughts she had had about Vero's murder and how it likely related to their investigation of the councilman's, and the doubts that would plague her whenever she started seeing a case unfold. Josie would question whether her imagination had

The Program

led her astray, and she would pause before announcing her ideas on a matter. She had come to think of this as prudence, though she knew she was perhaps a bit too guarded at times. But better to keep one's mouth closed and be thought a fool...

The phone stopped vibrating. She pictured Dickie with his eyes narrowed and one brow twisted up as he pondered the possibilities: Josie was with someone and didn't want to answer the phone—she wondered if he would think it were a man or a woman. Or he'd think she had overslept. Or he'd think of the worst-case scenarios: she'd been kidnapped again. She was dead. Worse yet, she'd found a new partner and was no longer speaking to him.

Josie let the call go to voicemail and began willing herself out of bed. What she'd give to sleep till noon and spend the rest of the day on the couch with a book, no matter the grief she would take from her partner for doing so. In Dickie's eyes, you had to be up early—preferably before the sun, but certainly before the masses. His favorite thing was arriving at the office before everyone else so he could have his coffee and go through his emails and voicemails without the distractions and interruptions that inherently came with being one of about eighty homicide detectives in a building the size of a skating rink. She'd call him on the way to the office rather than whiling away the time when Dickie would expect her to be cracking.

A half hour later she kissed her mama goodbye and wheeled out of her driveway with a coffee-to-go in the cupholder and a toasted bagel with butter and cream cheese wrapped in a paper towel. It wasn't exactly a breakfast of champions, but an appropriate substitute for a sleep-deprived big city murder cop. One thing for certain, she needed to get back to some type of workout routine. It always happened this way: she'd go back to running and just as she reached the point of being able to glide three or four miles or more while feeling relaxed and breathing easily, they'd get busy with a big case and the running would cease for a couple weeks or more, and before she knew it, she was back to square one, barely able to run a mile without stopping. It wasn't fair the way it took forever to get into shape and you'd lose it overnight. Lately, she'd been hitting the gym, incorporating a more balanced routine of weights and cardio. She had reached the point where she enjoyed the workouts and looked forward to her routine, though now she dreaded the return, knowing the pain that awaited her—a punishment for laying off. But there were only so many hours in the day, she knew, now punching the gas as she accelerated onto the freeway.

Her phone rang again, Dickie on the display. His *ESPN* must come with partner tracking software, and he knew that Josie was now on her way to the office—unforgivably late, but at least on her way. Josie pushed a button on the steering wheel and said, "I had a late night, give me a break."

"Yeah, I heard."

"Oh, is Lopes in already?"

"No, he's nowhere to be found either. But he sent me a text sometime last night after I'd gone to bed, some incoherent message about how I should be drinking with the two of you, not home in bed. I'm about to fire you both as partners. What'd you two do, tie one on last night? Please don't tell me anything I don't want to know."

"Don't worry, partner, I play for the other team, remember?"

"Yeah, well, Lopes doesn't—he plays *with* the other team, as often as he can."

"We were out having a drink when Miguel called to tell me about a case Luna and Wright caught in La Mirada, and you're going to die when you hear about it."

"Ohh-kaay... slay me."

"Well, I figured we'd talk at the office, maybe wait till Lopes is there too and we can step into the conference room or go outside or down the road for a coffee. I'm not sure I want to discuss this around anyone else yet." The truth was she hadn't even decided she wanted to declare to her partner her theory about how Vero's murder tied in with the councilman's. It was a stretch, she knew, but she had that gut feeling about it.

"What does it have to do with? Give me a hint at least as to how much worse my day is going to get."

"Uh-oh, what's going on with you?"

"It's what's going on with us," he said. "We have a one o'clock briefing with your boyfriend, McKnight, and your sister, Lieutenant Neely. And I have no idea what we're going to tell them about the direction of this case, since we don't yet seem to have one."

"We might now," Josie said, taking a sip of coffee before continuing. Thinking, here we go, sister, put it out there and don't hold back. "Vero got shot in the face last night in her own home, and I think Frankie did it."

"Really?"

"Yes, my love, really."

She waited in the silence, knowing Dickie's wheels were spinning. Knowing he'd come out with an opinion on the matter and hoping it would be along the lines of what she was thinking. Of course, he'd need to hear the particulars before he could render an opinion or agree with hers. Lopes hadn't been so sure about it. But if Dickie went down the same path she had traveled, thinking that Vero being shot in the face could be related to the councilman's murder, that Frankie was panicked with the gun being recovered and now Prada being locked up and possibly talking to the cops, then that would strengthen her resolve as to the new direction the investigation had to go: home in on Rudy and Frankie for the councilman's murder. That would give them something to tell Aunt Brenda. Josie smiled at her new nickname for Lieutenant Neely, suddenly seeing the correlation between the demeanor, dress, and attitude of the bureau's newest admin lieutenant, and her mother's (much) younger sister who fancied herself as a yet-to-be-discovered Jennifer Lopez, with her sizable hips and big hair, a body and voice that landed her gigs in seedy, smoke-filled night clubs from Hollywood to Mexico City. Josie would refer to her as Aunt Jen or sometimes Aunt Selena but her mother seemed to have never understood why.

If Dickie's wheels were spinning, he wasn't yet prepared to share his thoughts with Josie. All he said was, "Hurry up and get your ass in here."

She disconnected and took in a breath, seeing the sea of cars ahead of her and thinking, *This is L.A., Dickie; how do I hurry and get my ass anywhere in rush hour traffic?*

THE THREE OF THEM GATHERED IN THE CONFERENCE ROOM AT THE OFFICE an hour later, each with a fresh cup of coffee and that was it—no case files, no notepads, no laptop computers, and no phones. Leaving the cells out was Dickie's idea, his paranoia in full bloom this morning. "You never know what they do with these things now, turn 'em on remotely to listen in on your private conversations." He said he didn't even trust bringing them into the room and shutting them off; he had heard *they* can turn them on and listen in, *they* being Big Brother. Uncle Sam. The Enemy. Dickie was the most anti-government government employee Josie had ever known.

She briefed Dickie on Vero's murder, the crime scene, the evidence that indicated to her that the killer had been there and likely had consensual sex with Vero before killing her. Lopes just watched with his eyes narrowed, concentrating on every word she said, undoubtedly seeing the crime scene again in his mind. Occasionally he would nod. Dickie listened attentively, likely painting a fairly accurate picture of the unsightly scene in his mind. A moment of silent contemplation followed her briefing.

Dickie tugged at his tie, loosened the knot. Said, "Why shoot her in the face? That's rage, something you'd expect from a scorned lover."

Josie didn't answer. She knew he was voicing his thoughts, and there would be more. She was right.

"But with Rudy locked up, that eliminates him as a suspect. Was she sleeping with Frankie? Maybe. Probably. I agree with you that the sex was most likely consensual—you said there was no evidence of violence other than the gunshots—which makes you wonder why he killed her. Let's just say it was Frankie. Is he dumb enough to have sex with someone he plans to murder? Doesn't seem like a premeditated murder to me. Did something set him off after they finished?"

Lopes answered him. "Frankie is probably dumb enough, but I don't think he—or whoever the killer is—had planned to kill her. Maybe it was something she said that sent him over the edge."

"Like what," Josie asked, "that he was no good? That his manhood didn't measure up?"

Lopes grinned but Dickie stayed deadpan. He said, "I don't think so, Josie. I think it had nothing to do with the sex. Maybe he realized she was a threat to him, that she knew too much about something that could ruin him or put him away."

The room fell silent. Josie felt confident now, seeing her partner was on the same train of thought as to motive. It was a smaller step to seeing Frankie as the suspect, the councilman's murder a motive, once you saw

Vero's case as an attempt to eliminate a threat. If Frankie killed her, what —other than the councilman's murder—would be the motive? It seemed clear to Josie. The murder weapon was found in Prada's possession, and according to Prada, it was attributable to Frankie. Sure, guns were passed around, but something told her that wasn't the case this time. Maybe Frankie had held onto the gun as a souvenir—perhaps it had been his first murder. Maybe that's why there was also a missing cartridge case from the scene; he could have picked one up for a keepsake.

Josie heard faint voices from the hallway. She pictured Lieutenant Neely—*Aunt Brenda*—popping her head in and asking what they were up to while modeling her latest fashion trend, sure to be something straight out of Vogue. Suddenly she felt they needed to end the meeting and get out of the conference room before there were questions she was not yet ready to answer. Josie pushed away from the table and stood up from her chair to convey her feeling about it. She said, "We need to find Frankie, and I think we can justify paper on his grandma's home."

Dickie raised his brows.

She said, "The missing shell casing from the councilman's murder. The gun is attributed to Frankie. If he's held onto the gun all these years, it's a trophy. Maybe that other cartridge case that was never found at the scene is sitting on his dresser or hidden in his sock drawer. Give me an hour, and I can have an affidavit typed up that any half-sober judge would sign."

"It's a good enough reason to get out of the meeting," Dickie said.

26

Frankie Rosas had listed his grandmother's address in Pico Rivera when he applied for his driver's license, which was now suspended, and he had claimed her address as his own on each of his dozen arrests dating back as many years. Carter, from Pico Gangs, had told Josie that the grandmother's house, where the deputy-involved shooting occurred, was where Frankie lived, and where other homeboys hung out. But there had to be a link to East L.A. somehow, hadn't there?

Dickie was poring over the folds of paper that had spewed from the dot matrix printer that sat atop a table at the back of the squad room. This relic was dedicated to an old IBM computer with a blinking green cursor prompt and a monitor the size of a small stove or large microwave. Josie stood reading over his shoulder, looking for a connection to East L.A. while her partner remained focused on establishing current residency for the search warrant he was preparing. It had been her idea to write a warrant on Grandma's house in Pico on the premise that a shell casing from the councilman's murder might be found there. But since that suggestion, it had occurred to her that she wouldn't likely have any way to establish that a casing from the murder weapon, if found at his residence, was the one missing from that particular crime. For that matter, how would she even prove that any shell casing found was related to *any* crime? A good lawyer would suggest that it was saved after a day at the range, or an afternoon up Angeles Highway where the gangsters would often go shoot their weapons in order to be more proficient when they needed to spray lead throughout a rival gang neighborhood. Her only hope would be if DNA from the victim was found on the casing, a microscopic spatter of blood, perhaps.

Her partner pushed his chair back from the table, the folds of printout trailing behind him like a paper dragon's tail, looked her in the eyes and said, "It's Grandma's house in Pico. Nothing else comes up on him. We should be good to go for the warrant."

Dickie must've seen that her wheels were spinning, saying, "What? You've gone off in another direction, haven't you?"

She eased backward, her hand feeling behind her for the side of an unoccupied desk to lean against. Yes, she had, and with good reason. Josie said, "Here's the thing. If Frankie and maybe even Rudy *were* involved in that killing, we have somehow to put Frankie in East L.A. at the time. We know Rudy was living there at the time, but what about Frankie?"

"Seventeen years ago, two thousand five."

She nodded. "But all we're finding on Frankie is Pico."

Dickie eased back into the chair he had just stood up from, crossed his ankle over his other leg and sat for a moment thinking, the toe of his black wingtip making circles in the air. "He's related to Prada, so maybe he stayed up there with him at times. Maybe they grew up together, but Frankie moved in with his grandmother before he'd had any arrests or before he got a license or any other documentation."

"Right," Josie said. "So we need to find where he went to school. We need to put him in East L.A. in August of two thousand five if we like him for this murder."

Dickie shrugged. "I'm not yet convinced. It's a long-shot at best."

"But the trophy keeps me thinking," she said.

"The gun."

Josie nodded. "Frankie would've been what, thirteen?"

He glanced at his paperwork, seemed to do the math quickly in his head. "Fourteen."

"Okay, so no priors, and maybe his first murder. You keep your first home-run ball, right? And this one—taking out a city councilman—that would really be something to a young gangster, a real way of making his bones."

Dickie took a deep breath, let it out and said, "Okay, so you don't want to do Grandma's house?"

She pushed away from the desk she was leaning on. "*Au contraire, monsieur*," she said in her best French accent—which she knew didn't sound much like a *frog* when she said it. "We need to add some additional items of evidence to search for, basically anything that can establish his residency from that time in his life: school records, clothing, or memorabilia; letters, notes, receipts, photographs, et cetera. The possibilities are endless. This gives us even more of a reason to search Grandma's house."

"This might actually turn out to be a worthwhile effort after all," he said, "irregardless of that shell casing."

There he went again with his made-up words. "Regardless," she corrected.

He rolled his eyes. "Whatever, Sergeant. Finish your affidavit and I'll wrap up the warrant. We can get it signed and serve it tomorrow, if we can get a crew from Pico to assist."

"Carter's good to go," she said. "I talked to him an hour ago and let him know what we were planning to do. He said his team is at our disposal, especially if we're hitting *that* house."

"Have you ever noticed how all the dudes bend over backwards to help you out?"

"Don't be a jerk."

He grinned. "No, I'm just saying. It must be your charming personality, because everyone always wants to play on your team."

She smiled back. "But you're not sure which team I play for, remember?"

"Touché," he said, doing his own Frenchie bit.

SCHAUER ROSE FROM THE METAL DESK IN THE DINGY ROOM THEY CALLED the jailer's office, made his rounds of the holding cells and saw that all inmates being held at Norwalk station were accounted for, other than the four trustees. Williams, the designated gas pump trustee, was outside where he belonged, filling a black and white while a deputy sat inside behind the wheel, his head down and the motor running. He was likely checking his phone, this new breed of deputy and their addiction to social media. For all Schauer knew, the kid was making a *TikTok* video or doing a *Facebook Live* event, things he didn't really understand but had recently learned about during a training class he had been forced to attend that was designed to get the young cops to knock that shit off.

Montenegro, the car wash trustee, was working on some young deputy's pickup truck—a lifted black Chevy with tires the size of wrecking balls and ladders beneath the doors so the midget with his shiny black hair and mirrored shades could climb into it. He probably parked it on the street when he got home, no room in the driveway because he still lived with his mom and dad and two adult sisters. Monte would get it polished up, and for his efforts he'd get a couple bucks and maybe talk the kid into bringing him a hamburger from outside, so he didn't have to eat a jail bologna sandwich for lunch.

Schauer assumed that Trustee Brady was somewhere in the station, cleaning toilets or mopping floors, the soft-bodied middle-aged white guy doing another six months for drunk driving, a regular at the station. He must've known someone because he always showed up at Norwalk as a trustee and never had to do his time at the county where his daily routine would consist of staying in his cell hoping not to be robbed, beaten, or raped. Schauer would stroll through the station and check on him, just to be certain he was accounted for. Then there was Prada, who had been assigned to assist the station maintenance man, Jenkins, who had immediately placed Prada in charge of repainting the wood trim around the entire station, a task Jenkins had been putting off for a year.

After seeing Brady with a mop and bucket in the admin office hallway, Schauer headed outside to check on Prada. He'd been meaning to talk to him anyway, as he hadn't had a chance since Prada had started working long hours outside and only checking into the jail in the evening when his work for the day was done. By then, Schauer was long gone, usually bellied up to the bar at his local watering hole, a little dive he found not far from the station and where the activity was much more subdued than that of The Shack in *East Los*. Prada had been working hard, and Jenkins seemed to be pleased with his progress on the painting project, but

Schauer needed to start cultivating that informant relationship with him, and that meant he needed more access to him.

He remembered seeing Prada on the south side of the building this morning when he came in, a ladder propped against the building and Prada halfway up with a bucket of paint in one hand and a paintbrush sticking out of the back pocket of his green L.A. County Jail pants that were now speckled royal blue. He was obviously just getting started for the day. Schauer knew he had completed the north and east sides in the prior days, so he decided to walk around the west side of the building where he would see him if he had progressed, and if not, he would round the corner and try to avoid running right into his ladder on the corner of the south side.

The west side was void of Prada or any sign that he had progressed that far, so Schauer rounded the corner and found a vacated ladder with two empty paint cans lying on the grass beneath it. There were tarps and mixing sticks and rags speckled with paint, rolls of tape, and two empty Pepsi cans scattered about. Schauer stood with his hands on his hips that were much wider than they had been when he began his law enforcement career at twenty-one years of age, a wiry runner type who had wrestled at a buck forty-five in high school. The sound of cars whizzing past behind him barely registered as his eyes scanned the corners of the property and beyond, a bad feeling welling up inside him. Was Prada stupid enough to walk away? If he did, would that be something they'd hold against him, the jailer? He didn't see how they could. It was an accepted practice that station trustees were given free rein of the unsecured areas of the stations as they performed their duties with very little supervision at times. That's why they called them trustees—you were supposed to be able to trust them. But Schauer knew you couldn't trust any convict. Hell, you couldn't trust half the deputies you worked with. Maybe with your life, but you wouldn't leave your locker open with your gear inside, and you wouldn't leave your personal vehicle unlocked in the parking lot, and you wouldn't leave your wife or girlfriend unattended at a station party—especially at The Shack. Honestly, you couldn't fucking trust anyone.

Schauer huffed and started around the other side of the building, praying he would run into Prada coming back with more supplies or a sandwich. Praying the man hadn't turned rabbit on him and was now hoofing it through nearby alleys, looking over fences hoping to find some

The Program

civilian clothes hanging on a line—or prying open a window or two in search of fresh attire and a weapon to aid in his escape. He needed to keep a shorter leash on the man, and if he were so lucky as to find Prada tending to his trustee business, he'd do just that. Also warn him about checking in and not straying, and let Prada know he wasn't happy having to search for him when he needed him. The little bastard.

He made a complete lap around the building, the last two sides at a hasty pace with his heart rate up and his breathing labored, beads of sweat forming on his forehead and trickling down his back. Schauer's mind raced to see his next steps: search the interior building and then make another lap around the perimeter, just to be safe? Or sound the alarm and get all units searching for him? Jesus, this was going to be a disaster. It was worse than misplacing a firearm, or having an accidental discharge, or being caught with the captain's secretary in the bunk room. This was bad —really bad. They'd lock down the station, begin a search of the neighborhood, call in Aero bureau and SWAT and the boys from Metro who tracked escapees and other fugitives here and abroad. You might as well have pitched a tent because the circus was coming to town.

Where the hell was Prada!

27

The policy on search warrant service had significantly changed since Josie worked as a gang detective in East Los Angeles a decade ago. Used to be, you served your own warrants by assembling your team members and coming up with an action plan and hitting doors at seven in the morning, the earliest you could legally serve a search warrant that didn't have night service endorsement. Now there was a slew of paperwork and a conga line of administrators whose approval of your warrant and operations plan must be had before it could be served. Worse yet, it was no longer up to the investigator—who was most intimately familiar with all aspects of her case—to determine whether the warrant was considered high risk; rather, it was the inflexible calculation of factors determined through a checklist, things such as the nature of the crime. Well, at homicide, the so-called nature of every crime was determined as high risk. Josie recalled her partner arguing with his lieutenant on just such a matter not long after she had first come to Homicide. The case was a domestic murder, and the suspect was the surviving spouse. Dickie had gone to the suspect's home and interviewed him several times, just showed up and knocked on his door and did a Columbo *Just one more thing* deal, the annoying detective with another question. As he rightly had argued, the suspect would have no idea that on that day, Dickie was coming with an arrest warrant in his pocket. But now all of a sudden, the protocol was to surround the house and have SWAT call him out or bust through his door in their green pajamas and ninja suits? Dickie didn't think so, and Josie was with him on this.

Nonetheless, she wouldn't have a leg to stand on in this case, given that the suspect was a known gang member, the home where they intended to serve the warrant a known gang hangout, and that they were looking for firearms-related evidence in the slaying of a Los Angeles City councilman. She wouldn't even try to argue that they could serve the warrant themselves with the aid of Carter and his team of gang investigators from Pico Rivera—though she knew they could.

Josie stacked and straightened the ream of completed and approved documents required for their forthcoming adventure, pushed out of her office chair and started for the captain's office where he and Lieutenant Neely awaited her briefing. Along the way, she ducked into the kitchen where she knew Dickie and Lopes had met with Carter and two of his investigators. She caught their attention and hoisted the pile of cradled documents to indicate she was finished with the paperwork. "Heading in to see the skipper now."

Lopes nodded.

Dickie said, "Good luck."

Carter gave a quick wave of his hand as a greeting of sorts—*we're ready when you are.*

Josie finished briefing the brass and told them they would be meeting at Pico Rivera station at six the next morning, where all participants would gather for a briefing with the intent of hitting the door at seven. SWAT was scouting the location as they spoke, she told them, and she couldn't resist a parting shot: "Seems like a big to-do for a routine search for evidence."

Neely cocked her head, curious. Or maybe suspicious. Stover just shrugged, likely in agreement. He had his moments, but the truth of it was he was an old-school cop himself, and he likely agreed with her subtly stated point that the bureaucracy of the job had exceeded the limits of reasonableness, if not sanity.

As she started for the door, Lieutenant Neely asked, "What's the status of the guy you locked up for the gun—what's-his-name?"

"Prada. Rudy Prada."

"Right, Mr. Prada. Can we assume he's still in custody?"

Josie did a mental eye roll. "Yes, Lieutenant, we can assume he is."

SCHAUER HUSTLED IN THROUGH THE BACK DOOR OF THE STATION AND INTO the watch sergeant's office where an easygoing sergeant named Reynolds hovered over a report on his desk, a pair of reading glasses perched on the end of his nose. The abrupt entry startled him, then he met Schauer's troubled gaze.

"A trustee's missing."

Reynolds seemed to take a moment to digest the information as he leaned back in his chair and twisted a gold bracelet against his dark skin. "When you say 'missing'—"

"I mean gone. AWOL. The fuck outta'ere."

"You're a hunnerd percent sure?"

Schauer nodded, his face twisted like he'd swallowed a bug.

"Which one?"

"Name's Prada. He was painting the trim for—"

"Uh-huh," the sergeant replied, leaning forward now and jotting notes on a piece of scratch paper that lay on his desk. "Prada."

"—painting the station trim for Mr. Jenkins. But now he's disappeared, probably just walked off. The ladder was outside against the south side of the building where I last saw him working when I came in at about six thirty, materials scattered beneath it. I've searched the building twice inside and out, checked the basement. Hit up Jenkins and two trustees but nobody's seen him for at least an hour."

"Isn't he supposed to be supervised out there?"

Schauer blew out a breath. "Come on, Sarge, you know they give these trustees free rein. Every station does. I mean, Jenkins gives him an assignment and his materials, but it's not like he's going to stand guard all day. We're not supposed to have to do that with trustees."

Reynolds nodded, contemplating. "Yeah, well, and sometimes we get burned on it. Okay, go up and tell Dispatch to get every available unit to start searching for him. Let's get Aero responding and notify Special Enforcement Bureau, see if we can get a couple of canines to respond. I'll

The Program

let the watch commander know what's happened and call Major Crimes, inform them we have an escape. Notify DB, see if we can get some of our detectives out there to assist on the search till Metro gets here."

"Yes, sir."

"Hey—"

Schauer turned back to face the sergeant as he rose from his seat, hitching up his pants. "Please tell me this dude ain't in on anything too serious."

Schauer didn't answer him, because he knew the story about the gun and the unsolved murder case, and he knew that someone was going to get days off behind this caper. Him, or Sanchez? It was her case, and she was the one who wanted him to stay at Norwalk rather than going to County, but it was his decision to make him a trustee. Schauer had a bad feeling that his return to patrol had just taken another detour. At this rate, keeping his job as a station jailer would be a miracle. "I'll pull his package and see what he's in for after making the notifications," he said, starting for the dispatch center, his mouth suddenly dry and his stomach sour.

JOSIE WAS HAPPY TO BE HEADING HOME EARLY FOR A CHANGE. SHE'D BE up at four, four-thirty, and out of the house by five so she would be the first to arrive at Pico Rivera where she could get everything prepared for the briefing. She wouldn't sleep well tonight. She never did before these types of operations—not when she was the one who put it together. If it didn't involve SWAT, there wouldn't be a duty commander, two captains, a handful of lieutenants, and every other Tom and Harry. Just she and Dickie and a few volunteer gunslingers to help hit the door and cover the back. But now there would be the entourage, and that added stress and pressure that Josie could do without.

She idled through traffic with her thoughts on tomorrow, and realized that McKnight would be there too. Neely had volunteered to notify him, which had given Josie just a moment of pause. Wasn't the lieutenant a bit old for the strapping young prosecutor? She grinned as the word *cougar* came to mind. Oh well, she thought, it wasn't as if he would have anything to do with the operation or have any say about how it was handled. There was really no reason for him to be there at all, but Neely had argued that there could be evidence recovered that was directly related to a case that had been adjudicated, and wherein a man had been sentenced to life in prison. The District Attorney's office certainly had a vested interest in anything that might come from a search of Frankie's home, since that murder weapon had been attributed to him. At any rate, she was just about over the McKnight fiasco. Josie couldn't bring herself to believe that he had drugged her that night, and she had convinced herself that it was the creepy couple sitting next to her who had done it—Smiley and his loaded date. It made more sense to her that the swingers would be the type to slip her a mickey, not a clean-cut, all-American boy-turned-prosecutor.

Still, she wanted to resolve it with him. Ask him what happened. Hadn't he even wondered why she was so out of it that night? Something still didn't add up with the young lawyer.

Josie pulled into her driveway and saw her mother hefting a small suitcase into the trunk of her Nissan Sentra. Josie had bought her the car so she'd have reliable transportation that wouldn't cause Josie grief when her mother bounced it off curbs or scraped it against the three-foot decorative block wall that enclosed the front of her property. Josie never parked her county car alongside the Nissan, nor behind it.

"Where are you going, Mama?" she asked, shutting her car door and quickly scanning the street as she customarily did. She saw nothing that concerned her—no suspicious vehicles or lingering strangers—so she met her mother's gaze as she answered in Spanish, telling her that she and her girlfriend, Socorro, were headed to Vegas. Josie smiled as she moved in for a gentle hug, her mother feeling frailer all the time. "Mama, are you losing weight?"

"*No, mija,*" she said with a quick shake of her head, dismissive.

Josie held her mother's hands as she stood back and regarded her, certain that her paisley chambray top and slim-fit chinos she wore no longer fit her as they had when Josie had taken her to the Nordstrom Rack and bought them for her, several sets, and a nice cardigan sweater. It was all she could do to get her mother to spend money on herself, much less shop anywhere other than the thrift shops. "Okay, but you need to eat better. Take care of yourself, Mama."

The Program

Her mother pulled away and dismissed her with a wave of her hand. "*Tengo que irme, mija. Ya me voy.*"

Josie shook her head. *Ya me voy.* I'm out. Where did she get this stuff, her *El Cartel* shows? "Mama, you have your phone, right? And a charger?"

"*Sí, mija, tengo mi teléfono.*"

Josie appreciated her mother's carefree spirit, quite the change now that she was in her sixties and a widow free of her husband's rule. He had been a sick-minded man Josie had grown to hate as she reached her teenage years. Her mother, trying to protect her from him, had sent her to live in Mexico for two years. When she returned, her father was gone—presumed dead, her mother had told her—and Josie reentered public school a grade below the friends she had left behind. The two of them survived by her mother cleaning houses and Josie working assorted part-time jobs until she finished high school, and living in small, rundown apartments or with distant relatives when they were able. Now they lived comfortably on Josie's salary in a home that she was able to buy shortly after becoming a deputy sheriff. Esmeralda still cleaned houses a few days a week so that she could have her own money to spend as she pleased, which was something she had never experienced until their roles reversed and now Josie mostly took care of her. It was the reason Josie was reluctant to have a serious relationship. What would she do with her mom? She could never put her out nor could she leave her by herself. Sometimes Josie recognized the dilemma she was creating for herself; she would have no one when her mother passed on, no husband and no offspring to care for her the way she had cared for her mom. She tried to not dwell on those things and to remain focused on the present. Josie had her career, and for now, her mother, and it was all she really needed. It was all she likely could manage.

Josie kissed her mother goodbye and gave her the usual admonishments about not talking to strangers and keeping her purse clutched tightly and watching her drinks closely—especially watching her drinks!—while at the slot machines or sitting at the bar or standing at the roulette table, all of the things her mother enjoyed doing in Vegas. "And check in with me too!"

Her mother assured her she would be safe, and she backed out of the driveway with a string of rosary beads swaying from the rearview and the sound of a horn from a car she apparently hadn't noticed coming down the street. Josie shook her head and made the sign of the cross before reaching into her purse as her phone began ringing.

"Sergeant Sanchez," she announced. A moment later she said, "Oh my," and started back toward her Charger that sat ticking in her driveway, the summer sun glimmering off the windshield. "On my way," she added, shutting her door and firing the engine, then racing backwards out of the driveway to the sounds of another horn blasting. She flipped on her *excuse me, police business* lights on the rear deck, dropped it into Drive, and stepped on the pedal. Maybe she needed to move to a less busy street, perhaps find something at the end of a cul-de-sac.

28

Why would Prada escape? Because Frankie had killed Vero.

Josie had no doubt about it. But what was he going to do?

Rudy was trying to change his life around. She had witnessed his efforts, heard his testimony firsthand that day at the Alano, Rudy telling the other winos how the 12-step program had changed his life for the better, how he had turned his will and his life over to God, how, like the dude who had been lost at sea—referring, Josie knew, to Captain Eddie Rickenbacker, who survived twenty-four days at sea during World War II—he had found himself saved from death, but still floating on a perilous sea. Josie remembered sitting at the back of the room, hearing the reasonably elegant words from the former gangster, and believing him. She had wanted to call out Rickenbacker's name, a name with which she was quite familiar as the Homicide Bureau had been previously located on a street in Commerce named in his honor, giving the proper attribution to "dude lost at sea." She could appreciate the analogy—Rudy leaving the gang life behind had saved him from death, yet his world was a perilous sea that required thoughtful navigation if he were going to survive.

She had believed all of it, had fallen for his easy smile and soft eyes, an unexplainable charisma, and somehow overlooked his history—*their* history, even. Foolishly, she had taken some chances with him, believing his bit about the gun, and initially letting him walk. Then allowing him to stay at Norwalk under the guise of needing him close and convenient as they worked together on this case of a murdered councilman, knowing she hadn't actually needed him so readily available to her, knowing he would likely have zero information about the murder case from seventeen years ago she was working on, but still having some unexplainable soft spot deep inside her for him. Maybe she had always felt bad about shooting him, knowing in hindsight he hadn't drawn on her, that he hadn't intended her any harm. Or maybe it was as simple as his charisma, this former gangster who was handsome and smooth. Maybe she had been conned all along.

Or did she have it right? She couldn't dismiss the possibility of that.

Her instincts had kept her alive during many deadly encounters, and she had always been good at judging the character of people and getting below their surfaces with relative ease. Dickie had bragged about her skills to others. Right in front of her, he had said, "She's the best I've ever seen in an interview. People want to tell her everything, even if it's going to cost them a life sentence." Floyd told her Dickie had said to him, "I have to remind myself we're investigating a murder, to keep from confessing shit to her when she gets going." He had said, "Swear to God, she doesn't even have to ask these assholes what happened. They just start talking and won't shut up."

Dickie had also told her and many others that what impressed him the most about her was that she knew people better than anyone. He'd say, "If her gut tells her the dude didn't do it, you'd better put your money on the man being innocent."

Josie reflected on her hunch about the game warden, a real leap against the tide that nobody else had seen coming. By then Dickie had trusted her instinct, and he had encouraged her to run with it. Others were shocked when the case came together, and when they were able to charge Warden Jacob Spencer for kidnapping Josie and killing her boyfriend.

So how had she gotten so far off track with Prada?

Or had she?

Had she misread his intentions and motivations, fallen for his lies about changing his life? Or did she have it right, and something had altered his course?

Vero. That's what changed. The mother of Rudy Prada's child, murdered. Rudy was on the run not because he wanted to be free, but because there was something he had to do. She could feel it now, deep in her gut, that I-might-be-crazy-but-it-doesn't-mean-I'm-wrong feeling. Whatever it was that caused Rudy to break out of jail, go over the wall or walk away—whatever it was that happened at Norwalk station that resulted in his being free of confinement, if only temporarily—he had to have had a very compelling reason for it, something she felt could be understood once they figured it out.

Therein lay the question: what did Rudy have to do that was so important he escaped from custody? He would have to know that he'd catch a new felony case just for walking away, regardless of what happened on the gun case. He was making everything worse with his choices, and she wished he could see that. Maybe he did. What stupid thing was he planning to do? Was he going after Frankie? To what, commit a murder? That was in contrast to everything she saw in him, everything he was trying to change. She hoped he would see that, get a grip on himself before he destroyed the rest of his life. That's what she would tell him if she could talk to him now—Don't throw everything away because of *her*!

But what did Josie care? She shook her head at herself, pondering just that.

Josie was on the freeway now, her Charger pointed toward Norwalk, its red and blue lights flashing through the windshield, nudging people out of her way. Ten minutes now she'd been on the road, knowing she needed to call her partner but not yet prepared to tell him they'd fucked up—*she'd* fucked up. Josie could hear him in the future, a new tune: *Yeah, she's okay in the interview room, but her instincts can be off when it comes to men.* Citing McKnight and now Prada as two examples. Maybe she wasn't that good. Maybe her instincts had seen better days, she was past her prime, all used up.

For the love of Pete, she was only forty-two, twenty-one years on the job.

Everyone makes a mistake.

She called him. "It's me. We've got a problem."

29

Rudy had been raised knowing only his mother, Marianna Prada Hernandez. A prominent businessman from her hometown, Cholula, Pueblo, Mexico, had financed her trek across the border of Mexico and through the deserts of Southern California, and he had accompanied her on the journey, Rudy learned as a teenager. He heard the story of how this businessman had assured his mother's mother that he would care for the young, attractive *doncella* as if she were his own. And it had been during a short rest on a still night—nothing to be heard but the song of distant coyotes—when he took her as his own, stealing the once-hopeful teen's innocence on the cold desert floor beneath a blanket of stars. Her dreams of a flourishing future in the lights of L.A.—Hollywood, even—had turned into a nightmare. Her eyes darkened and her carefree spirit vanished and her heart turned to stone as her "guardian" took everything from her, time after time, night after night.

She never should have told her son about him.

Rudy remembered the day well. He had come home with scratches and scrapes on his hands, arms, and neck, swollen red knuckles, and dried blood crusted inside his nostrils. His clothes were soaked from his walk home during an unlikely September rainstorm, the blood on his oversized white T-shirt blotted and streaked with shades of red and pink, a failed

The Program

Halloween tie dye experiment. His injuries were minor, and he had known that the pain would only last a short time, so he had walked proudly through a neighborhood he could then claim as his own, his bloody face and clothing a badge of honor. Rudy had been jumped into the Maravilla gang.

"I'll jump your ass right back out of it," his mother had said.

She understood the significance of what had just happened; after all, she had been a "homegirl" for many years. She would have known that it was about acceptance, recognition, and a so-called family. That's what appealed to those who were lured in.

One of the *veteranos*, Scrappy, would be the older brother he'd always wanted, or the father he never had. Scrappy had been the one who initiated the jump-in, knocking him down quickly with a combination of punches from lightning-fast, hard fists. Scrappy was known then as one of the toughest kids around. Fifteen at the time and he had already been to juvie twice. Everyone knew him as a fighter *and* a shooter, a burgeoning leader of the gang. Rudy's mother hadn't wanted that life for him, but it wasn't as if she had led by example, so what could she say?

Scrappy had taken him under his wing, made him a good fighter, given him respect among his peers, and had become the only male influence Rudy ever had. Taught him about the ladies, too—hooked him up with the whores and made him a man. He had put the first gun in Rudy's hand and drove him to a rival's neighborhood where they found some *cholos* hanging out on the street and rolled on them, Rudy busting caps and *vatos* scattering for cover. Rudy didn't think he had hit anyone—he actually had hoped he hadn't—but then he, too, was a shooter, a peewee gangster but one who wasn't afraid to pull the trigger, Scrappy had told the others.

The day he had been jumped into the gang, his mom had said about Scrappy, "He's not your father. He's just another dumb kid like you."

She said, "Fact, he's dumb enough, he could practically be your father, if I weren't old enough to be his mother."

Said, "Maybe I'll take a bat and beat that little gangster myself, show him how boys like him were dealt with in Mexico."

It went on and on, his mother going from anger to despair, knowing instinctively that her son would never be the same. At her most vulnerable point, Rudy, already a master at manipulation, said, "So, mama, who *is* my father? Why do I know nothing about this man, and why has he never been a part of my life? Why do we struggle to eat, and I have to steal from the *mercado* to have the things I need, and you have to be alone in the room with the fucking *propietario* when you don't have the money for rent?"

She had slapped his bloody face—hard—and sent him to his room. She had seethed for a long while before going to him and telling him the things she never should have told him. Things no son ever wanted to know about his mother, the terrible things that had happened to her during her journey across the border all those years before.

"Where is he now!" Rudy demanded.

"When did you last see him?" he asked.

Rudy, a gang member with vengeance on his mind. "Did he go back to Mexico, or is he here? Tell me!"

She hadn't answered any of his questions, and Rudy had wondered why. Finally, after hours of badgering, threatening to leave home—he had a new family now, the Maravillas, and he could go live with any of his homeboys—she told Rudy his father's name. She had likely reasoned it couldn't hurt anything to give him the name of his biological father. Maybe she felt he deserved to know. Or maybe she wanted him to take his anger and find him, and then who knew what. But more than likely his mother had reasoned that neither of them would ever see the child-molesting son of a bitch again. She probably hadn't expected to ever hear his name again, not in this City of Angels with its population twice that of Mexico City, a vast sea of immigrants where paper trails were vague, and the name Juarez was as common as Ramos and Rodriguez.

She probably had never imagined that just two years later his face would be on their television screen, a clean-shaven, nicely groomed man in a business suit, something your attorney would wear to court. But he was no attorney—he had been elected as a Los Angeles City councilman. A leader of the community, this rapist, child-molesting piece of shit. And she hadn't been able to lie to Rudy when he asked if that was the same Raymond Juarez, the man who had raped her repeatedly when she was a young girl. His father.

Rudy, now hunkered low in a stolen Nissan he had parked half a block from where his cousin Frankie stayed in Pico, reflected on all of these things while contemplating his next action. He knew, instinctively, that it was Frankie who had murdered Vero. Oddly, it made sense to him. You tied up loose ends when it was clear the rope was beginning to unravel. And that is exactly what Rudy would do now—tie up a loose end. Only a handful of people knew everything about that gun, about that night, things the cops were about to discover that would change everything for several people, Frankie among them. Well, and his mother too. She knew. But would Frankie also kill *her*? Rudy didn't think so, but as he pondered it, he really couldn't be certain. He never would have imaged that Frankie would have killed Vero, but Rudy was sure that he had.

Gangsters had come and gone from the pad, but there had been no sign of Frankie. As the shadows grew long and the sky turned to darker shades of gray-blue, Rudy became more anxious with the idea that Frankie might have gone to East L.A.—might have gone to find Rudy's mother. He pulled his cap lower since now he needed to remove his shades, darkness hindering his vision, and he reached beneath the steering column with both hands and sparked two wires together, starting the car. It was one of many skills he had learned from Scrappy, may he rest in peace. With a glance over his shoulder, he pulled away from the curb and whipped a bitch, the tires squealing against the blacktop as he reversed directions and headed toward his old neighborhood with murder on his mind.

30

Josie told Dickie everything she knew about the escape, which wasn't much, just that Prada was gone from Norwalk, and that's all that really mattered. She told him she was almost to the station, and that when she knew something more, she'd call him. In the meantime, she said, he'd better grab Lopes and Floyd and get their asses to East L.A.

"What's your thinking on that?" Dickie asked.

"His mama. They always go back to their mamas."

"What about Pico?"

It wasn't a bad question. If Frankie had killed Vero—and Josie had made it clear to her partner that she believed he had—and if Rudy had escaped from custody because of it, wouldn't it be to track down Frankie and exact his revenge?

She said, "I agree, Pico is in play. But you guys are closer to East L.A., and I'll be closer to Pico. After I get an update and some details on the escape, I'll get Carter and his gang unit to give me a hand over at Frankie's place."

"So are you thinking we should contact Prada's mother, or just sit on the place and see what happens, see if he shows up?"

Josie thought about it for a moment, thinking of the timeline and wondering what the odds were that Rudy had already made it home. She didn't see that as his first priority. Yes, he would go there eventually, if for no other reason than to tell his mother goodbye. But first he would hunt down his cousin and take care of that situation—whatever that meant—if she was right about why Prada had walked away in the first place.

"I'd say set up on the house, see what's shaking," she said. "I'll call you when I leave Norwalk and head to Pico."

"You watch your ass, partner."

"That's your job, partner."

"I'm a married man."

"Don't be a pig," she said. "Also, tell Floyd not to shoot Prada on sight."

"Right," Dickie said, "because that's *your* job."

"Shut up. I'm serious. I don't think he's a threat to any of us. I think he's caught up in a bad mess, and he's trying to sort things out the only way he knows how. Plus, we won't learn anything if he's dead."

"Roger that," he said.

Josie glanced at her sideview mirror and began moving to the right, ready to get off the freeway now. "Okay, I'm rolling up to Norwalk. I'll be in touch."

31

Rudy Prada was born at the Los Angeles County Medical Center, LCMC, or General Hospital as it is known by locals, and raised in East Los Angeles just a few miles from his birthplace. What family he had in the States could be found in the area: aunts, uncles, and cousins, a mixture of immigrants and their first-, second-, and third-generation American offspring. He had many friends there as well: Mikey, whom he had known for as long as he could remember, was one of the few he knew he could trust with his life. Hopefully, it wouldn't come to that. There was Harry, the barber, where Rudy had always gone for his haircuts. The barber shop was still there and Harry, his thin, dark hands not as steady as they had once been, still did a dozen cuts a day. He would help Rudy with anything he needed, having always called Rudy "*mi hijo*," projecting a fatherly image to him. Jose, and his wife, Lucia, ran the thrift shop where, back in the day, chinos could be bought for ten bucks, white T-shirts for half of that. They, too, were like family to him. Helena, who owned the hardware store where Rudy had worked the first time he was released from prison, had been an inspiration to him, having come from war-stricken Argentina with no education and only the clothes on her back. She would tell stories of *guerra sucia*—the dirty war—where tens of thousands were killed or disappeared as the state's death squads hunted

The Program

the communist guerillas. Like many from Rudy's community, she was accustomed to death and violence, yet her heart was soft, her soul pure. Rudy thought about the many places he might seek refuge until he could resolve the issue at hand, but as he did, he eliminated each as a possible refuge, one by one. Some problems you didn't take to the doorsteps of others.

Vero's family, other than the grandparents who owned the property in La Mirada, all lived in the East L.A. area as well. Rudy thought maybe he should stop by and pay his respects to them. But how would he be received? Would they know, as Rudy instinctively knew, that his cousin Frankie had killed Vero? Rudy didn't think so. They would be shocked that she had been murdered, but they wouldn't likely know about Rudy being arrested with Frankie's gun, nor that it was red hot, having come back on a high-profile murder case.

Rudy wouldn't take the chance though. The fewer who saw him back in the neighborhood, the better. From the safe distance of the small house in which he was raised, Rudy would watch for Frankie, and if he saw him, well, he'd do what needed to be done. There would only be one reason Frankie would go to see Rudy's mother.

For seventeen years, the councilman's murder had haunted him. Almost daily something would remind him of that night, one that Rudy would give anything to have back, to undo the terrible deed that had left his father dead. But a bullet fired can never be taken back, so Rudy had focused on the harm the man had done to his mother, his way of justifying what had happened. Somewhere deep inside, he had always known this day would come, where everything would unravel and more blood would be shed as one of those who were involved might scramble to silence the others, self-preservation always the primal instinct.

Rudy thought about his program, the words of his sponsor, Bobby Young: "If I could take back all the bad things I've done over the years, I wouldn't. If it weren't for sober reflections of a life ruined, I wouldn't see the path before me."

Living with what had happened that night hadn't been easy. Especially during the past year of sobriety as he tried to reconcile his past life with various steps of his program: turning his will and life over to the care of God; making a list of those he had harmed, and setting out to make amends to each of them; admitting to God, to himself, and to one other person the exact nature of his wrongs.

Vero, God rest her soul, couldn't keep her mouth shut. Especially when she was drunk or high, which is to say that she never shut up. She had said to Frankie, "It's one thing to whack a gangster, but if they catch you killing cops or politicians, they'll see to it you get the chair." Once, while in a particularly drunken stupor, she had said to Frankie, "You ever fuck me over, I've got that shit on you. You *puto*."

Frankie might have killed her that night if Rudy hadn't been there to stop him.

If Vero could've kept her mouth shut—well, she couldn't, so it wasn't worth Rudy's contemplation of how things might have been.

Now look at him, on the lam, the cops no doubt searching for him, Frankie on a killing spree and likely waiting for him to slip up. Maybe waiting at Rudy's mother's house, knowing that's where he'd go sooner or later.

The cops would probably know it too. Especially Sergeant Sanchez, he thought, picturing those almond-shaped outlaw eyes that looked through him, deep inside him. She knew him, instinctively. He knew that about her.

Rudy thought about the encounters they had had, and now he pictured her leading the charge to find him. After all, he had really fucked her over this time, gaining her trust only to betray her, to make her look like an idiot for taking a chance with him. He hadn't meant for it to be that way—he really hadn't. Rudy wanted to be clean and sober, to live a normal life, to make amends for the things he'd done, and to help others avoid the dangers, heartaches, and pain of a life on the streets. He wanted his and Vero's kids to see his example. They were all adults now and mostly floundering with no direction or discipline, destined to be losers like their parents. Rudy didn't want that for them. He needed to show them a better way. That had been his intent, but he could see it all coming undone now.

He again pictured the lady cop, and he saw her putting him down. A movie-like ending of a gangster's life, the cop coming to him during his last moments, holding him in her arms, telling him she was sorry she had to kill him. Or maybe cursing him for making her do it.

It was all bullshit though. Rudy knew he'd likely surrender after

The Program

finishing his business with Frankie—if he survived that. He'd admit to everything and ask the court for mercy, but he knew it would be hard to stay clean and sober in the joint. He'd probably die someday curled on a steel-framed bunk bolted to a concrete wall, a needle in his arm. Or maybe he'd catch a shank in his jugular, someone putting in work for the Mexican Mafia, taking out a rat.

Rudy slowed as he passed Angel's market, seeing homies out front—youngsters he didn't recognize—and thinking about the man and woman inside, two people he needed to go to before it was over if he were serious about making amends for the harm he'd done to others. But not now. He'd have to wait for the cholos to leave, because he couldn't take the chance of word getting back to Frankie that he was in the hood, not until Rudy finished his business with him. He could feel that Frankie was near—he knew the end of all this was near, and there was a sense of relief to knowing it.

And as that realization set in, Rudy decided he had to take one big risk if he were going to survive this mess: he needed to get a heater, something small enough to stick in his pocket but big enough to put a man down. To put Frankie down, if it came to that.

Somehow, he knew it would.

32

Josie clicked off with Dickie, her sights now set on Norwalk station. She glanced at her phone to see there were numerous text messages that had come in during her conversation with her partner. Her eyes darted back and forth from the road to the screen as she scrolled through to see if any of the messages were urgent, or if they could all wait until things settled down. One was from her mom:

> I put $40 in the tank and it's not full. ¡Ay, caramba!

Another was from McKnight:

> Call me when you get a chance.

What the hell did he want? She had to assume it was all business, likely looking for some update on the councilman's murder, having no idea how far off track they were on that case now that her boy, Rudy, had gone rabbit on them. There were two or three texts from friends that she'd read later, and there was one from a local area code, but she didn't recognize the number. It obviously wasn't programmed into her phone's address book. She opened the message and frowned as she read it:

The Program

> I'm going to confess everything to you when this is over. Don't shoot me.

Stunned, Josie pulled to the side of the road and read it again. It was Rudy. On the run but sending her a message. She looked up from the phone and glanced around at her surroundings as she thought about what this meant, and how to react to it. She saw the station half a block away, abuzz with activity. Her mind raced to think of a response. Or say nothing? She wasn't sure yet, so she wheeled into the parking lot of Norwalk station.

She made her way past the conglomeration of cops and their vehicles from various assignments who had responded to assist in the search. There were SWAT cops everywhere, fit men and women in army green tactical wear, black shoulder patches and badges sewn onto their shirts. They wore pistols in low-slung holsters, and some cradled automatic weapons while others had rifles propped in the crooks of their arms. There were canine handlers, their black and white Explorers with dark tinted windows and dog head decals on the side doors, the handlers also dressed in SWAT attire as they, too, were part of the Special Enforcement Bureau. The difference was that these deputies carried leashes around their necks or draped from their belts while their furry partners waited in the air conditioning of their running vehicles. There were plainclothes detectives too, cops who looked more like bad guys with their long hair or shaved heads and bushy facial hair, pistols on their belts and badges hung around their necks. These were the Metro cops, Major Crimes Bureau. Josie knew a few of them, and they were the ones who would take the lead on the investigation and search for Prada. And there were the brass, unmistakable executives in their suits and loafers milling about smartly while they likely focused on damage control, finding fault, and handing out discipline, while the real cops were set on finding the escaped prisoner.

Again, three rings and a tent for the show.

Josie would get what she needed, provide whatever information about Prada that she could, to whomever needed it, and get the hell out of there as quickly as possible. But before she braved the crowd, she sat in her car with the air conditioner running and called Ty Couture, the phone man at Homicide. Ty, an experienced detective, had found his niche in mobile phones, learning the ins and outs of cell phone identification, tracking, and even cloning. He could get you information you weren't supposed to have, but he was careful about for whom he would go out on those limbs.

She said, "Ty, I need info on a number. I think my escapee just texted me."

"Your escapee?"

"Well, it's complicated. But yes, we were working with a dude on an unsolved, and I had him housed at Norwalk. He's walked away. I just got a message and I'm sure it's from him. Probably picked up a burner."

"Ah," he said, "gotcha. You want to see if we can find him through the phone."

"Is it possible, even with a burner?"

"Everything's possible, sweetheart."

"You're the best," she said. "I'll text you the number when we hang up. Hit me up on my cell if you come up with anything. Oh, and also—Ty?"

"Yes?"

"If the captain or his girl, Neely, ask about what you're working on, tell them anything other than the truth."

"That's my standing policy."

She knew she could trust him, and she hoped he could come through for her. The sooner they found Rudy, the better for all involved. And now he said he was going to confess to her… Confess what?

PRADA DIDN'T KNOW IF THEY COULD TRACK A BURNER PHONE OR NOT, BUT he hoped they could.

He had gone around the block and waited for the *vatos* out front of Angel's to wander off before he went inside, knowing he could pick up a couple things and also take care of something that needed to be done, something that had been weighing on him for the last several months. Inside, he asked the proprietors for their forgiveness for his past deeds, and assured them he was a changed man. When he finished, he began shopping for the things he needed with two pairs of unconvinced eyes

The Program

following his every move. A customer came in, a string of keys in one hand, a cell phone in her other. Rudy hurried to the counter with his roll of black duct tape, pointed to a burner phone behind the counter, and paid the tentative lady at the register for both. He nodded his goodbye and walked briskly through the door, where he immediately spotted a car along the curb that hadn't been there when he had gone inside. It was a compact white car with fuzzy seat covers and strings of beads hanging from the mirror, a plastic Jesus on the dash. It had to belong to the woman who had just walked inside the market, which meant he had at least five minutes to accomplish his task. It was perfect.

He had memorized Sanchez's cell number from the business card she had provided him when they met at Norwalk after the gun incident and before she let him go. It wasn't weird that he had committed it to memory, because it was an easy number to remember. The area code was 323, the second most common area code for the L.A. area after 213, and the prefix happened to be the same as Mikey's. The last four digits, the only numbers that might have been a challenge to remember, were 1998. Rudy's birth year was 1988, so close he had done a double take the first time he saw it printed on her card. It was lucky that he did commit the number to memory, since he had left the card on a table in Vero's house and didn't remember to retrieve it the night he left. He typed her cell number into a new text message along with a short and poignant message, hit send, and left the phone on. He peeled off a couple footlong strips of tape and placed the phone in the middle against the sticky sides.

Rudy didn't bother checking the doors to see if they were unlocked. This was a sketchy-ass neighborhood, thieving little *vatos* to be found everywhere, and nobody would leave their car unlocked, out of view. Rudy had been a victim many times before he joined the gang, having his bicycle stolen, having his tennis shoes taken from him, and being beaten badly when he took a stand against two thugs trying to take his jacket. He hadn't done so out of bravery, but because it was fucking cold that month, and Rudy couldn't stand being cold. At the back of the car, he knelt down and placed the phone beneath the bumper, smoothing the tape out in both directions until he was satisfied that the throwaway phone was secured to the car well enough to buy him a couple hours, and however many miles he would be lucky enough for her to travel. Then he slinked back toward the alley behind Angel's where he had left the hot car he was using to get around, hoping it hadn't been found by the cops or re-stolen by one of those youngsters who had been hanging out earlier.

33

HER CELL PHONE RANG. IT WAS TY, PROBABLY CALLING BACK WITH information on the burner phone already—the man worked miracles and he did it quickly. But Josie couldn't answer, so she hit the ignore button, hoping she would be able to call him back in the next few minutes. First she needed to get rid of this captain and his lieutenant who were incensed that she had requested Prada remain in their jail at Norwalk rather than go downtown, knowing he was a dangerous felon and a flight risk.

"Honestly, I don't consider him either of those things."

The captain cocked his head, incredulous. "He's in on a gun charge, and the weapon he was found to be in possession of was used to kill a councilman, but you don't consider him to be dangerous or a flight risk?"

If this man with his hundred-dollar silk tie had even the slightest inkling about her and Prada's history, he'd shit his Brooks Brothers or flip his toupee. Josie sometimes wondered how these people were promoted through the ranks, and how much police work they had actually done before becoming brass. This guy was so soft there was no way he could've survived working the streets anywhere other than Malibu, maybe, or out in San Dimas in the days before Section 8 brought actual crime to parts of that jurisdiction, real capers like armed robbery and the occasional shooting, not just petty theft and vandalism. Wherever he had put in his patrol time, he likely hadn't spent more than a year or so on the streets. She could see him as the type to quickly take a desk assignment on dayshift where he could brown nose the admin and start working on his upward mobility strategy.

She said, "No sir, I don't, honestly. No more so than any of the other trustees at your station." Josie indicated a muscular black trustee not far from where they stood, filling a radio car at the gas pump. "You don't think that man over there has been to the joint? I'll bet you lunch he's got violent felonies on his sheet, probably more than Prada."

The lieutenant, heavyset, with the gaze of a man who had worked the streets, and meaty hands that had no doubt been around the throats of a few bad men in his day, picked his chin up and shook it slightly as he loosened his tie. Josie could see him doing the same thing in an interview room before he came across the table at someone. She could see the soft captain choosing a goon like this as his admin lieutenant, not a real smart guy maybe but the type who could keep too many people from arguing with the captain or showing him too much disrespect. Josie looked him in the eyes, said, "I know you from somewhere. Have I handled one of your shootings, or met you on a murder case?"

That put him at ease, the simple recognition that he wasn't an actual house fairy, though that was where he found himself. The man probably took the promotion trying to bump the pension a few percentage points before pulling the plug in the next year or two, his wages likely garnished by an ex or two already, the poor bastard just hoping for a few years of retirement before stress and high cholesterol took him down.

He grinned. "No ma'am, I don't believe you have. Fact I don't recall any lady cops at Homicide back when I was working the streets."

So still a bit of an asshole even after trading in his boots for loafers. Josie grinned back. "Ah, the good ol' days, you mean."

He smiled, knowingly. Probably seeing she wasn't the type to back down, and maybe not too sure he wanted to take her on. She'd give him credit for being smart enough to not underestimate her as many of her colleagues initially had. Her days of proving herself were far behind her though, and those who thought otherwise played with fire.

Josie, now addressing the lieutenant as if the captain was no longer there, said, "Either way, you know what I'm saying. None of these trustees

The Program

are trustworthy. Prada was no more an escape risk than anyone else you have here. His girlfriend was murdered, and that's what set this in motion. Like how Cool Hand Luke got rabbit in his blood after his mama passed away, escaped from that Florida prison as soon as the boss man let him out of the box and allowed him back on the chain gang."

The lieutenant let out a breath, folded his arms across his chest and shifted his weight. The captain's head was on a swivel, likely looking for media or anyone he might have to answer to, the commander or a chief—you never knew who would show up at these types of incidents.

"That's the whole thing right there, gentlemen," Josie said. "Something we couldn't have seen coming. If Prada's girlfriend hadn't been murdered, he'd be a model prisoner and trustee—ask Schauer. And I can assure you I'll have him back in custody in twenty-four hours." God, she hoped she hadn't bitten off more than she could chew with that declaration.

"I hope you're right, Detective." The captain had stepped toward her, and she could smell his coffee breath and Old Spice cologne. "Because otherwise, this deal is coming down on you and Homicide, not us. Also, don't bring him back to my station. Take him to County, or better yet book him at LCMC with a split noggin or bullet wounds."

She frowned at him. Talking big, but probably the type of captain who hammered his deputies whenever force was used, sent everything off to Internal Affairs for review. And it wasn't likely that he, himself, had ever used any type of force to effect an arrest—if he'd ever made one. Her cell phone vibrated, and she glanced at the screen. Ty Couture again. Perfect! She was about done with these two buffoons anyway.

Josie exaggerated a smile and held up a finger while lifting the phone to her ear. "I have to take this." She turned and took several steps away from them.

"Ty, what've you got?"

"I've got your boy, and he's in East L.A."

"Where!" she exclaimed. Josie pictured Prada on Third Street, hanging out at Belvedere Park—a stone's throw from East L.A. station—or outside Angel's Market, a beer in his hand that he would thrust into his jacket pocket when the cops rolled around the corner. But it wasn't cold, and he couldn't be wearing a jacket, and he wasn't a dumb kid with a gun in his pocket anymore. Hopefully. She saw him getting off a bus at Third and Arizona, or was he driving a stolen car? How did he get from Norwalk to East L.A.? Was he with anyone? Not Frankie. Not yet, anyway. That would be the finale, she knew.

"A few minutes ago, I had him at Third and Atlantic, the McDonald's. Waiting for an update."

McDonald's. She guessed that until she did time, Josie would never understand the craving for a Big Mac or a Quarter Pounder with Cheese, and fries. She hadn't eaten lunch at a Mickey D's since high school, though she had, on many occasions, grabbed a sausage McMuffin with egg for a quick on-the-go breakfast, knowing well how full of fat and high in calories they were. But a few weeks of jail food would probably make anything sound good, so she saw Prada scarfing a couple of cheeseburger snacks on his way to handle his business, maybe fries and a Coke.

But how would he have acquired money already? Hopefully he hadn't robbed someone or pulled a burglary. She turned back to the captain and lieutenant, who were now speaking with Schauer, and none of them appeared happy about anything. She said, "Hey, did you guys check with Dispatch to see if anything interesting has been called in since he disappeared, a carjacking maybe, or a burglary? Stolen car?"

They all looked at her for a moment and then at one another. The lieutenant shrugged and said to his boss, "I'll look into it," turning on his heel.

She turned her back to them again, Ty saying into her earpiece, "Okay, hang on, no longer at the McDonald's... looks like he's down on Amalia now—hang on... Fourth Street and Amalia."

"Fourth and Amalia?" She tried to picture it in her mind. "What's there? Is he moving or stationary?"

"I don't know, sister. You're the one who worked East Los."

"I'm trying to think. Residential is what I remember."

"Hang on, I'm pulling up a Google map... okay, yeah, some residential but it looks like a school takes up the whole block."

"Fourth Street Elementary," she recalled. "Shit, what's he doing there?"

Ty said, "I'll keep watching to see if he moves, and let you know. But for now, looks like your boy is at the school, maybe picking up his kid or something."

Josie clicked off, confused now about the school deal. He didn't have school-aged kids, as far as she knew. But maybe Vero did? Or grandkids? Maybe a niece or nephew. But still, that's not why Prada walked away—she was certain of that. Could he be there to say goodbye to someone? None of this made sense.

She called Ty back. "Tell me there's no chance you're on the wrong phone."

"I'm on the number you gave me," he said, reading it back to her.

Josie looked at the text message Rudy had sent her, and confirmed it was the right number. "Okay, sorry. This just doesn't make sense. My partner should be up in East L.A. by now, so let me get him this information."

"Good luck," he said. "*Hasta luego.*"

She clicked off and called her partner.

34

Rudy passed by his mother's home slowly, taking in the cars on the street and looking for any sign of Frankie being there already. It was a small older home with a patchy lawn in front and broken walkways yielding to the roots of a hundred-year-old poplar that shaded the front of the house. A couch sat empty on the raised wooden porch, and Rudy reflected on the many hours he had spent there. With Mikey. With Frankie, who had lived there with them for years. With Vero, the two of them snuggled under a blanket, her head on his shoulder as they stared into the night, oldies on a boombox, familiar sounds of the city the backdrop: traffic, horns, bursts of gunfire, wailing sirens...

His mother's car was in the driveway. The front door was closed, and the window shades were drawn, a few lights glowing inside in the early evening hour. Rudy pictured her in her chair, the TV turned up loud to be heard over the droning of the air conditioner blasting cold air from the dining room window. He saw her dithering about while watching her soaps, folding clothes or dusting the timeworn furnishings and cheap frames encasing yellowed photographs of nearly forgotten loved ones and better days. But that was a lie. Those were images of *her* mother, the woman who raised Rudy while his mom was out doing who-knew-what and coming home days later smelling of booze and cigarettes, cheap perfume and cheaper sex. A more accurate image came to him now, his mother passed out on the couch, a bottle nearby, maybe even a syringe on the coffee table, the plunger to the bottom, its barrel empty. His *abuela* would likely be alone in her tiny room, sewing or reading a dog-eared paperback, the frail woman in a threadbare dress, her gray hair tied in a ponytail by a strip of ribbon—grandma just doing her time too. Everybody doing their time. Rudy remembered when she came from Mexico. He was just a young boy then, but his memories of her were some of the best of his childhood. She had raised him, not his mother. It was she who saw that he had something to eat before school and when he came home, and she who put him to bed at night after a bath. His mama was seldom around.

Abuela used to say, in Spanish, and with great sorrow, that she never should have sent her *hija* to America. Not at that early age. Not in the care of bad men. Rudy would ask her to tell him more, but she would dismiss him with a wave of her small, calloused hand. She'd say, "*La vida es dura en México*," as if to justify sending her daughter away at such a young age. "*No hay denero in México—no hay trabajo*." As if life wouldn't also be hard in America. As if the money would flow and there were jobs for everyone, even a teenage girl. Though he loved his *abuela*, he could never understand how she had sent her daughter—*his mother*—off to a foreign land with strangers.

As he reflected on his life, the path seemed more clear to him now than it had when he traveled it. He reasoned that many of his poor choices had been made due to circumstances he was born into. He had no family structure, only an absentee mother and an ignorant grandmother—neither of whom imparted direction nor discipline. Each day he faced danger: being robbed, beaten, chased home from school; at times he was certain he would be killed. He joined the gang for protection, and for a short time he had felt a sense of safety, and even invincibility. But soon he realized he had become a target of many rival gangs, and the more he "banged," the more they banged back. Soon he experienced juvie, then jail, and eventually prison. It was the same there as it was on the streets, in some ways safer to be part of a gang, but in other ways more dangerous. You couldn't just do your time, and certain things were demanded of you that you wished you didn't have to do. It was a life he had chosen, one from which it was difficult to escape—some said impossible. But Rudy knew he had

had a legitimate chance once he had committed to the steps of his program, and once he decided to distance himself from the neighborhood and his bad influences.

But you couldn't escape your past. Until you made amends for the wrongs you had done, you would never fully realize the spiritual awakening that is the foundation of a renewed life, free of guilt, and no longer reliant on the numbing effects of drugs and alcohol to face each day. You had to confess your sins.

Maybe he would call Sanchez and tell her he'd surrender but only to her, do his time on the escape and tell the whole story about the councilman. She'd put her handcuffs on him for the third time since they first met, and he'd take the sensations of her touch and fragrance to the joint with him. He'd spend his time in solitary where snitches were less likely to be killed, with thoughts of better days and a brighter future, the lady cop forever on his mind.

Rudy felt an emotion welling up inside him as he gave a final glance at the place he once called home, and continued on with a heaviness in his soul. But he knew he couldn't keep a foot in each of the two worlds he now knew, so it was time to say goodbye to the hood and all that went with it, including family. It was time to take a big step in the opposite direction from where he had come—twelve of them, actually—and never look back.

35

Dickie sat behind the wheel as they crept south on Amalia Avenue, his eyes scanning everything on his side of the car while Lopes watched the passenger side through mirrored aviators. Floyd was in the back with his head on a swivel, saying, "How the fuck are we supposed to know what to look for? Is the dude on foot, or is he in a ride? For all we know he caught a bus. What's he wearing? Probably not anything fashionable. Probably dressed like Dickie here, wearing raggedy seconds from the Salvation Army."

"Really, asshole?" Dickie said without looking back, his focus on a small group of adults standing outside the school, likely waiting for their little angels. One man, certainly not Prada, a heavyset twenty-something who probably worked around the corner at McDonald's, sweated in his black slacks and white short-sleeved button-up.

"I'm just saying," Floyd continued. "I mean, you know he's not going to be standing out here on the corner in a county jail jumpsuit flagging us down saying, over here, come and get me. This feels like a needle in a haystack, like chasing those fucking gypsies way back when."

Dickie glanced at him through the rearview mirror. "He's going to look like every other *cholo* out here on the streets, only he'll have an *ah shit* look on his face when he sees us. If he's in a car, I don't know what to tell you. Look for someone trying to be invisible."

"It'd be nice to know what he's driving," Lopes added. "For all we know, dude got picked up by a homie, and that asshole was told by his ol' lady to go by the school and pick up their little shithead kid on the way home—try not to do a drive-by with the kid in the car."

"He's out of homies," Dickie said, "far as I know. At least that's the way I understand it. Josie says he walked away from the gang life, and now everyone probably thinks he's a snitch, beings how he got popped with a heater and hasn't hit the county yet."

"What about this clown over here," Floyd said.

Dickie stopped the car and turned to see who he was looking at. It was a *veterano* sitting on a bus bench across from the school. He looked fresh out of the joint with his creased khakis hanging over his state-issued prison shoes, the sun gleaming off his large-frame black plastic shades, dark black and gray ink covering his body. When the tattoos come up the neck and onto the face and cover the backs of one's hands, you needn't see them without a shirt to know what you would find beneath the clothing. But this guy also looked like he was ready to doze off, not what you would expect from a recent escapee on the run. He was probably under the influence of heroin, with his head on the nod, a long-sleeved shirt in the heat of the day, there to cover his tracks, old and new puncture wounds from intravenous drug use. In the old days—when the laws had allowed it—cops like Dickie, Floyd, and Lopes would be jamming the dude, checking his arms, checking his pupils, asking when he last used, did he have a needle in his pocket—"You better not fucking lie to me. If I get stuck while searching you..." The hype would be hooked up and he'd go to jail for 11550 H&S, Under the Influence of a Controlled Substance, because every good cop knew that when you took a heroin addict to jail, you took a burglar off the streets. But now, the laws of California's Health and Safety code had been rendered generally useless due to "progressive" laws in the Golden State. It didn't escape Dickie that he and his type of cops were following suit, being rendered generally useless, while the City of Angels headed to her ruin.

"Dude's a hype. Plus, he's too old, and a smaller dude than Prada."

The Program

Dickie glanced back at Floyd. "Don't you have a photo of him? Didn't we give you a booking photo?"

Floyd held his gaze a moment, staring at him through designer shades, his windswept hair dancing on his forehead. "Yeah, dickhead, I've got that ten-year-old piece of shit booking photo your partner gave me, the one that half the cholos in East L.A. resemble. Sorry I fucking asked."

Dickie turned back and continued idling down the road, scanning his side for anything or anyone who looked suspicious. He knew Lopes would be watching his side of the car, Floyd a wild card, a free safety who would cover wherever the action took him. It was a learned skill and habit from their days in patrol at Firestone station where your training officer would tell you that everything on your side of the car was your responsibility, and you had better not miss anything. There was no reason for two sets of eyes looking in the same direction—or for that matter three, in this case—because that would leave the other direction unseen. That's how you patrolled, back when cops aggressively looked to take bad men to jail in order to keep the streets safe for women and orphans.

Lopes said, "Hang on."

Dickie stopped.

"Back up a second."

"What've you got?"

"You're going to think I'm nuts—"

"Shit, we already know that," Floyd said.

"—but this little white compact car…"

Dickie was backing toward it now, seeing it was unoccupied, seeing it had fuzzy seat covers and necklaces hanging from the mirror, a little car that fit into the neighborhood nicely. What about it had grabbed Lopes's attention? Dickie said, "Yeah, the little Ford here… what about it?"

"Keep going," he said.

Now all of them had their heads craned to the right, all eyes on this car Lopes had an interest in, but not the type of interest that called for alarm, a quick stop-the-car-and-let's-all-jump-out-with-our-guns-in-hand type of interest. It was more like something was off and they needed to check into it. Maybe Lopes had seen a punched lock, a broken rear window—car thieves would sometimes break a window to get into a car, but always a rear one so they weren't sitting on glass while driving away. Dickie didn't see any broken glass or punched locks, so there must've been some other anomaly that a good street cop would spot, and others never would.

Dickie, side by side with the car now, said, "What're we looking at here?"

"Back up further—all the way. Get behind it."

He did, and now the three of them were looking over the hood of their car and at the back of the Ford Escape, a Fourth Street Elementary sticker in the rear window boasting a student's good grades.

Floyd said, "Expired tags?"

"What are you, a traffic cop?" Lopes said.

"Dude, the car obviously belongs here," Dickie said to Lopes. "Look at the sticker in the window."

Lopes said, "For a couple of ghetto cops, you two aren't very fucking bright."

Dickie looked back at Floyd and grinned. Floyd shrugged and ran his fingers through his hair, bored with it now.

Lopes said, "What's that taped to the bottom of the bumper? Does that look like a cell phone to either of you geniuses?"

ON THE PHONE, JOSIE WAS SAYING, "WE HAVE TO KNOW WHO'S DRIVING that car, where they've been, if they know Prada. Or if they've seen him. Show 'em his picture and see if they remember crossing paths with him."

They had already confirmed it was, in fact, the burner phone that had been used to send a text to Josie, Josie making a call while the boys sat next to it and listened to it ring. Then they had driven off, or so they had told her, looking for a place to sit and watch the car and see who came out to it. Josie knew she'd been had. The text message was meant to send them in the opposite direction of where he was headed. Rudy knew—or had correctly guessed—that as soon as they had a cell number, they'd start tracking that signal, using technology to run him down. The little bastard. But where had he gone, Pico? Josie thought of Frankie's grandma's house, and her pulse raced a little with the thought of him being nearby, Josie still at Norwalk. But no, he wouldn't be in Pico. She needed to get ahead of him and stop chasing the obvious clues. First, unless whoever was driving that car in East L.A. had just happened to have previously been in Pico, how would Prada have been able to put the device on the car? No, he was in his old neighborhood. But where? Not Fourth Street Elementary—that was for sure. He was looking for Frankie, and that's what they needed to be doing as well.

Or was he?

Josie considered other possibilities. What if he was just going to tell his mother goodbye, and head for Mexico? No, he wouldn't go to Mexico, he was born in East L.A. Now she had the jingle in her head, *I was born in East L.A., man, I was... born in East L.A.*—Cheech & Chong's parody of Bruce Springsteen's "Born in the U.S.A." But to the point of the song, Prada belonged here, not in Mexico, and she didn't see him going south of the border. Maybe he'd go to Fresno, or Texas, but not to T.J.

But would he escape from custody without a good reason? No, she didn't think he would. So either he was hunting down Vero's killer, or she was missing something else. She had a feeling it was the latter. There were times during an investigation when she'd get the feeling they were on the wrong track or missing an important part of the case, and she had learned to pay attention to that intuition. Was it as simple as Rudy going after Frankie, or was there something more to it?

Lopes said, "We'll hang out here for a few, but I don't think you're going to learn anything from whoever's driving this car."

She knew he was right.

Dickie said in the background, "What about Rudy's people? Who's he got here?"

Lopes began to repeat it, "Yeah, he got any family—"

But Josie was answering, saying, "Just his mom that I know of, but Jesus, he lived there all his life. I'm sure there's other family and friends who would take him in. But I don't think he's there to hide out."

"Right, you think he's hunting his homie, dude you think shot his 'ol lady."

Dickie in the background: "Frankie Rosas."

Josie said, "Yes, that's what I think. Listen, I'm pulling into a parking lot right now where Carter and the gang guys from Pico are staged, waiting. We're about a block from Frankie's grandma's place, so we'll hit it to see what we can find out. I don't think either one of them will be there, Frankie or Rudy."

Dickie's faint voice, "Sounds good."

Lopes said, "Okay cha-cha, keep us posted. And watch your ass!"

Before clicking off she heard Floyd in the background making some comment in response to that. She didn't even want to know.

36

They cleared Frankie's house with little resistance; only a couple homegirls were there to curse them and grumble about illegal searches and police harassment. There wasn't a gangster in sight anywhere—everyone in the neighborhood likely sensing what was coming down. A cop had been shot at this location just a few days before, and now Frankie was hot for a murder, and Rudy was on the lam. It hadn't surprised Josie that everyone was in the wind, but it did surprise her that nothing of value was recovered from Frankie's bedroom during the search. Since she had the signed warrant in hand, there was no sense in not serving it while they were there, which allowed her to cancel the operation that had been planned for tomorrow.

Josie made the notifications, notifying SWAT with a phone call and sending a text to Lieutenant Neely. She had replied, Oh, you hit the house without SWAT? Josie didn't bother pointing out that there was a loophole in the stringent new policy that covered search warrant service, and that loophole was a term all good cops knew and embraced for the purpose of expediency and efficiency: exigent circumstances. In fact, Josie didn't bother responding to her at all. She was too busy to engage with administrators about procedural issues when she was on the hunt for an escapee, and almost parenthetically, his murderous cousin.

She said her thanks and goodbyes to Deputy Carter and his team of gang investigators, and started for East L.A. with a feeling that everything was coming to a head, and that East Los Angeles was where the story would end. If Frankie was looking for Rudy, and Rudy was looking for Frankie, and neither of them were in Pico, it made sense to her that both would be found in their old haunts—*her old haunts*, as it happened. Josie would be more at home there than in Norwalk or Pico, having intimate knowledge of the streets and still knowing many of the players. But so would the two she sought. Still, she felt the advantage would be hers, at least in her quest to bring in Prada, if for no other reason than that she had the support of a small army of hard-hitting and savvy street cops to assist her. Rudy would be on his own, estranged from his gang at best, and possibly even being hunted by them at this point—word of having a rat in your hood traveled swiftly.

On her way, Josie dialed Dickie for an update.

"Nothing yet," he said, the answer to the all-encompassing question she proffered when he had answered his phone: "What's new in the zoo?"

"You're still sitting on the white car?"

"Yes, the Ford Escape. Floyd is bored and Lopes is hungry. How long do you think we need to sit on this? I don't think whoever's driving has a clue about what we need to know."

Josie thought about it for a moment. "That's true, but if nothing else, I'd like to know where she's been—where Prada might have put that phone on her car. That might give us a clue as to where he is."

"We should be checking his mama's house and any of his homies'. Maybe get a black and white to come sit on this parked car."

"I'm a step ahead of you on that, partner. I've got two detectives from East L.A. headed to mom's house in a slick, and they're going to sit on it for us until further instruction. I've got a radio car headed your way to relieve you there."

"Okay, good. Thank you."

"Just make sure you give them a list of the questions we need answered by that car's owner."

"Yes, dear."

Josie didn't bother remarking on the tone. "You guys meet me at East L.A., back in DB. That's going to be our command post for the time being, see what happens over the next few hours. I've got a feeling he's not far."

"You might be right," Dickie said, "but what's your plan? Other than mama's house, where are we going to look for him?"

Dickie always had to have a plan—he was hard-wired that way. Josie was comfortable running and gunning, so to speak—bobbing and weaving until she had her opponent's timing and reach measured, then going in for the knockout. But to appease her partner, she offered some low-hanging fruit. "I'm going to see if I can get the gang detail to do a saturation patrol of Prada's old turf, hit up anyone on the streets and jam any gangsters rolling around, see if they can get someone to talk. I've got Ty trying to get a cell number for Frankie, and then he can start tracking him. I feel like if we find Frankie, we'll find Rudy, and vice versa. And if Rudy doesn't show up at his mama's house in the next hour or so, I think you and I will go over and talk to her, let Lopes and Floyd oversee the gang detail's efforts. What'd'ya think?"

"I think you're flying by the seat of your pants again."

Josie sighed. "I'm open for suggestions, partner. What've you got? I know this whole thing is my fault and I'm trying my best to claw our way out of it. I need your support more than ever, partner."

Dickie took a moment before responding, and Josie heard him let out a breath. She could see him with his fedora pushed up on his forehead, his eyes darting about while he fiddled with his mustache, deep in thought. He said, "How about putting a trap/trace on mama's landline? He has to know we'd go there to look for him, probably knows we've got someone watching it, but I don't think he would consider that his mom's phone would be hot."

Josie liked it. They wouldn't be able to hear any conversations—you had to have an electronic monitoring warrant to do a wiretap. They didn't just hand those out, either. There were many criteria that must be met before the presiding judge would even entertain the idea of one, and truthfully, the implementation of a wire was an enormous undertaking, legally and logistically. However, a trap/trace was a much simpler process that could be done with minimal probable cause in an exigent case like this, and the existence of one could potentially provide them with a phone number to work with. If it were a cell phone, they could track it. If it were a public phone or a landline, they'd have his location, for however long he stayed put. There was certainly no downside to it. She said, "That's a great idea, partner. Do you want to get started on the paper, or maybe see if Lopes or Floyd will?"

"Floyd would be happy to do that for us, I'm sure."

She heard Floyd in the background grumbling, calling Dickie an asshole and something else. "Perfect," Josie said. "I'll see you guys in a few."

37

Prada drove around in his hot car, sitting low, avoiding eye contact with the *vatos* he passed who would eye his ride from their own rides or from the various street corners where they loitered. One of which was occupied by King Taco, where Rudy had hoped to get something to eat while trying to think of how he was going to turn himself in. But as usual, the place was full of people from all walks of life: families, workers on their breaks, cops, and of course, gangsters. His hope for a good meal before he went away had been a fantasy. He might pull off going through a Jack in the Box drive-thru, but he knew better than to think he could stand on the sidewalk of Third and Ford waiting for his order of tacos—too many people were hunting him now. He needed to get to a phone somewhere and make the call. He had walked away hastily without thinking things through, only thinking about Vero being killed and knowing instinctively that Frankie had done it. He had made his escape with a hazy head and murder in his heart.

But now he'd had time to cool off and think things through. Why he had run, he had no idea. What was he going to do? He was no killer—he wasn't going to track Frankie down and put a cap in him. In fact, it was far more likely that Frankie would kill him. He'd take Frankie any day in a fistfight, but he would never want to face him when Frankie had a gun in his hand. Some people were killers, and most others were not. The killers never hesitated when it came time to pull the trigger, and usually they were exacting in their missions. Frankie had been killing since he was fourteen. He was born a cold-blooded killer. Rudy knew better than to challenge him to a gunfight.

Rudy had to come clean with Sanchez about his father's murder. It hadn't been his idea to kill the man, but he felt at the time his father had it coming for what he had done to Rudy's mother. Perhaps at some point, after learning about the man and what he had done to his mother during her journey to America, Rudy fantasized about confronting him and bringing him great harm. But that was all any of those thoughts had been —fantasy, homicidal ideation. Although Rudy had earned the reputation of being a shooter among his fellow gang members, having fired a few errant bullets toward groups of rival gang members on a couple occasions, he would always aim high or low, away from the target because he never wanted to kill anyone. When he'd shot the chino at the market, Rudy had reacted instinctively when the man pulled his pistol. He regretted shooting the storeowner, and he accepted the time he was given for doing it—a dime in the big house for robbery and assault. Rudy was no killer.

He knew it was time to call her. Ditch the stolen ride and walk a few blocks away from it before making the call—there was no sense in adding a G-ride to the list of charges he was now facing. Rudy wondered if they would put the burglary on him too, if it had been reported and the cops put two and two together on it. Shortly after walking away from Norwalk, and only a block from the station, he had found an unlocked back door to a home that was, at that time, void of residents. He went in and found a change of clothes that would do until he was back in a county jail jumpsuit, and he took about sixty-five dollars from an envelope he found in a nightstand, a collection of small bills probably kept there for savings. It was enough to get him something to eat and buy the burner phone, which now he wished he still had. You couldn't find a payphone anywhere nowadays.

Rudy considered just walking into East L.A. station and turning himself in, but then he might not even get to talk to Sanchez. That had to be part of the deal. Talk to her and tell her his side of everything and hope for some consideration on her part. She'd be pissed at him for escaping—

there was no doubt about that. But there was something that Rudy saw in her that told him she could be empathetic when she heard the whole story. With his luck, if he turned himself in at the station, he'd never see her again. Her asshole partner would come down to interview him and he'd be on the warpath after what Rudy had put them through.

He drove down Third Street, thinking about where to use a phone, and it struck him. He could go back to Angel's and get another burner. He was sure he had enough money left to buy it, and if not, maybe the chino would let him use his phone if he asked nicely.

Rudy drove around the block and through a graffiti-covered alley that was perfect for dumping a stolen ride. No doubt others had been dumped there before, and no big deal would be made of it. Someone would call the sheriff in the next few days or weeks and make a complaint, and they'd send the cops out along with a tow truck to take a report and haul it away. Nobody ever got busted for stealing cars anymore—it was as if there was just too much other crime for the cops to worry about the small stuff.

As he walked to the market, a kid rode by on a bicycle, a youngster maybe fourteen but sporting the gangster apparel and trying to look hard as he eyeballed Rudy. In the old days, Rudy would have challenged him, or flat punked him out—ask him what the fuck he was supposed to be, like he was wearing a costume, trying to be a grownup. Ask him what the fuck he was looking at, was he trying to get himself killed? Tell him he looked like a bitch Rudy had had in prison, ask if they called him Peaches. Laugh at him when he peddled away. But today Rudy avoided eye contact and hoped the kid would mind his own business, not worry about who Rudy was, why he was in the neighborhood. The kid rode by, and after a few moments passed, Rudy glanced back at him. The kid's head was on a swivel, riding the other direction but continually glancing back at him. Rudy didn't like the amount of interest the kid took in him, and he had to consider that the kid was a neighborhood lookout.

He looked back once more before veering toward the market, and the kid was nowhere to be seen. Rudy felt a sense of relief, but he remained wary of the situation. He knew as well as anyone how a stranger in the hood drew the attention of the gangsters, and Rudy was now that in his old neighborhood, a stranger. Most of the homies of his era were locked up or dead, maybe some of them had moved on like he had. And the only way

Rudy would be able to walk freely here would be to claim this neighborhood as his own again, profess to be an OG—which he would certainly have been considered to be, had he not walked away from his hood—and to boldly challenge anyone who doubted him. He wasn't willing to do any of those things. How stupid was it, he now considered, to live for claiming a territory as one's own when the truth was you didn't "own" any of it. It was less your neighborhood than the chino who owned the market or the old couple who lived on the small lot down the street and had been there since the sixties. It was pathetic to risk your life for a geographical area where you happened to live.

Inside he was met by the familiar, skeptical gaze of Mister and Missus Chino—or whatever their names actually were—so he smiled and nodded and said, "Good evening, I'm back for a phone," with his hands raised as if surrendering, showing them that he had no weapon in his hands. Rudy could see relief in the man's eyes, uncertainty in those of his wife. He paid for the phone, thanked them, again told them how sorry he was for the pain he had caused them, told them he was a changed man, and that he regretted his past behaviors more than they would ever know. Neither of them responded or showed any expression of acceptance or gratitude. They were likely grateful that he spent some more of his stolen money with them, but they would be more grateful when he walked out the door and if he didn't return.

He went around the corner and paused to reflect, the bad memories of that sunny day when he stood along this very wall drinking a beer with a gun in his pocket. The mural of Our Lady of Guadalupe had been refreshed with the addition of a prayer, or perhaps part of one, attributed to —according to the unrecognized urban artist who had likely covered a decade of graffiti and perhaps even spattering of blood with his renewed piece—Pope John Paul II. Rudy lowered himself to the sidewalk, near where he had fallen with a gunshot to his abdomen fifteen years before, and leaned against the wall in heavy contemplation. Perhaps, in retrospect, for all of the bad things he'd done in his life, for all the pain he had both caused and endured, maybe it would have been better if he hadn't survived the bullet fired from the lady cop's service pistol. Most of the years that had passed had been spent in physical prisons; the others had offered nothing more than confinement, if only in his mind. Confinement to a life he had been born into and had had few chances to escape, an existence bound by societal edicts that were hesitant to fully sanction freedom of convicts like him. Maybe it had all been a façade, and the truth was that he would never be free.

Rudy stood, walked back into the store. The eyes were upon him again, but this time he didn't smile or greet them. He walked past the two proprietors and went straight to the cooler along the back wall. He returned to the counter where the couple stood near their register. Looking at the man, he said, "Do you have a coat?"

He did, the man indicated with a nod, his eyes glancing toward the back room.

"May I buy it from you?"

He and his wife looked at one another, apprehensive. It wasn't exactly jacket weather.

"You'll be fine. Please."

Moments later Rudy walked out of Angel's market, a beer stuffed into the pocket of his newly acquired, ill-fitting jacket. He returned to the place it happened, slid down the wall next to the prayer once more, and turned his new burner phone on. It was time to make a call—two of them, actually.

38

Josie walked into the rear door of East L.A. station, down the narrow tile hallway to the detective bureau. The room was about the size of a tennis court, filled by metal desks that held large computer monitors with blinking cursors or revolving photos, and stacks of files and miscellaneous paperwork. In the old days, there would've been ashtrays scattered about and fedoras and London Fog raincoats on the old wooden coat trees, heavy steel sedans littering the parking lot outside. The building had stood there for a hundred years, and generations of sheriff's deputies had proudly served the community. Some were witnesses to the Sleepy Lagoon murder of 1942 and its infamous trial of seventeen Mexican American defendants, and the resulting Zoot Suit riots of 1943. Or the Chicano movement of the sixties and seventies, and the ensuing Young Chicanos for Community Action—the Brown Berets. In 1970 there were protests of the Vietnam war, its organizers and some of the participants declaring that Hispanics were overrepresented in the conflict and dying disproportionately. The demonstrations turned to riots, and activist Ruben Salazar, a news director of a local Spanish television station and former L.A. Times reporter, was killed. Salazar had gathered inside the Silver Dollar saloon on Whittier Boulevard with some of the protesters when he was struck in the head by a tear gas projectile fired by a sheriff's deputy. Josie recalled that when she was first assigned to the station, her training officer had filled her in on some of its history, drove her around to different sites, the place Salazar had died among them. The Silver Dollar had, by then, become a theatre by the same name which hosted an annual play in tribute to the Chicano Moratorium and the death of Ruben Salazar. But the theatre didn't last long, and soon the historic saloon was transformed into a church.

Her cell phone rang, *unknown number* showing on the screen. She sent it to voicemail because she didn't have time right now to deal with anything other than the thing on which she was currently focused—namely, finding Prada. If it were something important, they'd leave a message. Even burners showed some type of number, unless the caller blocked it before making the call, so she had to assume it was probably someone from the office, or just another spam call.

Dickie was angling across the room with a cup of coffee in one hand as he studied the face of his Apple watch on the opposite wrist. The watch was his most recent toy, a birthday gift from Emily. But it was Josie who had been burdened with helping him learn how to use it, Dickie not being the greatest with technological advances that many of his younger colleagues enjoyed. He had wanted the watch so that he could track his steps and record his workouts, again committed to dropping a few pounds and getting back in shape. The problem was the job. It was difficult to stick to a routine at times, and Josie couldn't imagine having a spouse and child to share her time with also. Nonetheless, Dickie found his new toy offered other conveniences, such as the ability to take a call like Dick Tracy, or to check an incoming text message or email. He had asked Josie if there was a way to reply to those messages using the watch, and she said there was not, hoping he never noticed that she did it all the time. The last thing she wanted was to try to instruct him on how to do that or to tutor him on any of the other advanced features. She said, "Checking your messages, or the weather?"

"You can get the weather report on these too?"

Josie knew that had been a mistake. "No, I was kidding you. What's up?" she said, a nod toward his current fixation.

He glanced at his watch again. "Nothing, really... just checking my texts. Emily had to stay late at the office tonight too, so I'm just making sure everything is squared away with Rosalva, our nanny. She just texted me back."

Josie knew who Rosalva was—she'd even met her. She didn't bother mentioning it. She glanced around the office to accentuate her next question. "Where's everyone else?"

Dickie turned around to have a look as well, as if he, too, had just arrived. "Well, Floyd went back to the office to write that warrant for the trap/trace, and Lopes headed out with a couple of the gang guys a few minutes ago. The two night car detectives are sitting on Prada's place—or I should say, his mama's house. What's the plan?"

Josie drifted toward a desk and pulled out the chair. She was looking at her phone now, seeing a new voicemail message had arrived. The message was quickly transcribed for her to read, but it hadn't deciphered much of it, just a few words: *...at the market... was... anyway... call the station*—Josie knew she'd never get the gist of the message with this translation, so she hit Play and put it on speaker so that Dickie could listen also. It was Rudy, and his speech was slow, his tone serene, maybe glum. The reason his message hadn't transcribed well was that at times you could barely hear him speaking, as if he hadn't held the phone steadily to his face, maybe turning his head side to side, looking around.

Hey, uh, Sergeant Sanchez... it's me, Rudy—Rudy Prada... Listen, I was going to turn myself in to you, and tell you about everything that's happened... about the gun, and about some other stuff, crazy shit you can't believe. But, I don't think that's going to work now.

It sounded as if he were choking back an emotion.

I've fucked everything up for me, and for other people too, and now it's over. I can't go back to the pen, eh... you know what I mean?

Dickie said, "Where is he?" with urgency in his voice.

Josie shook her head. How would she know?

Dickie said, "He's gonna off himself."

She frowned.

There are some things I need to tell you though—

Dickie said, "Give me that number. I'll get Ty working on a location."

The Program

"Unknown caller. He might be on a payphone. Remember he dumped his burner."

"Shit."

Rudy was saying, ...*was Frankie who killed him. He was my father.*

Josie frowned more, said, "What the fuck?"

Dickie was shaking his head now, both of them leaning over the phone, Josie's forehead nearly touching the brim of his hat, hints of a woody floral aftershave a contrast to the feel of the moment. Dickie saying, "Who? Who was his father?"

"The councilman?" she wondered aloud.

...*shot him twice, then my—*

"What did he just say!"

Josie shook her head again. I couldn't tell.

...*put one in his head.*

His voice was still fading in and out. Josie had toggled the volume up high, and she and Dickie were both still crowding over the phone, trying to catch each word.

...*shot him too*— and his voice faded off.

"What'd he say? Who, Prada?" Dickie demanded of the recording. "Who was the other shooter!"

Josie lifted the phone closer to her face. "Rudy!" she snapped at the phone, commanding him to tell them more.

"The background noise, is that traffic?" Dickie asked.

Josie nodded. "Sounds like it."

"Okay, a major street." He grabbed the landline next to him, dialed the front desk.

Rudy's voice was quivering now, sniffles and unintelligible words. ...*gonna kill me.*

Dickie, into the landline: "Get your units to start canvassing Third Street, ASAP. Have the gang units start checking payphones. I know there's one at King Taco. Also look at liquor stores. We're looking for Rudy Prada, male Hispanic, early thirties. He's the escapee from Norwalk. There's a countywide BOLO with his picture—you should have it up there."

Josie had turned away from Dickie and had the phone at her ear now, trying to hear his rambling message.

209

Rudy saying, *...but before they kill me, I just wanted you to know. I'm sorry.*

Dickie was saying into the phone, "Angel's Market? That might be him."

The message had ended. Josie spun back to face her partner. "What about Angel's!"

He told the desk they were rolling and said into the phone before dropping it back in its cradle, "He might be good for a one eighty-seven... tell your units to use caution."

Josie said, "Fuck, he might be suicidal. What'd they say?"

"They just took a man with a gun call outside Angel's Market on Third."

She pushed out of her chair and started for the hallway. "Jesus, partner, this sounds like a suicide by cop situation now."

They hurried out the back door and ran to her car, Josie thinking she could've run to Angel's from the station, if she hadn't stopped jogging several weeks ago, and if she were wearing a good pair of running shoes, not these flats she had on her feet.

Dickie had grabbed a portable radio, and he had it set on East L.A.'s frequency.

The call came out:

East L.A. twenty-two, twenty-one, twenty-two to handle, twenty-one to assist, possible man with a gun outside of Angel's Market, described as a male Hispanic, thirty-three, wearing blue jeans and a black jacket... Twenty-two?

A series of beeps could be heard now, the configuration of the sheriff's radio system allowing for all units to hear the dispatchers, but not the traffic of other units, not unless the dispatcher put you "on the patch," meaning everyone on that frequency—and sometimes all over the county —could hear your transmission. The beeps indicated that a unit was transmitting, likely, in this case, it was Unit 22 acknowledging the call and giving his ETA to the location.

As Josie closed her door and turned the ignition, Dickie was settling into his seat and pulling the door closed behind him. Gunshots rang out, seven or eight in two separate volleys just moments apart, and not far away. Their eyes met, and Josie knew her partner saw in his mind exactly what she envisioned in hers, but without the personal experience of having once seen Rudy lying on the ground clutching himself, Our Lady of Guadalupe looking down on him.

Josie peeled out of the parking lot and slid sideways onto Third.

The dispatcher was saying,

East L.A. unit with emergency traffic, go, you are on the patch.

Twenty-two, ten thirty-three! Ten thirty-three! Nine ninety-eight, shots fired! Shots fired!

Dispatcher responded:

Twenty-two, what is your location?

There was no response.

Twenty-two... your location?

Josie had the corner where Angel's Market stood in her sights. She bore down on it with her throttle wide open, lights flashing and the siren wailing.

Dispatcher:

All units, East L.A. twenty-two had ten thirty-three traffic, nine ninety-eight at Angel's Market. Any units to respond in less than one?

The sounds of multiple units attempting to transmit at the same time clogged the air. The dispatcher commanded all units to clear the air, and said:

Twenty-two only, what is your traffic?

It's code four at our location, McDonnell and Fourth. Need 902R for a gunshot victim. Request a supervisor to our location, deputies involved in a shooting. You can drop the patch.

The soothing voice of the dispatcher came back, a contrast to the excited voice of the deputy on the other end:

Ten-four, twenty-two, code four at your location, rescue responding to Angel's Market. The patch is released, frequency clear.

39

It took less than a minute from the time they heard the gunfire to arrive at the scene. In those moments, Josie had processed everything she knew to be fact and filled in the blanks with supposition. Rudy had left a despairing message that led her and Dickie to believe he was planning to commit suicide. Dickie had called it first, and Josie agreed with his assessment. The rambling message had one almost incomprehensible revelation: the councilman was Rudy's father! How could that have been? Was it even true? Why would he say it if it weren't? Maybe Josie misinterpreted it; she'd have to review the message again when everything was over to see if that had been, in fact, what he told her. He had also put the murder on Frankie, saying it was Frankie who put the last shot into Juarez's head. So Frankie was one of two shooters—who was the other? Had Rudy been the other shooter?

She hoped that whatever had just happened down the street wouldn't prevent her from getting more detail from him. But she feared it might. Shortly after Rudy had left her the message, the station received a man with a gun call at Angel's Market. How coincidental could that have been? If he was going to commit suicide, would he for some reason choose to do so at the very place she had shot him herself? How crazy would that be, and what would it really mean? Josie didn't want to even think about it.

Had he orchestrated a repeat of their first encounter? Had he stiffed in the call about a man with a gun so that deputies would respond and shoot him? With the number of gunshots she had heard fired, she could picture one or two deputies opening up on him.

The description of the *man with a gun* included the exact age of Rudy —thirty-three. People didn't guess ages when describing a suspect. They might say, thirty to forty, or early thirties, or I don't know, he wasn't young, but he wasn't old, either. You never had anyone say, he appeared to be thirty-three. Of course, when this was all over, and when Josie had the time to review the recorded call to the station, she would know for certain if it had been Rudy who made the call. At this moment, she would bet the house that it was.

And the description of the suspect also said he was wearing a black jacket. Nobody would have a jacket on tonight, when the highs were reaching a hundred during the day and maybe, if they were lucky, it was cooling to seventy-five overnight. Everyone else on the streets was wearing shorts or chinos with wife-beaters or T-shirts—nobody had a jacket or even a hoodie on tonight.

She flashed back to that night, Rudy leaned against the wall with his hands in his jacket pocket as she came around the corner, got out of her car and drew down on him, told him to show her his hands. She remembered it like it happened yesterday. He'd come out with a beer can that reflected the sun, and in that instant, she had thought it was a gun. After all, the call that day had been like the one that came in tonight, a male Hispanic with a gun outside Angel's Market. Only that day he had been described as eighteen to twenty, not "thirty-three."

They were pulling up on the corner now, Josie's heartbeat thumping in her ears, her vision narrowing to focus on the man on the ground, a uniformed deputy over him, a radio car parked on the street, both doors open. Where was the other deputy?

Josie knew it was Rudy, and she hoped he'd survive this time too. There were too many questions that needed to be answered, and truthfully —she knew in her heart—she had come to like the friendly convict. She had come to believe in him, to see him as one of the few who could walk away from The Life and be a productive citizen who would spend the rest of his days giving back. She knew, instinctively, that had Vero not been murdered, Rudy would still be on the path to serenity. But that was what made it so difficult for people like him to turn their lives around—there were too many influences from their pasts, too many skeletons in their closets. It was a steep climb from the gorges of gang life to the planes of righteousness.

As Josie and Dickie hurried from their vehicle and came alongside the deputy on the sidewalk, he turned to see them coming, said, "You got 'im? I've got to go check on my partner. He went after the shooter."

With that, the deputy took off at a run, down the sidewalk and disappearing around the corner. Dickie said, "I'm going with him," and was gone before she could respond.

Rudy moaned, and Josie knelt beside him, careful not to disturb any evidence near him, always with crime scene preservation in mind. It would drive her crazy to watch shows where someone came upon a murder scene, found a loved one perhaps, and the first thing they'd do is run to them and take the dying or dead person into their arms, transferring trace evidence from their person to that of the victim's, and vice versa. Did they not realize the complications that could create? His eyes fluttered and he winced in pain. He was on his left side, crescent shaped, his legs crossed one over the other, his left arm beneath him and the right clutching his stomach. Blood pooled on the sidewalk, the acrid smell of the crimson slick taking her mind to the service floor of the coroner's office where corpses cooled on metal gurneys awaiting their final examinations. She pictured Rudy on the slab, and it saddened her, but she could see it all the way through.

At this moment, though, she had to focus on her work. Most importantly, she needed answers from him, if he were able. It wasn't a dying declaration she sought, because she already knew instinctively what had happened here tonight—it had been a replay of what had happened fifteen years ago. Although maybe he could answer the one question she and Dickie had been left with after listening to his rambling phone message: Who was the second shooter of the councilman?

The sirens were approaching, paramedics and an ambulance on the way. She didn't know if they could save him or not—he had lost a lot of blood, and she had to assume he suffered from multiple gunshot wounds, and that significantly decreased the likelihood of survival.

Josie said, "Rudy, stay with me."

He opened his eyes and met her gaze, held it for a long moment before closing them again, his face a mask of agony.

"You need to tell me about your father's murder."

Again, his eyes opened, but only for an instant, and without the connection she had felt when he looked into her eyes a moment before. There had been recognition, even a feeling, something between only the two of them that she would never be able to explain to anyone else, and she'd never even try.

"The councilman, he was your father," she clarified.

Rudy winced and gave her the slightest nod of his head, but it was unmistakable. Yes, he was telling her, the councilman was his father.

The sirens drew nearer.

She said, "Rudy, this is important. They're going to take you and try to save you. You need to be strong, and fight to stay alive. Do you hear me?"

Again, he nodded, almost imperceptibly.

"You said Frankie shot your father."

A nod.

"Who else? Who was the other shooter?"

He opened his eyes again and regarded her for a long moment before they closed.

"Rudy?"

His mouth opened, then closed, and his head fell to the side.

The sound of footsteps pulled her away, and with it the emotion that had started a moment before disappeared—she had stuffed it away in a dark recess of her soul, where it would only reappear when there was an appropriate time for her to process it.

Dickie was coming, no urgency in his pace. He stopped next to her and contemplated the body at his feet for a long moment, then cut his eyes to meet hers. "He gonna make it?"

She shrugged. "How's the deputy?"

"He's fine. It's Frankie."

"Wait, what?" she exclaimed.

Rudy groaned.

She looked at him, then back to her partner. "What do you mean?"

The Program

"Deputies came around the corner as it went down. Frankie's the one who shot him."

"Did they catch him?"

"He's dead. Apparently, he turned on the deputy who chased him around the corner, gun still in his hand. The deputy lit him up."

Josie looked at Rudy. "Frankie did this to you?"

Rudy, his eyes still closed, didn't respond.

Dickie said, "Deputies saw him do it, Josie. And they lit his ass up for it."

She reached for his head—to hell with the evidence—and touched him the way you might lay your hand on a resting loved one. He looked at her again, his eyes darker now, his stare more distant. She said, "Who else shot your father, Rudy?"

His gaze grew fixed, and she knew he was gone.

40

THERE ARE STAGES OF DEATH, AND EVERY COP KNEW IT.

Dickie remembered sitting at a local cop bar having this conversation with a handful of other ghetto cops, back in the day when he worked Firestone station in South Los Angeles. Two other Firestone deputies were with him, the three of them hoisting grog and telling lies of sailing those radio cars, the topic of death and near-death and the luck of the bad man the topic du jour. An LAPD cop who worked neighboring 77th Street Division—a legendary place in its own right—had chimed in:

"We had a rescue call just the other night, man not breathing over on McKinley and Seventy-Eighth. We get there just as the paramedics arrive, and an old woman is on the porch, directing them through the front door. I walk in and my partner stays with her to get some information for the report. The dude's in bed, blue. Paramedics pronounce him dead, and I walk out ahead of them to give my partner the word so he could record on his report the time he was pronounced. Before I could speak, the woman looks at me with pleading eyes, says, 'Is he dead bad?'"

They all laughed and swigged their beer and then Dickie and Frank, this LAPD copper from 77th, waxed philosophical on the topic.

"What do you suppose she was thinking, that there're stages of death?" Dickie asked.

The Program

Frank pondered it over his Jameson. "Yeah, maybe. I mean, they see people gunned down and rushed away in ambulances, and a month later they're back on the corner, slinging dope."

"So there's dead bad," Dickie pondered aloud.

Frank said, "Dead, dead bad, and maybe something in between also, like fairly dead."

"Fairly dead," Dickie had said to his beer.

Frank rattled his ice and finished off his drink, pushed the glass toward the well and told Tommy he'd have another double. "Yeah, I guess, man. Who knows?"

Now Dickie stood in the security office of the Los Angeles County Medical Center, LCMC, waiting for word on Prada. One of the officers had gone to check with medical staff to see if there was any update. As he did, Dickie pondered Rudy's fate. Would he make it? What were the chances? Shot four times, three to the torso and one to his leg. But the question that lingered in Dickie's mind was, had he been barely dead, fairly dead, or dead bad? Because Dickie was certain that Rudy had, at the very least, seen the tunnel of light in those final moments on the sidewalk before the paramedics had whisked him away.

Josie had gone for a coffee. She seemed to need some alone time, and Dickie contemplated that now too, though not to the extent he had pondered with Frank the stages of death. But he had known for a while that Josie had become fond of Rudy Prada in the short time that they had been dealing with him now. And not in the way a girl falls for the bad boy, or the way a lady loves an outlaw. This was something other than that, more like championing the underdog, respecting the earnest effort put forth by a man who had come from the streets and who was fighting against the odds to change his life. Dickie suspected there was something about Josie's upbringing that made her empathetic to his plight. He had seen her this way with others too, Josie making extra efforts to help those who were willing to help themselves. He'd never told her so, but Dickie admired this quality in his partner. She had this aura about her that drew people in, when she allowed it. You could see it at times, the way a child would fall into her arms, or how a grief-stricken parent would let down their guard with her, allow their emotions to gush from the depths of their beings as they would share with her things about the loss of a loved one they might not have ever told the cops. Dickie had seen it tonight, when Josie had lain her hand on Rudy's head, how he suddenly seemed at peace with whatever was to be. It was as if her touch alone could comfort even the fairly dead.

The security officer returned, told Dickie that the patient was still in surgery. That was a good sign, Dickie knew. There were too many times where the efforts of emergency surgery were short lived because there really was no chance at all, but they had to try. They had to at least go through the motions though the paramedics had brought the patient in already flatlined. Dead bad.

Outside in the fresh air, Dickie sat down on the concrete steps and looked out over the inky summer sky, not a star in sight. You couldn't see the stars most nights, not from the city, not with the illumination from the downtown skyscrapers, the streets and bridges, the glowing—and sometimes flashing—billboards and signs along the roadways and freeways throughout the southland. The faint glow of stadium lights to the north from the not-so-faraway Chavez Ravine brought him the simple joy of knowing he'd be headed home soon, and he'd be able to catch the rest of the game during his drive, listening to the voices of Steiner and Monday, whom he respected although they were no Vin Scully. If the game lasted long enough, he could watch the rest of it on TV, hear his old buddy Eric Karros recounting the action. Not that Karros was truly a buddy, but he was a friend of a friend, and Dickie had had the pleasure of speaking with him a couple of times. Many years ago when Karros was the Dodgers first baseman, Dickie had met him and got him to sign a baseball card for him. Those things somehow made Dickie feel a connection with the baseball icon, though their worlds were far apart. Maybe this was how Rudy felt about Josie, and perhaps the other way around, a small but meaningful connection between two people whose paths had been otherwise unlikely to ever cross.

The charcoal-colored Charger roared around the corner and came to a stop at the curb, Josie obviously getting Dickie's message that he'd be waiting out front. He didn't have news for her, one way or the other, but at least she could still hold on to hope.

Dickie got in the car, and she offered him a cup. "Hot and plain, nothing sweet about it. Like you."

He smiled and Josie smiled back. He said, "No news. They're still working on him."

She nodded and pulled away, one hand on the wheel, the other on her own cup which no doubt contained mostly sweetness and goodness, like her. They rode in silence to East L.A. where she wheeled around the lot and stopped in the aisle behind Dickie's old Crown Vic, a relic—like himself, she'd probably say.

"Okay, partner, tomorrow morning in the office?"

"Unless something changes," she said. "I'm going back to the hospital to wait. If he pulls through this, I want to be there to try again."

Dickie sat for a moment, his right foot having found purchase on the blacktop, but his butt still nestled in the bucket seat. "I'd be surprised if you can talk to him tonight, Josie. Why don't you go home and get some rest."

She was staring at her coffee, likely in agreement but arguing with herself about it rather than with him. After a moment, she broke her trance and looked her partner in the eyes. "You're probably right. I'll go by and check on him once more, maybe hang around for a while just to see that he pulls through, then head home."

"Either way, partner," Dickie said, now reaching over and placing his hand on her shoulder, "We did all we could do. You did what you could do, and you were good to him. And most importantly, he did the best he could do to walk away from it all. It's just that sometimes we can't run far enough to escape our pasts."

She nodded. "Okay, get out of here. Go home and kiss Emily and Angelo and tell him Aunt Josefina loves him. Besides, you leave now, you can listen to the game, and I won't have to cry in front of you."

Dickie smiled and stepped out of the car, stood there as her taillights disappeared from the parking lot. He could hear her gunning it down the road. The woman drove like Mario Andretti, though the time he had told her so, she had frowned and said, "Who?" She was apparently no fan of motor sports.

As he placed his suit jacket on a hanger in the back of his car, Dickie noticed the relative silence. It was as if the town had shut off the lights after the evening's crescendo that left two men shot, one dead bad, the other still trying. He pictured the scene, knowing it would be adorned with yellow tape, the perimeter lined with black and whites and unmarked sedans driven there by homicide detectives, and an assortment of other county cars that had carried the nonessentials to the scene: namely, Internal Affairs and the brass. It would be an all-night affair for whoever from Homicide caught this case, and Dickie was glad it wasn't him. It was times like these when working Unsolveds had never appealed to him more.

Dickie pulled out of the parking lot with his radio tuned in to the game, the Dodgers up by two in the top of the sixth, two runners on and one out. Before he reached the freeway, he learned that Roberts had pulled the starter in the fifth and was on his second relief pitcher already. Dickie shook his head at one of the two things about new-age Dodgers that drove him nuts, the other being that nobody knew how to bunt. They were going to the bottom of the sixth still up by two when his phone rang. It was Josie.

41

Rudy spiraled into an infinite black hole. Miles away he could see a pinpoint-sized light, intense and motionless, beams of green and blue reflecting off the cylindrical walls of glazed white tile. It was a tunnel, not unlike the Second Street tunnel downtown, a passageway the length of five football fields cutting through parts of Los Angeles. Only this tunnel seemed much longer, the light at the end perhaps unreachable. His arms and legs were outstretched, pulled by the gravity of his spin, like a spinout ride at an amusement park, only Rudy didn't feel sick. In fact, he didn't feel anything at all. The pain of searing bullets ripping through his flesh had gone, and he no longer felt the icy cold sensation that had enveloped him as he lay on the sidewalk. Even the mental anguish that he had carried throughout the day was no longer with him. He began to embrace the end, the bright light drawing nearer, albeit slowly. How bad could it be to reach the other side? It couldn't be worse than his last day on earth had been.

But now he was being jostled about, his arms no longer stretched out, but pulled tightly along his body, his legs now together, fixed somehow but not tightly bound. His sensations had returned, the coldness replaced by a warmth that coursed through his body like gulps of hot chocolate. There were the sounds of speech, muted but rushed, snappy spurts of unintelligible sentences that seemed urgent, the voices of both men and women.

Rudy remembered the tunnel and its beckoning light, but he could no longer see it. Had he gone through it, or had something pulled him out of it from the direction he had entered? A sense of sadness came over him, as he had yearned to cross through the light.

He dreamed of a lady cop stroking his head, her warm touch a piercing contrast to the cold darkness that had returned. Her voice, soothing yet commanding, repeatedly telling him to hold on—he was going to be okay. More darkness came but he still felt her touch, and as the tunnel spun and the light intensified, she reached for him with both hands, her arms outstretched, her eyes brighter than the light at the other end. She commanded him to come back, and she pulled at him against the force that drew him deeper into the darkness.

Then it all stopped. His dream was over, and nobody was fretting over him. It was quiet now, only a tone beeping steadily somewhere beyond his view, behind him, perhaps. He was warm, and relaxed. At peace now with himself, with all he had done, and all that had happened. His odyssey through the hereafter had been a spiritual awakening, and he was now prepared to *actually* turn over his will and his life to God.

EXHAUSTED AS SHE HAD BEEN, JOSIE TOSSED AND TURNED THROUGH THE night, all that had happened playing on a continuous loop in her head: the escape, the manhunt, Rudy's suicide voicemail. She couldn't sleep because there were parts that still didn't fit together, things that had been left unresolved. The second shooter, primarily. Josie was thrilled when she called LCMC, and they told her Rudy was stable and recovering in ICU. Now there was a chance she would get the answer to that question, and others. Like, why was Vero killed? Did Frankie kill her? Had she been involved in the murder of Rudy's father? Or did she just know too much, and Frankie had to ensure she wouldn't talk?

What would happen to Rudy now? Josie had a bad feeling that he had been the other shooter, but she had a difficult time reconciling it in her mind. She didn't think he could do it. Shoot his own father to death?

Sixteen years old? But until she heard it from him directly, that he had or had not participated in that murder, she would likely never know. With both Vero and Frankie dead, there was only one other person she had a hunch might know what happened that night.

There was another problem: what about Macias, the man who had the councilman's blood on his hoodie, and who had been convicted of the killing? What part had he played in the murder? It occurred to Josie that no matter what Rudy might tell them, they would need to visit Macias in the pen and get his story too. He had refused to speak with Robles, Neely's deceased ex-husband, or so his report had said. But now what would he have to lose? Josie would need to research the case through the DA's office to see if there were any pending appeals. If so, they would have to notify Macias's attorney before they spoke with him, likely have the counselor there when they did. And McKnight. He would have to be in on that as well.

It was no wonder she hadn't slept, Josie realized, now willing herself from between the sheets and into the start of a new day—likely a long one at that. As she showered, Josie reflected on Rudy lying on the sidewalk flirting with death. She thought he had died when he finally stopped responding and his gaze darkened and his stare had become fixed on something far away. Josie had watched others die, and that was exactly the way death looked when it came slowly, when one was fighting it off for as long as they could, but lost. Had Rudy died and come back from the dark side? She believed in that happening, and she had heard stories of others that it had happened to. For that matter, there were those who had been pronounced dead by a paramedic or even a doctor, who suddenly came to life. One occasion of which Josie was aware involved a body being taken to the coroner's office before the person came to life, likely scaring others half to death. There was another occasion when a man killed his wife, rolled her inside a piece of carpet for the purpose of disposing of her, but had been unable to do so in the following days. There she stayed, in the garage, maggots infesting her corpse. The discovery was made, Homicide called, and it was during the scene investigation when the woman came back to life. One of the two detectives on scene that day soon after joined the rubber gun brigade, and left her job at Homicide. The prevailing thought on the matter was that the woman hadn't died—but did anyone really know? Josie would never know if Rudy had crossed over and come back, but in her gut, she believed that he had. It was that stare.

On her way into the office a short time later, her partner called, asked how she was doing. She had called him on his way home last night, shortly after they had parted company, thanked him for being a great partner, and maybe got a little too mushy about it. She had been in an emotional state.

But Dickie didn't mention any of it. He asked how she was, she told him she was fine. That was it. Dickie then told her that they had a meeting at ten with the skipper, Neely, and McKnight. Mandatory, he said. This wasn't the way she hoped to start the day, but okay. She called LCMC after hanging up with Dickie, and checked on Rudy's status. Still critical, not thought to be able to speak yet. There you had it, nothing better to do anyway than to spend the morning entertaining three of her favorite people.

42

McKnight had called the captain and told him he'd be late, tied up in court. Josie expressed her disposition on the matter when Neely had poked her head into Unsolveds to let them know. "Hmpf." As the lieutenant departed, Josie considered Neely's wardrobe today, a J.Crew blazer and slacks in heather graphite, and a low-cut white silk blouse. "Hmpf," Josie uttered again. Her partner chuckled, likely knowing her thoughts. Dickie was good like that—or bad like that, depending on your situation. He pushed out of his chair and walked to the office door. Stopped and looked back, "You want a coffee?"

"No, thanks," she said.

He allowed that to hang there a moment, then asked, "Do you want to go get drunk?"

Josie grinned. "That I can do."

"Okay, we'll consider it after the meeting."

"If I make it through without committing a felony."

She watched him leave, then sat back in her seat, exhausted. Lack of sleep and the stress of the job—two things that went together like Neely's pantsuits. It was silent now, Josie alone in the Unsolveds office, willing her phone to ring. She'd given the hospital all her numbers: her cell, her office, the front desk… Josie didn't want to miss an update on Rudy's condition. She thought about calling again, but she had just checked during her drive to the office, and she didn't think there would've been any change in that short time. She could call once more before the meeting, or maybe wait until it was over.

What she needed to do was chill.

But how could she chill when the key to solving the councilman's case lay in a hospital bed in critical condition? It wasn't just about the "solve," either—there was the situation with Anthony Macias doing twenty-five to life, perhaps in Frankie's place. The question now was, should Frankie have been there in his place, or there with Macias? If in his place, who would it be? Frankie and who else?

And that was the question that haunted her. Had Rudy been one of the two shooters? For whatever reason—likely a multitude of them—Josie prayed it wasn't so.

Dickie came back with a steaming Styrofoam cup, a grin on his face. Josie asked, "What're you laughing about?"

Rather than continuing past her desk to his, which butted up to hers and was within spit wad range, he took a seat at the guest's chair that sat next to her desk, putting them nearly face to face at an arm's length. He set his coffee on the edge of her desk and said, "Oh, fucking Ghan. Dude kills me with his stories."

"I'm surprised he's still around."

"He's been retired six years, just doing the hireback deal to stay busy, and to have a new audience to tell his stories to."

"That's what he was doing," Josie guessed.

"Yeah, in the break room. He was talking about the Riordon brothers. You ever hear of them?"

Josie shook her head, glanced at her cell phone.

Dickie said, "These two brothers worked here way back when. One of 'em was tall and skinny, had a droopy face like a hound. The other had short little legs and a long torso, couldn't keep his shirts tucked in. Both of 'em country boys. And the weird part was, they pronounced their last names differently."

"Two brothers," Josie said.

"Yeah, one would say his name was *Rear*don, and the other would say

Riorden, like *rye,* and then really annunciating the '*or*' part of it. *Rye-or-den.*"

"And that cracks you up," she said, a statement, not a question.

Dickie took a swig of his coffee, set the cup back on her desk. "No—I mean, yes—but that's not what I was laughing about."

She gave him the nod to go ahead, but then Lopes stuck his head in the door. "Your boyfriend's here, we're ready to start the meeting."

Josie knew he was referring to McKnight, so she responded with a middle finger salute, then began gathering her things: her phone, purse, case file…

Dickie stood as well, coffee in hand again. "Anyway, Ghan was telling this story about an interview he was doing with one of the two Riordens, this dude they had in on a murder beef, a juvie, and of course the dude's swearing he didn't do it. Dude says, 'I put that on my mother.' Riorden says to him, 'Well, your mother is in the lobby, I'll go get her,' and the kid starts singing a different tune, spills his guts on himself *and* his homeboy."

Josie forced a grin, more focused on the meeting she was dreading than Dickie's so-called funny story. She pushed by him, and she could feel him following behind her.

Dickie saying, "You'd probably have to hear Ghan tell it."

"Uh-huh."

"The point is, this was one of those cases where the kid'd rather go to jail than take the ass whoopin' his mama was about to give him."

She glanced back. "I get it, partner."

They continued in silence. Dickie passed her in the stretch just in time to get the door for her, proving chivalry hadn't died, at least not where dinosaurs still roamed.

CAPTAIN STOVER LED OFF WITH A GESTURE AND NOD TO DICKIE AND SAID, "Well, fill us all in on the councilman case—I understand there have been some major developments."

Everyone was seated around the rectangular table, plenty of room to spare. Dickie, Lopes, and Josie together at one end, McKnight at the other. Stover and Neely between them, Aunt Brenda paying more attention to

McKnight than anything or anybody else in the room. Josie thinking, Uh-huh, that's why the J.Crew today. *Cougar.*

Dickie took off with the story, beginning with the escape and finishing with the latest update Josie had gotten from the hospital a short time before they gathered. McKnight had been taking notes feverishly, his pen zipping back and forth on a yellow legal notepad he had before him, flipping pages and rolling one at a time beneath the pad every few minutes. He must've taken ten pages worth of notes, and Josie wondered how he could write so much about so little information. In a nutshell, Rudy escaped, Frankie found Rudy and shot him, Rudy was in the hospital fighting for his life. Oh, and Rudy said Frankie was a shooter on the councilman case, and the councilman happened to be Rudy's father. Nowhere near a dozen pages, even with the genealogy detail.

Stover had a couple questions: Why would Frankie kill Rudy? Do we know why Rudy escaped—what had his intention been? Is there any reason to think Rudy isn't the other shooter? How does Macias tie in with all of this?

Dickie and Josie exchanged a glance, but Lopes weighed in before they had to silently resolve who was going to field those questions.

Lopes said, "Everything we've looked at, going back several years before the murder, there is nothing that puts Macias together with either one of them, Frankie Rosas or Rudy Prada. So, I think we're looking at the case against Macias completely unwinding."

McKnight was quick to defend his office. "Let's not jump to conclusions here. Just because nothing comes up on paper, doesn't mean they weren't associates. Also, Prada saying his cousin, who had just shot and tried to kill him, was a shooter on his father's case, doesn't make it so."

"He said it on the voicemail message, before Frankie tried to kill him."

McKnight cut his eyes to Josie. "You've saved the recording, I hope."

She rolled her eyes and didn't bother answering.

Stover caught the eye roll. "Okay, good, so we have him saying it on a recorded message. But to Mr. McKnight's point, what do we have other than that statement to tie Rosas or anyone else to that murder?"

Dickie said, "I mean, we've got the gun, Captain."

Stover glared at him, picking up the sarcastic tone.

He lightened his tone when he continued, Dickie knowing when to tamp it down. "My point is, you've got a guy who is caught with the murder weapon seventeen years after the killing, and now you have his own cousin telling us that it was Frankie who shot his father."

McKnight corrected, "You actually caught Prada with the murder weapon, so what you really have is the one who is truly in the hot seat pointing the finger at somebody else."

"But we have Frankie's prints on the gun, and not Rudy Prada's," Josie argued, "which corroborates Prada's statement from the very beginning, that it was Frankie's gun, and that he had stashed it in Rudy's car."

Stover held up his hands, "Okay, okay, let's not argue the case here. Let's get all the facts and argue it in court."

Lopes said, "Someone needs to go beat Macias's balls."

Neely shot her daggers at him. "Excuse me?"

Dickie chuckled. "It's a manner of speech, Lieutenant. He's just saying we need to interview Macias and get his story."

"Was that not already done?" she asked.

Josie looked at Dickie, knowing he wouldn't allow that opportunity to pass. He didn't disappoint. "We don't know, ma'am. The detective who handled this case originally said Macias wouldn't talk."

She seemed to gather herself for a moment before replying, the room silent as snow. "Well then, there would be no reason to think otherwise, would there?"

Josie could feel the tension between them. She almost wanted Dickie to retreat, or at least to bow out of the fight gracefully. Nothing good could come from his calling into question the integrity of another homicide detective, not in this forum—not in this company.

Dickie let his breath out through his nose slowly, reminding Josie of Selleck as Chief Reagan in *Blue Bloods*, and suddenly the story about the Riorden brothers seemed funny. Josie snickered and everyone looked her way. "Sorry, just had a funny thought. Go ahead, partner," she said, her eyes on Dickie and praying he would step right in.

He did. "No, Lieutenant, there would be no reason to doubt that Macias had lawyered up back when they were putting this case together, but now that he's been convicted, it could be a whole other story. Meaning, maybe he'll talk to us now—what does he have to lose?"

McKnight said, "I'll see if he's got any appeals pending. If not, we'll go talk to him. Even if he does, I'll find out who's representing him now, make a call and ask him or her to join us."

Josie couldn't help but to silently question his use of *we'll* and *us*. It wasn't as if McKnight was going to take his ass up to Tehachapi to interview Macias.

Stover looked at the three of them, his focus seemingly on Josie. "Okay, who's going?"

She didn't hesitate. Josie wanted to put this case together, and until Rudy could carry on a conversation, there wasn't much else she could do here. Maybe interview Rudy's mom, but that would probably need to wait a day or two also, his mother being at the hospital the last time Josie had checked. "I'll do it. I'll go today."

Josie looked at Dickie, assuming he was going to throw his hat in the ring, say there you have it, we'll go now. But instead, he just looked at her for a long moment, glanced at his watch, and said, "I can't do it today, but—"

McKnight said, "Perfect. I'll go with Detective Sanchez." He now glanced at his wrist, only he was looking at something that probably cost five grand, not an Apple watch. He said, "I'll have my clerk find out who the attorney is, make a call, and see if today works for everyone. If not—" he cut his eyes to Josie again, "I'll let you know when we can go."

Josie was speechless, but she held his gaze.

He then said, "I assume you'll drive? I don't have a county car."

She said, "If I can stay sober."

The captain frowned at her.

"I'm joking," she said. "Inside joke between the counselor and me."

43

Back in Unsolveds, Josie said, "But I'm not actually joking. I'm going to start drinking right now."

"I don't like it," Lopes said. "Do you want me to go with you?"

She considered it for a moment, hooked her purse over the back of her chair, and sat down in it. "No, I'll be fine."

Dickie said, "I can move some things around, call Emily and see—"

"It's fine," she assured them both. "As I've been saying all along, I don't think he drugged me. I really don't. Besides, even if he had, do you think he would do anything stupid now? With everyone knowing I left here with him?"

"You could kick his ass anyway," Lopes said, "the little weasel."

"There's that," she said.

She checked her phone and then turned her attention to the computer screen on her desk. Dickie took a seat at his desk across from her and Lopes settled into his, over in the corner. The room fell silent other than the sounds of keystrokes, slurps of coffee, and the occasional clearing of a throat. Even outside their office, it seemed subdued. Josie had noticed it more and more lately, whereas the floor used to be equal parts serious and Animal House. The newer investigators didn't seem to openly joke with one another and taunt each other the way everyone had when she first arrived at Homicide. She didn't know what had changed, but it was different. Maybe it was that this newer generation were the ones who grew up texting their friends that were sitting next to them on the couch, technology having turned many of them into recluses. Maybe they were having just as much fun as her generation of detectives had had, but not showing it. Sending memes and GIFs to one another and laughing hysterically inside.

Her phone vibrated against her desktop, and she saw a message had come in. McKnight. A trace of nausea overcame her. She read the text.

> We're good to go anytime this afternoon. If you could pick me up at my office just after noon or so that would be great.

It was time to establish the big dog-little dog relationship with the lawyerly gentleman. Josie took a couple deep breaths, sat up a little straighter, and thumbed her response.

> I'll be double-parked on Temple at noon. Be out front. Don't make me wait.

There.

JUSTIN MCKNIGHT WAS STANDING ON THE SIDEWALK IN FRONT OF 210 W. Temple Street, a contrast with the masses in his deftly tailored Armani, a tea-colored slim-fit affair with a mint shirt and matching paisley tie. It was no wonder Neely couldn't keep her eyes off him at the office this morning, the two fashion models of L.A. law.

The two-hour drive to Tehachapi had been uneventful, two professionals behaving as if they were otherwise strangers, the only conversation centered on what they hoped to accomplish with Macias. McKnight had been the primary contributor of the dialogue, going through files and taking notes as he formulated his plan for them, Josie thinking it was just what she needed, a lawyer to tell her how to talk to convicts. Between the strategy sessions there were long periods of uncomfortable silence, specked with awkward spurts of extraneous conversation. He liked her car.

It was comfortable. How fast have you had it going? Man, this is a long boring drive. Josie with a lot of uh-huhs and yeahs and only answering questions that required more than that with concise responses, all along resisting the urge to brace him about That Night. But she knew nothing good could come of broaching that topic when they had an important interview ahead of them and a two-hour return trip. On the way back, maybe... after they were halfway home with only an hour or less to go. Or wait until they were ten minutes out. She'd wait to see how she felt after the interview.

In the prison, Josie checked her gun, then she and McKnight exchanged their IDs for visitor badges. A sumo wrestler in a prison guard outfit escorted them through a series of polished concrete hallways among roaming inmates until they reached the visitors room, a sign on the entryway marking the spot. He keyed open the heavy metal door and stepped aside, signaling their path toward a desk where what might have been his opponent waited. This other man, not quite as large but with a neck like a whiskey barrel and arms and a chest that suggested he could bench press a Buick, motioned them forward as if they were holding up progress, checked and logged the numbers of their visitor badges, and then nodded to the Sumo. He took them across the lobby and placed them in an interview room that appeared very much like the hundreds of other interview rooms wherein Josie had spent a sizable portion of her life.

McKnight shuffled through his notes and kept himself busy while Josie sat in silence, contemplating the potential outcome of this interview. How much would they learn that had never been told in seventeen years? Would there be any revelation, or would it be a dry run, half a day sweating the tension that hung in the air between her and McKnight? But if not—if it wasn't a waste of their time, and Macias sat down and told them a story—what might they learn? That Macias and Frankie shot the councilman? Probably not. That Frankie and someone else did it, and he just got caught up in some bad shit? Maybe. Who might that someone else be? Would Macias even know?

Josie still believed that the other shooter hadn't been Rudy. If there were two shooters, and one of them was Frankie, as Rudy stated in what was essentially a dying testament, who was the other? Would Rudy have admitted to it if he had been the other shooter? Why wouldn't he have?

She didn't want to believe it was him, and she didn't, if for no other reason than to reaffirm her instinct on these things. She hadn't been wrong very often, not when it came to crime scenes and theories and having a feel for who did what and why.

The sounds of footfalls in the hallway and jangling keys at the door snapped Josie from her reverie. Sumo was back, and this time he had with him a man in oversized prison blues: dark pants and a lighter colored pullover shirt, the young man appearing older than his age, with graying hair and haggard eyes. Prison takes its toll.

Three of Macias could have fit inside the man who had escorted him.

Macias was shown to his seat as his attorney appeared behind them, a portly man wearing an ill-fitted cheap suit and glasses that sat crooked on his head, framed by disheveled wiry brown hair. Once settled, the attorney provided McKnight a business card, said, "Okay, my client is willing to talk to you, but with the stipulation that nothing is recorded. There will be no formal admissions or testimonies until such time as an exoneration hearing is scheduled, and an agreement is made between your office and mine. Agreed?"

McKnight nodded. "Fair enough. We're here to ask a few questions based on some new evidence that has come to light, relatively critical information that may have bearing on the status of Mr. Macias's conviction. This is very preliminary, but given the fact that we've driven here to speak with your client, you can assume these developments are significant and compelling."

"Very good," he said, "have at it."

McKnight turned his eyes to Josie. "This is Detective Sergeant Sanchez, and she is the lead investigator on the case now." He pushed his chair back slightly, crossed his legs, and placed his legal tablet on his lap, his pen hovering over it. "All yours, Sergeant."

44

Josie walked into Rudy's hospital room and found him awake, alert even, and in the company of a woman who Josie suspected was his mother. She was in her early fifties with loose wrinkly skin, graying hair, and droopy eyes set against heavy blue shadowing. Josie had seen her before. Not Rudy's mom—but *this* woman. Hundreds of times. You saw them living in tents, at the homeless shelters, and in rehabs. Jail and prison. Women who had lived hard and whose organs were on the verge of failing from a lifetime of drug and alcohol abuse, and you knew they were already at the last few inches of their rulers. They both set their eyes on Josie. Rudy's gaze was soft, perhaps hopeful… maybe humbled by yet another chance at life. His mother's eyes told a different story—fear, maybe apprehension. Was it from nearly losing a child? Or was it something else behind those yellowing eyes, something more nefarious? Josie tried to read her, but she looked away, careful not to show much. Poker players wear sunglasses during tournaments to shade the windows to their minds. Josie, a fan of the game, would often think of the unfair advantage it gave those who did, and she was thankful that those she interviewed weren't generally afforded the luxury of hiding behind mirrored shades.

Josie went to the opposite side of Rudy's bed from where his mother sat, the woman still averting her eyes downward. Was she hiding something, or was she just uncomfortable around the cops? There was no doubt a woman like her would know a cop the moment they exchanged their first glances, and she had likely already heard about Josie.

She turned her attention to Rudy, looked into his eyes for a long moment before beginning. Josie could see kindness in his eyes, the soft eye of a horse, a sign to the horseman of willingness, or submission. Partnership. It was a sign you'd want to see before stepping into the stirrup of one that had the potential to buck, and Josie knew that men like Rudy—for all his charm, for the goodness that rested somewhere deep in his soul—had to be respected for their ability to buck.

She considered the rambling message he had left on her phone not long before he was shot. Surely a near-death experience would play into one's disposition. His message had been replete with despair, words of a man set on ending his life. Yet here he was. Had anything changed? Some who failed at suicide would continue until they succeeded. Others experienced awakenings, and they would commit themselves to new beginnings. Rudy had been found with an unopened can of beer in his pocket, and Josie knew why. She was likely the only one who knew instinctively what he had planned to do, and it wasn't that he had fallen off the wagon, or that he had wanted one more drink before the end. It was to force the end, a simulated weapon when the cops arrived to confront him. Suicide by cops. A replay of what happened between them fifteen years ago, but this time with a deadly consequence. Theatrics? Maybe. But there was no doubt in Josie's mind that Rudy had wanted to end his life. She didn't see that in his eyes now, not a single trace of it.

There was another aspect to the diffidence of Rudy's disposition this morning, Josie considered, and that could be the trauma of being a victim to violence. The plan to end his life, though poetic as it might have seemed when he set it in motion, was disrupted when Frankie found him, walked up on him, and started shooting before Rudy even recognized the mortal danger he faced. He had been taken out, and that was a difficult pill to swallow. Josie knew all too well the disgrace and self-loathing that came from being a victim—especially for those who were far from being the victim type. It was mortifying, terrifying, emotionally devastating. Humbling, truthfully—the recognition of one's vulnerability, mortality even.

She put her hand on his arm and held it there a moment. It was all she needed to establish a connection with him, or perhaps to solidify what was already there between them. It was part of the interview process that many investigators shunned, as it was every bit as awkward as the moments leading up to a first kiss. Josie had seen her partner place his hand over the clasped hands of a woman who had killed her husband, and she had watched in amazement how the simple act had broken through barriers and led to a confession. Josie was a fan of touch.

She said, "Hey there."

There was a slight smile beneath his bushy mustache and the oxygen tubes that sat upon it.

"You've had a few rough days."

Rudy closed his eyes for a moment, then opened them slowly as if waking from a long, hard sleep. Morphine will do that to you, and it had crossed Josie's mind that he would have more of a battle staying clean when he left here with a supply of pain pills to go.

He took his time with the words, saying, "I got lucky, Sergeant."

Josie nodded, contemplating just how lucky he had been. She smiled back at him, shifted gears. "This is your mother?"

He shifted his eyes toward her, and Josie's gaze followed. There she sat, quietly watching the show with a ringside seat. The cop and the outlaw, about to get to the business at hand. The haggard woman offered only a quick glance of acknowledgment to Josie's assumption. Yes, she was his mama.

Rudy said, "Yes, my mama," and lifted his hand in her direction. Josie believed he was wanting his mother to take his hand in her own, but she didn't move from her position, her frail hands clutching the handbag on her lap.

Josie touched him again, bringing him back to her. She waited for that connection before saying, "Rudy, we need to talk."

"I guess you got my message."

She nodded.

"Damn," he said. "I wish I hadn't left it now. It's kind of embarrassing, you know?"

Josie pulled her hand back. "I know."

"It was like, all crazy, just everything that's happened, and then suddenly everything was unraveling. I didn't see any way out of all this. I knew that I was a dead man walking, either way. Know what I mean?"

She shook her head. "No, Rudy, I don't. Tell me why you believe that."

His eyes cut back to his mother. There was something to it. Josie said, "Should we finish this talk alone, just you and me?"

Josie looked up to see his mother's eyes more intense now, a look Josie knew was her trying to will her son not to talk. Not talking to the cops was part of their culture, truthfully, and Josie understood that. But was that all this was, or was there more to it?

Rudy hadn't looked away from his mother's glare. It was a standoff of sorts, though a short-lived one. Rudy said, "Mama, it's time to tell her what happened."

She shook her head. "*No, mi hijo,*" she pled, her eyes now showing apprehension. "*No digas nada. Traerá problemas.*"

Josie, fluent in Spanish, knew what she had told him. *No, my son. Don't say anything. It will bring us trouble.* Rudy's mother had just unknowingly corroborated Anthony Macias's statement, one that had seemed unbelievable to Josie when she heard it yesterday in the cold concrete room at Tehachapi State Prison. It was a statement that would soon be repeated in closed chambers with a judge, his court reporter, and counsel for both the People and Macias all present. And that would lead to a public session where the judge would exonerate Macias of the murder charges for which he had now served seventeen years.

Without taking her eyes off the woman and her clutched purse, Josie raised her voice slightly, said, "Partner?"

Dickie came in, and Josie signaled him with a slight nod as to what needed to be done. He went to Rudy's mother, took the purse from her hands, and held it behind his back without taking his eyes off her. Josie received the handbag, and Dickie assisted the woman from her seat, guided her to turn and face away from him, and asked her to put her hands behind her back. There were no words, no prodding—it seemed to be an expected part of a day she always knew would come.

45

They booked Marianna Prada Hernandez at the East Los Angeles sheriff's station on the charge of murder, California Penal Code section 187(a)—*the unlawful killing of a human being, or fetus, with malice aforethought.*

Afterward, they grabbed lunch at Manny's, carne asada tacos for them both, Josie saying now that this case was over, she needed to get back to running, or something, and stop eating like a dumpster rat. She said, "It's no wonder I'm still single." And, "Even my mother asked if I had gained weight—my mother!" Dickie, obviously smarter than to engage in the conversation, had sat quietly chewing his food, averting his eyes even, watching the door, scanning the street beyond the paned window, advertisements of *especials* in bold letters and bright colors. Josie saying, "Thank God for pants suits with jackets that cover my big ass." Dickie chortled, then retreated in preparation for an assault. It didn't come. Josie smiled and said, "After we brief the captain—"

"And your buddy, Neely," Dickie said.

"—yeah, Aunt Brenda. Anyway, after we fill them in on everything, I'm taking off. Might take the rest of the week off."

Dickie was getting after his tacos, Josie taking her time. He finished chewing a bite, said, "So you haven't filled me in on the details about Macias."

Josie hit the highlights of Macias's story, told Dickie how Macias said he had come from the liquor store, heard three gunshots—two, a pause, then one more—and he came around the corner and saw a kid—that's how Macias had described Frankie, *just a kid*, which he had been that night seventeen years ago—with a woman who could have been his mother. Each of them with a pistol. The kid, Frankie, made eye contact with Macias before he and the woman started away. They ran into the street as a small car pulled up, a girl driving, and they fled together.

Dickie guessed, "Vero?"

Josie nodded. "Rudy confirmed it. He knew it then, and that's how he knew instinctively that it had been Frankie who killed her."

"Makes sense," Dickie said. "It's just amazing that his mother was in on it."

"In on it? She set the wheels in motion." Josie set half a taco back on her plate, looked outside and off at nothing in particular, thinking about being in her shoes, thinking about Jacob Spencer. She came back to Dickie and changed the subject. "Macias said he saw the councilman slumped at the side of his car, the passenger door open, and he saw a briefcase inside. Just as he reached in to grab it, the getaway car had turned around and was coming back. He knew by the way they were coming at him that they were there to finish their business, take out a witness. He left the brief case and ran, over a fence and through a yard. Someone from the car fired several shots at him as he fled. That's how the blood got on his sweatshirt, leaning across the councilman as he reached for the briefcase."

He agreed with her, a slight nod as his gaze seemed a mile away, maybe seventeen years back, Dickie likely putting the scene together with the new information. "Okay, I can see that. Would've been nice if he had mentioned all this to Victor Robles."

Josie smirked. "Macias said he did."

"Jesus," Dickie said, shook his head and sighed. "I mean, I get it, you don't believe the guy, but you could at least document the statement somewhere. Wouldn't that have been nice, a couple paragraphs in the murder book that would corroborate what Macias is saying now?"

She agreed. "Still, we've got them. Rudy gave me everything, the shocker being the story behind his biological father."

"The councilman," Dickie said, disgustedly. "I'm not going to say he didn't have it coming."

"Well..."

"Sorry, but a child rapist... I don't have any sympathy."

Josie didn't respond. Some things were better left unsaid.

Dickie moved on. "The thing I worry about is that everything Rudy gave us is hearsay. I get that he lays it out, but he wasn't at the scene, right? He's not an eyewitness."

"No, he wasn't there. But as far as exonerating Macias, it doesn't matter. Frankie and Vero are both dead, so it's just Rudy's mom, Marianna, as far as going forward with prosecution. She'll likely take a plea, given that the gun she had in her purse when we arrested her is supposed to be the second murder weapon, according to Rudy."

"Yeah, maybe," Dickie said. "But we can't prove that with ballistics, right?"

"I don't think so, no." She had another thought. "So let her plead to a lesser charge—fifteen years would probably be a life sentence for her."

Josie pushed her paper plate to the side, took a sip of her water. They had both finished eating but neither of them seemed in too big a hurry to return to their office where their captain waited to be updated about the arrest of Rudy's mother.

"McKnight coming down for the briefing?" Dickie asked, a slight grin on his face.

Josie knew what was coming, so she got right to it and answered the next line of questioning before it was asked, the elephant in the room being the long car ride she and McKnight had shared to and from the prison.

There had been no misconduct on McKnight's part, she assured him.

"How can you be certain?"

"I believe him."

"Yeah?"

She waited a minute, not sure how much she wanted to tell her partner about what McKnight had told her. Josie knew she could trust him, but she wasn't sure that Dickie wouldn't round up Lopes and Floyd and take matters into their own hands with the new information.

McKnight had told her that he had only avoided her at first because he thought she was a blackout drunk. At some point, he had confided this to his investigator, who happened to know Josie well enough to tell him it wasn't the case. As the two discussed what had happened that night, they concluded she must have been drugged—but by whom? The couple next to them. McKnight had replayed the evening in his mind and realized how uncomfortable Josie had been with the couple who sat next to her when he returned from the restroom. McKnight and his investigator returned to Brandy's, the sports bar downtown, several times until McKnight recognized the couple from that night, there again, at the bar, next to a pretty woman and her male companion. They watched closely—intensely when the gentleman left her alone for a few minutes and went to the restroom—but the woman wisely guarded her drink throughout the night, never giving them an opportunity to slip her something, if they had even thought to do so. McKnight noticed the man would crowd the young woman, and it appeared to him that the man was copping cheap feels. Josie knew when he told her that part of it that Smiley and his girlfriend were, in fact, the likely culprits.

But feed that type of detail to Dickie, and he'd be on a mission. Josie felt it was best to let it go, especially since McKnight and his investigator had waited until the couple left, followed them out, and copped the license number of his car. Now McKnight had his name, his criminal background —which included domestic violence, stalking, and an indecent exposure charge—and he had flagged the name so that if he were to be entered into their system again, as a defendant, McKnight would be one of the first to know. McKnight had also contacted LAPD's Central Division, spoken with a sex crimes detective, and told her about the man, in the event any similar cases were reported.

There was no way this naked dog-owning former football jock would come up with all that just to clean himself up. Even if he was viewed as one of the top prosecutors in the DA's office, an up-and-comer who would no doubt soon be trying the county's highest profile cases, he wasn't *that* clever.

Josie said, "You'll have to trust me on this one, partner. I know for a fact McKnight did nothing wrong, and now I regret having suggested otherwise."

Dickie pondered it a moment. "Well, at least we didn't kill him yet."

46

They sat with a view of the pier, a hundred-foot affair with a Mediterranean-style building that sat at the end. Josie's date had told her it was the Roundhouse Aquarium, a marine study lab that was open to the public and featured tanks of baby sharks, lobsters, and brightly colored, non-native fish and invertebrates. It interested her, and she told him so. He said next time they should go see it, perhaps a notion about the future.

Josie had asked him what invertebrates were, feeling a bit unscholarly in doing so, but explaining that she had never studied much about marine life. He was happy to explain, telling her that invertebrates were a paraphyletic group of animals that neither possess nor develop a spine, like snails, clams, jellyfish, and squid—even corals. The man suddenly sounded like a marine biologist, not at all like a dumb jock. In fact, Josie began feeling rather ordinary—if not ignorant—as he went on, educating her about corals, how they were living organisms, how a quarter of all marine species lived in and around a coral reef, how they were invaluable to our planet's biodiversity...

Josie sipped her margarita, a house specialty of the StrandBar, their waiter had said. She found it refreshing, a bouquet of bitter and sweet across its chili-salted rim. It was a nice way to end an afternoon at the beach and to segue into the evening, Josie eager to distance her thoughts from the councilman case and all the lives destroyed because of it. She'd seen Rudy at Chino yesterday, and he was in good spirits, holding on to the tenets of his program, *one day at a time*. He'd pled guilty to the escape and was given a year, of which he'd likely do half. He'd said, "Six months ain't nothin', just enough time to heal, get my mind right, and get off these pain pills they've got me on." He had thanked her for all she had done, and told her he wanted to see her again someday, clarifying "not like that."

The summer sun slowly slipped into the Pacific, a blue horizon streaked with yellow and red and burnt orange. Wetsuit-clad surfers sat astride their boards, bobbing up and down as they waited to catch one more wave before darkness befell them. Tourists peppered the pier, snapping photos and taking in the sights, and seagulls circled above them, cawing over the sounds of waves crashing against the shore. Sunbathers packed their beach bags and brushed sand from their sun-kissed bodies, while scantily clad volleyballers hurried to finish their game.

"You're distracted," McKnight observed.

Only a little, she thought. Josie couldn't help reflecting on her work, even at times like this. She had moved on from Rudy, having just pictured him in his prison blues walking the yard or leaning against a cinder block building, soaking in the last moments of sunlight, and now she was thinking about a rifle scope and DNA. The little boy killed by a sniper was a case she couldn't let rest, and here she was, looking out over the ocean but imagining just how that scope might have been dislodged from the murder weapon during the killer's hasty escape. Figuring that case out would be her priority when she returned to work—unless, of course, Stover and his fashion model lieutenant had some other demand of her.

Josie cut her eyes back to him, proffered a smile, then allowed her gaze to settle on the frothy seawater rolling onto the beach. She could almost feel the coolness washing over her bare feet, the wet sand oozing between her toes, and she embraced these more pleasant thoughts over her deliberations of the dead and dying.

"I'm relaxed," she said, changing gears, "just taking in the beauty of all this." Josie's gaze spanned the horizon before she met his eyes again. "I didn't realize how much I needed a day like today. Thank you."

He lifted his old fashioned to offer a toast, and Josie clinked her glass against it. "To the sand and sun and briny sea," he said.

"Cheers," she responded.

Josie felt the coolness of the evening setting in, and she pictured ending the day with a small fire on the beach, toasting marshmallows on a stick. Maybe next time, she considered—and she liked the idea of seeing him again.

"Have you been to Hawaii?"

He nodded. "A couple of times."

Josie said, "I'm overdue."

"You've never been?" McKnight asked, his cadence one of surprise.

"I've never been. I've been to Mexico—Cabo, Cancun, and even Chihuahua."

He chuckled. "I know that's not on the beach, Chihuahua."

She smiled. "I know, just thought I'd throw that in to show you how well traveled I am. I even speak the language."

A string of lights had come to life against the darkening patio, and a reflection in his eyes seemed an answer to her smile.

"Is that where you're from, Chihuahua?"

"It's where my family is from. I was born here—well, not here, but in L.A."

"So you've been back to see family," he guessed, not a question.

"You could say that," Josie said, as she looked across the Pacific and thought about those years when her mother had sent her away. There hadn't been anything terrible about it, per se, nothing that left her damaged mentally or physically, but she had always felt as if it were a theft of her childhood, like being sent to jail for two years when you're a kid. She remembered coming back, her mother telling her that her father had gone, and never really explaining anything else about that. Rudy had had a similar experience, hadn't he? She wondered if that was one of the reasons she felt a connection to him. Josie pictured him now, probably already transferred out of Chino, a Level I state prison where inmates like Rudy were processed through and sent out to any of the other thirty-some facilities spread across the state. He had probably gone to one of the level II or III facilities, such as Avenal or Ironwood, or he might have been sent to Mule Creek, a segregation facility where gang dropouts, sex offenders, and cops were sent. Or maybe he went to Tehachapi to take Macias's place now that Macias was home, likely sitting in the plush office of a high-dollar attorney who was promising to make him rich.

McKnight said, "Well, why else would anyone go to Chihuahua?"

Josie pushed Rudy aside—so much for being unburdened by reflections of work—and decided she also didn't care to speak about her family. She said, "I'm going to take some of my vacation time in the very near future, do some of the things I've always wanted to do but have never taken time away from the job or my mother to do them. Maui is a must. But I'd like to see some other islands as well. I could take a month off, no problem, with all the time I have on the books—but it's a matter of financing the trip itself. More than a week or so of being a beach bum can get expensive."

"It definitely can in Hawaii," he said.

Josie hadn't realized how hungry she was until the tiger shrimp and horseradish cocktail sauce with lemon arrived, but then it occurred to her that she hadn't eaten anything other than a bagel with cream cheese for brunch, having allowed herself to sleep in for a change.

They each spooned a helping onto their plates, and started in. Around a bite, Josie said, "It's perfect!"

"One of my favorites," he said.

"Shrimp cocktail, or this restaurant?"

"Both," he said, showing her that boyish grin. "I'm a seafood kind of guy, to be honest about it. Don't get me wrong, I like a medium-rare cut of beef as much as any Texan, but I could live on a diet of yellowfin and halibut and pretty much any whitefish they catch."

"One thing about Mexico, if you like fish tacos..."

"Oh, I know," he said, "I'm a fan."

She set her fork down. "Are we going somewhere with this, or is this all just small talk until you've taken me to bed?"

He reached across the table and took her hand. "I'm not in any hurry to do that, Josie. But I do hope to spend more time with you. I'd like to someday take that vacation to Hawaii with you."

"You hardly know me."

"Hardly know you? I've carried you through the threshold of my castle and disrobed you, my dear. Fluffed your pillow and put you to bed, roused you in the morning with a slice of toast and a cup of gourmet coffee, then swapped that out for a sprite when I realized you had an upset tummy. Those things alone could consummate a marriage in some cultures."

Josie smiled as she recalled what a gentleman he had been—the circumstances notwithstanding—and she pictured his orderly and well-appointed home, the little naked dog he called Chappy, the linens and guest accommodations readily on hand. He certainly had longterm potential.

He smiled back at her. "What?"

"Nothing," she lied, not willing to share any part of her thoughts about that. Not just yet, anyway. Josie said, "Let's see how this date goes, and the next one—"

"So we'll be seeing each other again."

"—and then we'll talk about vacations and sunsets on the beach."

McKnight pushed out of his chair, came around to her side of the table, and joined her there. He put his arm around her shoulders, and leaned into her.

Josie breathed in his crisp, cool fragrance, a splendid pairing with the fresh ocean breeze, and every bit as satisfying as the radiating warmth of his touch. Feeling more content in his arms than she had felt for a very long time, she knew there was something between them. She sensed that this was the beginning of something special.

He snuggled closer, and the two of them gazed off into the last moments of the day, the ocean suddenly calm, the crowds all gone. He whispered, "Until we do, this sunset will do quite nicely."

Josie nestled into him, thought, *You'll do quite nicely as well, Counselor.*

ALSO BY DANNY R. SMITH

"The sharp, hardboiled prose you would expect from a detective novelist... Smith shares vivid details, hard-earned insights, and stories of courage and terror, told with crisp, raw dialogue, a feeling for the drama of potentially violent confrontations, and an undercurrent of despair, despite many heartfelt tributes to cops he trusted and the mentor whose murder he had to look into."

- BookLife Review

NOTHING LEFT TO PROVE

A LAW ENFORCEMENT MEMOIR

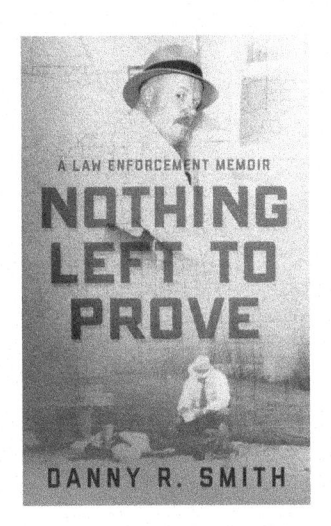

Get your copy today!

ALSO BY DANNY R. SMITH

THE DICKIE FLOYD DETECTIVE SERIES

- A Good Bunch of Men
- Door to a Dark Room
- Echo Killers
- The Color Dead
- Death after dishonor
- Unwritten Rules
- The Program

THE RICH FARRIS DETECTIVE SERIES

- The Outlaw

DICKIE FLOYD SHORT STORIES

- In the City of Crosses
- Exhuming Her Honor

AVAILABLE AUDIOBOOKS

- A Good Bunch of Men
- Door to a Dark Room
- Nothing Left to Prove

NON-FICTION – MEMOIR

- Nothing Left to Prove: A Law Enforcement Memoir

SUBSCRIBE TO MY NEWSLETTER

I love staying connected with my readers through social media and email. You can also sign up for my newsletter at murdermemo.com and receive bonus material, such as the Dickie Floyd short story, EXHUMING HER HONOR.

As a newsletter subscriber, you will receive special offers, updates, book releases, and blog posts. I promise to never sell or spam your email.

Danny R. Smith

Dickie Floyd Novels

BOOK REVIEWS

Independent authors count on word-of-mouth and paid advertising to find new readers and sell more books.

Reviews can help shoppers decide about taking a chance on authors who are new to them.

I would be grateful if you took a moment to write a review wherever you purchased the book.

Thank you!

Danny R. Smith

ACKNOWLEDGMENTS

I'd like to thank my editor, Patricia Barrick Brennan, for her ongoing support, her relentless pursuit of editing perfection, and most of all, her friendship.

My beta team provides me with terrific insight and feedback before my stories are published, and they are terrific at catching typos or grammatical errors, the manuscript gremlins that plague all writers. I would like to recognize and thank each of them for their continued commitment and dedication:

Phil Jonas, Deac Slocumb, Moon Mullen, Bud Johnson, Michele Carey, Scott Anderson, Andrea Self, Teresa Collins, Heather Wamboldt, Kay Reeves, Michele Kapugi, Jacqueline Beard, Fred Reynolds, Schauer, Daryl "Deedub" Knight, Lesli, and "the girls."

ABOUT THE AUTHOR

Danny R. Smith spent 21 years with the Los Angeles County Sheriff's Department, the last seven as a homicide detective. He now lives in Idaho where he worked as a private investigator and consultant until retiring from his second career in 2022. He is blessed with a beautiful family and surrounded by an assortment of furry critters whom he counts among his friends.

Danny is the author of the *Dickie Floyd Detective Novel* series and the *Rich Farris Detective* series. He writes about true crime and other topics in his blog, The Murder Memo.

He has appeared as an expert on numerous podcasts and shows including True Crime Daily and the STARZ channel's WRONG MAN series.

Danny is a member of the Idaho Writers Guild and the Public Safety Writers Association.